Chicory Island

Jennifer Lanzilotti

ISBN 978-1-61225-475-3

Published by Mirror Publishing
Fort Payne, AL 35967
www.pagesofwonder.com

Printed in the USA

Thank you to Mike Walker for lighting the fire under me to share my book. You were the first helper to get this journey started.

Thank you to John Lesko for your hours of editing and polishing.

And a very special thank you to Judy Crabb whose talents with the English language have been a life-long source of teaching and inspiration. This book would not exist if it weren't for her continuous encouragement and help. I will be forever grateful.

Chapter 1

Mark Williams knew they were going to kill him.

He glanced at his hands. You never know what will go through your mind when your time is up, especially when you aren't expecting it. Maybe if he were about to die of old age, he'd be thinking about the trite things; bucket lists, regrets, accomplishments, maybe even whether he'd go up or down? But instead, Mark stared at his dry, cracked hands, thinking he'd never get the chance to heal them. His hands were bothering him the last few weeks. The scaly, cracked skin kept him up nights itching. He planned to order a special cream with vitamin E and coconut oil. *Why am I thinking about this? Strange. Focus.*

The ship tipped slightly, but his body held the familiar stance that kept him upright. For a moment he simply stood in the middle of the room where he'd spent weeks. He ran a shaky hand through his hair, feeling the rough grain of his skin. He'd never dreamed his life would turn out this way. He spent years obtaining his degrees. He was a skilled microbiologist, a geneticist, and a hydrologist, holding two PHD's. He loved the study of life organisms, as well as the study of water and its cycle. When he was offered a lucrative job that involved both areas of research, he quickly suppressed the thought it might be too good to be true. He was paid more than he'd ever dreamed of, with nearly unlimited resources at his disposal. No expense was spared building his lab onboard the elaborate vessel. He let the glory of his ambition and opportunity obscure his common sense. In hindsight, the 'should haves' were adding up. Mark knew it was too late, the damage done. The company was corrupt, the boss a complete psychopath. But seeing that now did little good— about as much as being stuck on a ship with no hand lotion.

With his life at stake, time was of the utmost importance. He stared at the papers lying on the long metal table. He'd overheard his boss, Steven Malek, saying there couldn't be any loose ends. Mark was clearly a loose end. There was no way he'd keep quiet about his research, and of course he'd warn the authorities about what Psycho Steve (a fitting nickname for his boss) had in mind.

Mark eyed the large plastic zip-lock bag holding his lunch. After tossing the food in the trash, he gently blew in the bag to check for holes. When no leaks appeared, his heartbeat quickened. There were six documents most vital to mankind. He quickly searched through the pile of forms and found what he needed.

The ship's rocking increased, swaying back and forth. Not so much like a cradle now, but more like a seesaw. At least with death, he wouldn't miss the constant motion-sickness from living on the eight-hundred-foot vessel. He'd been onboard the ship for nine months, including its journey from the Atlantic Ocean to Lake Superior through the St. Lawrence Seaway. It seemed a bit ironic to be facing death at the tail end of a massive storm. *Figures*, he thought.

He carefully folded the documents, sealing them inside the zip-lock bag, praying the papers would stay safe. A shiver ran through him. He hated the cold winter months. The wind rattled the loose window of the spacious cabin. He glanced up as the storm sprayed water over the railing on the ship's starboard side. October wasn't cold enough to freeze the water, but it would easily cause hypothermia. And yet somehow, he knew that in a matter of minutes, he'd be out there, swimming for his life.

"There you are."

At the sound of Psycho Steve's slow-winded voice, Mark carefully pulled his shirt down over his pants. He'd tucked the bag inside his underwear band, hoping the elastic would keep the documents secure. He'd hidden the evidence just in time.

"I know what you're planning, and you're making a huge mistake. This organism is too advanced and dangerous for you to release. I'm begging you to reconsider." Mark backed away as his boss, Steve Malek, stepped inside the cabin.

Psycho Steve offered a slow, wide smile, with the perfect white veneers that were slightly too large for his mouth. "For a brilliant scientist, I'm surprised you can't see the big picture. Everything in life comes down to money, doc."

"The organism is extremely dangerous. I told you I need more time to study it. I had no idea you were breeding it!" His chest tightened at the thought of the ballast water, containing thousands of the dangerous life-forms. "Aside from the fact it could make fish extinct, we don't know what it will do to humans. An entity like this can't be allowed to live." The regret he felt created a wave of nausea. What he'd created was so morally and ethically wrong, the devil himself must have had a hand in it.

Malek scanned the microscopes, petri dishes and flasks, surrounded by scattered papers and other lab materials. "You really are a messy worker, doc. It's fortunate none of this needs to be preserved. I have what I needed from you, and there's nothing more to do. You truly are brilliant, and it's a shame you won't get credit for this. However, I'll always admire you for it."

Mark felt his stomach churn. The word 'Apocalypse' flashed through his mind last week when he discovered the reason Psycho Steve had him experimenting with genetically altered organisms, and why his work was done onboard a ship holding thousands of gallons of ballast water.

"Killing you brings me no pleasure." Malek pulled a revolver from his jacket pocket. His right-hand man, Shawn Sharconnon, was angry he'd not been given the job of ending Mark's life.

Normally Malek preferred Shawn do his less desirable work, but not this time. This time, Malek felt Williams deserved better than having his life ended by an ignorant sociopath. Malek didn't mind Shawn killing unimportant people, but Mark Williams was far from that. He'd earned Malek's respect and admiration. Not just anyone could do what Williams had done. He'd proved God-like with his unique ability to create a new life form. Malek appreciated those who could accomplish monumental tasks. No, he thought with a sting of regret. Williams deserved to die by someone equally superior, quick and painless.

"The fact you're so uniquely intelligent, and I unfortunately have to kill you, makes me somewhat sad." Malek tipped his head to the door. "Let's go."

"If you shoot me, there will be a murder investigation. They'll discover I was working for you." Mark felt panic, knowing if he screamed, there was no one aboard the ship to help him. He could jump overboard, taking his chances with the frigid water, but he needed to get past Malek first.

"That might be true if your body were found. But did you know Lake Superior is the largest, deepest, and coldest lake in the world? Did you know it contains 500 shipwrecks, and probably more yet to be discovered?" Malek liked the confused look on Mark's face. Was it possible he knew something the brilliant doctor didn't? "Your body will be at the bottom of this Great Lake, never to be seen again."

"You're insane." The idea was terrifying. Mark couldn't allow that to happen. He suddenly pushed through the cabin door, shoving Malek into the wall. The gun went off, but he kneed Malek forcefully in the groin before vaulting the ship's railing.

"No!" Malek yelled, firing the gun at Williams as his body splashed into the angry waves. The ship tipped as he shot, water spraying over the railing. Malek brushed his wet hair from his eyes. He should've shot the doctor inside the cabin, rather than trying to walk him to the bow of the ship, where the cement weights were. With the gray sky casting dark shadows over the water, all Malek could see were black, rolling waves. Williams was swept clear from sight.

Shawn ran toward Malek along the ship's slippery, narrow bridge. "What happened?" he asked, noting Malek's enraged face.

"There's going to be a body washing up somewhere. You're going to find and dispose of it before anyone else does. I don't care if you have to scan every inch of this lake with the lifeboat, you must find the doctor's body." He was pretty sure he'd shot Williams, but if not, there was no way he'd survive the frigid water.

Chapter 2

Doctor Jessica Bennett swiped the digital thermometer across her forehead and sighed. The flashing green numbers read 102.4.

"I'm going home, Wanda. Please tell Dr. Brown I'm sick and he'll need to see the rest of my patients today. Have Claire contact my afternoon patients and reschedule those who aren't urgent." Jessica's energy was draining fast. She remembered the mother of three who'd sat in her office looking like a corpse while her little, runny-nosed children touched every surface of the exam room. Jessica informed the extremely ill woman that she had the flu. That was two days ago, perfect incubation period.

"Yes, Doctor." Wanda handed her a small cup containing two Motrin tablets and a water bottle. "I'll start your car for you."

"Thanks." Jessica rose from her leather chair, feeling the rush of fever taking over. She could sense the virus hijacking her body, viciously attacking her muscles and throat. Her winter jacket hung from the wrought-iron coat tree, next to the piles of blue charts on her desk. Her work would have to wait.

"Call Greg and see if he can pick her up," Dr. Brown said from the hallway, as he entered her office. "Geeze, Jess, you look terrible. How high is your fever?" He placed his hand on his colleague's forehead. "Welcome to flu season. Maybe you better lie down and rest until your fever breaks."

"No." Jessica glanced at Wanda. "Don't call Greg. He's in surgery all day. I'm dying to get home to my bed. I'll be fine." She offered Dr. Brown a weak smile. "It's only a few minutes away." She lifted her phone to let her fiancé know she was heading home, but remembered his busy day, and decided not to bother him. Before tucking the phone away, she noticed a text from her sister Janie:

Need 2 talk 2 u, r u free Sat? It's important. TXT me soon. Xoxo

The thought of responding quickly passed as she felt chills run through her body. She needed to get home immediately. Besides, Saturday was just two days away, and if this was the flu, she wouldn't be seeing her sister then.

"Please feel better, Dr. Bennett." Wanda offered a sympathetic pat on her shoulder.

Dr. Brown held up Jessica's car keys. "Drive safe and don't worry about things here. I've got it under control."

She saw the concern on her friend's face. She called him Mike when they were alone, but always "Dr. Brown" out of respect when others were around. "I'll text you later and let you know how I'm feeling." She forced herself to stand up straight. If Mike had any idea how truly sick she was, he'd refuse to let her drive home.

Mike was the kind of guy whose amenable charm made him immediately well-liked. He was a great doctor, and even better at calming/soothing people with his relaxed disposition. She never had to worry about stressing him if he had to take on extra patients alone. It was one of the things she loved about him, and the reason she enjoyed working with him. They'd shared a medical practice for five years now. Being 17 years her senior, and happily married to his beautiful wife, Jessica viewed him almost like a father. Or perhaps, with his goofy grin and shaggy long hair, he was more like the big brother she never had. And more than that, he was a true friend whom she valued.

Snow fell softly outside, the cold making her body ache even more. She never used to mind Michigan winters, until the earth suddenly seemed to revisit the ice age with heavier snows and longer winters, with wicked cold. The hair on her arms stood up as chills shook her body. Weakening by the moment, she silently thanked Wanda for starting up her Land Rover. The warmth inside was a welcome relief.

The salted roads crunched under her tires, and she realized, halfway home, that she'd been speeding. Her forehead was now perspiring, with the fever overwhelming her body. She was nearly ready to collapse, and probably shouldn't have been driving.

Approaching the house, she noticed Greg's car sitting in the driveway. Parked in the street was a red Tahoe exactly like her sister's. Those details didn't really register, as all that mattered right then was finding enough strength in her tortured body to make it into the house. Everything ached with the kind of pain that makes you want to curl into a ball and die. With Greg's car in the middle of the driveway, she couldn't pull into the garage, so she parked her car behind his. He could move it for her later.

It took every ounce of energy she had to push herself out of the car and stagger to the front door. Fumbling for her house key, her fever was raging, and she could barely stand. The moment she opened the door, she felt her heart drop, blood rushing to her head.

"Oh my God, Jessie, let me explain!" Janie stood up frantically, pulling her sweater down.

Jessica swallowed as her eyes took in the scene, settling on her fiancé pulling up his pants. A wave of nausea had her gripping the door for support. Her mouth was watering as she tried to hold back the gall rising in her throat. The room was spinning, and she could feel herself ready to collapse to the floor.

"Jessie, what are you doing home?" Greg asked, tension in his eyes. "Are you sick?" She didn't look well. Her face was pale with red blotches. Her eyes drooped as he made his way toward her, catching her around the shoulders.

"Sis, I love you so much, I never wanted you to find out this way. I was planning to tell you Saturday. You have to hear me out. I—"

"Not now Janie!" Greg turned an angry glare toward her. "Can't you see she's sick?" He placed his hand over her forehead. "You're burning up, Jess. Come lie down on the couch." He guided her to the leather sectional.

She chided herself for having to lean on him for support. She was relieved to be lying down, unable to keep her eyes open. She felt Greg's hand on her forehead, brushing down to her cheek.

"I'm getting the thermometer. Have you taken anything for this yet?" He'd never seen her seriously ill before, and if her fever spiked too high, he'd need to get her to the hospital.

Jessica lay on the soft leather couch, listening to the voices fade in and out. She wasn't trying to hear what they were saying. She didn't really care. Her body was in agony. Bile shot up her throat as she leaned over the couch, letting it pour out on the hardwood floor. *Good. Greg can clean it up*!

Janie gasped. "I'm so sorry Jess. I feel terrible you had to discover us when you're this sick. I'll get you some water." She came back with a glass and watched as Greg laid a damp cloth across her sister's forehead. "Greg, explain that it was an accident. Tell her how when I came over that day, you thought I was her when you kissed me." She glanced away from the chunky bile splattered near Greg's foot. The idea she should clean it up entered her mind, but she quickly dismissed the thought. Seeing someone else's vomit would only make her throw up too, and her stomach was already churning.

With her eyes closed, Jessica could imagine the tears streaming down her twin's face. She'd heard that same desperate rattling in her sister's voice the day their parents were killed in a car crash. Janie was truly distraught, and no matter how betrayed Jessica felt, she still had a strong urge to comfort her sister. If she wasn't lying on her death bed, she might have tried to do just that.

"Jessie, you don't love Greg the way I do. He's everything to me," Janie continued. "I know you feel betrayed, but you don't really love him!" She didn't think it right that Jess agreed to marry Greg, knowing she wasn't all that crazy about him. Janie tried to hand the glass of water to her sister, but Greg took it from her, slamming it down on the coffee table.

"Enough Janie, just shut up! Jess is sick as hell, and now isn't the time to confess everything."

Jessica felt the bile shoot up her throat again and forced her eyes open. She leaned over before Greg could move, successfully emptying a large amount of liquid on his lap.

Greg quickly sat back, watching the pool pour from his pant leg onto the hardwood floor, where it spread and joined with the other puddle. "You did that on purpose," he said in a tone that sounded more astonished than disgusted. He stood up slowly and carefully removed his pants. He glanced quickly at Janie who was finally quiet and looking as if she too was about to toss her lunch. "I can't catch this." He'd need a shower and even then, he'd be lucky if he didn't get her flu. "Get the trash can from under the sink," he told Janie. "Quick! And grab the roll of paper towel."

Jessica wanted to smile but was in too much pain. Every bone in her body felt like someone hit it with a sledgehammer. She thought about the old days when people got high fevers, lost consciousness, and then became delirious saying things that didn't make sense. She thought the agony she felt could make her pass out, and perhaps she was already delusional, because she imagined Janie holding a sledgehammer, while Greg pointed out which parts of her body would make nice clean breaks. She felt something on her forehead, and wanted to bat it away, but heavy weights were pinning her arms down.

"Her fever is 104.5." Greg glanced from Janie back to Jessica. "How much higher has it risen since you left work, Jess? If it reaches 105, I'm taking you to the hospital."

"No." Jessica's voice was weak, and she could barely open her eyes. "Just give me more Motrin." She wanted to move to the bedroom and get under the blankets, because now she was shivering. "I only took 400 milligrams, and I've probably thrown it up." Her jaw was quivering, her words strained and low. "I just need more... and to sleep."

Greg swore under his breath, quickly grabbing the two throw blankets they kept in a basket next to the TV. He draped them over her before heading to the medicine cabinet for the prescription

Motrin 800.

"Jessie, I would never intentionally hurt you, you know that. We are in love, and it happened by accident. I didn't do it on purpose." Janie grabbed her purse from the table and shot Greg a pleading look before he headed to the bathroom. She needed to make her sister understand. "He's everything to me, Jess. I'm sorry." She stared at her sister lying helpless on the sofa, while feeling a tremendous weight of guilt and sympathy. Wiping the tears from her eyes, she watched as Greg walked back to Jess, holding the pill out to her. "Take good care of her, Greg. I hope you feel better soon, sis. I'll come back later so we can talk, and I'll bring you some soup."

When the door shut, Jessica forced her eyes open again. "Greg." She could barely get the words out, and she hated having to ask him for anything.

"Yes, baby?"

"Will you please carry me to my bed?" *And don't baby me, you two-timing SOB.* She knew it didn't matter though, because after today nothing would ever be the same. The life she had, and thought she was going to have, was abruptly over. She wasn't going to marry Greg and have a family with him. She wasn't going to live in his house anymore or add her name to the deed.

Greg's arms went under her shoulders and knees, lifting her. She was forced to wrap her arms around his neck for support. She could smell the cologne she'd gotten him for his birthday last week. He laid next to her on the bed, pulling the blankets up to her shoulders. She wanted him to leave and never come back, but the warmth he offered was more important. As her mind drifted, she heard Janie's pleading words, 'He's everything to me.'

Chapter 3

"I got you some ginger ale." Greg turned on the bedside lamp, handing Jessica a cool glass.

Her mouth was dry, her tongue felt like cardboard, and she could still taste her sickness. Her eyes adjusted to the light as she slowly sat up and took a sip. "How long did I sleep?"

"It's been about fifteen hours." He rested his hand on her forehead. "Your fever is down now. How do you feel?"

She noticed he was using his gentle, contrite tone of voice. The voice he used after they argued, and he wanted to apologize. It was a voice she once appreciated. Now, it seemed condescending. "I think I'm over the worst of it, thank God. I thought I was going to die." She took another sip of the soda. She wished she felt more anger, but it just wasn't there. Closing her eyes for a moment, Janie's words ran through her mind. 'He's everything to me.' "Greg, do you really love my sister?"

If it had been another woman, a stranger maybe, she would have compared herself to her. She might say to him, 'how could you choose her over me? Her hips are too wide, or her eyes are too close together or her hair sucks.' But Jessica couldn't say any of that because her twin, Janie, looked exactly like her. They shared the same thick blond hair, which they both complained about on humid days. Janie's long lanky body was the same size as hers, with the same small chest and bony butt. Jess thought maybe her sister's legs were nicer because she had more time for Pilate's classes. They shared the exact same smile, since both their braces were removed at the same time. When Jessica looked at her sister's green eyes, admiring her eye shadow, she'd know that color would look good on her too. Janie was basically her carbon copy.

"Jessie, I don't love Janie the way that I love you. I've made a terrible mistake and I know that now." Greg's voice broke, as he set his hand on hers. "I don't want to lose you. I will do whatever you ask of me, whatever it takes to win you back."

She looked down at the silver band with a single large sapphire diamond on her left hand, and again heard Janie's voice. *'He's everything to me.'* Jessica said yes when Greg placed the ring on her finger months ago, but she hadn't been entirely thrilled. There was a part of her that wasn't completely sure she was doing the right thing. *'He's everything to me.'* Jessica slowly began to take off the ring, knowing those were Janie's true feelings… not hers.

"Please don't do this baby. I've made a mistake, but—"

"If you want to do what's right and fix this, then here's what you'll do." She looked directly at his pleading eyes. "Make Janie happy. She loves you, and she won't be able to handle a broken heart." Their relationship was over, but she couldn't stop hearing her sister's plea. Janie was in love and there was no reason for both of them to lose the man wiping tears from his eyes.

"I can't commit to Janie. I'm still in love with you."

"She thinks you love her. Janie would be devastated if she lost you."

"And you won't be?" He gave her a questioning look.

"The difference is I can survive the loss, but Janie might not. The damage is done, Greg. I'll never be able to trust you, and more importantly, I can't stay with you and let you break my sister's heart." Janie was needy, more sensitive, and far too vulnerable to be cast aside. Jessica's chest felt tight and heavy. Wasn't it supposed to be a secretary or some nurse from the hospital that he would cheat with? She remembered the day she'd met him, at a doctor's convention for the hospital. All the other women were drawn to Greg and were immediately attracted to him. That fact alone made him less desirable in her eyes. She'd ignored him, and twice turned him down, with the excuse that she wouldn't date a fellow colleague. Finally, she agreed to date him after he'd pursued her for weeks. She chose to quit doing surgery and join a private practice with Mike.

Greg displayed a passion for the medical field. It was that common interest that pulled her into a relationship with him. She thought about them reading medical journals together, sharing the work and knowledge of their profession. Would he enjoy listening to Janie talk about her career as a schoolteacher? Jessica felt her sister was a gift to children. Janie's career was equally important, but she somehow didn't think Greg would feel that way. Janie didn't have a PHD, but she could've had one. Jessica knew her sister better than anyone, and Janie was smart, funny, and sweet. Aside from being with Greg, there was nothing bad she could say about her. She loved her sister more than anything, even more than the tearful man sitting beside her. "I feel like I stepped into a soap opera." She felt a twinge of the anger she needed and wanted to feel. "My sister, Greg? It's so cliché. Mistaken identity? Give me a break."

"It's not like that, Jess." He got up to pace the floor. "I came home from work one day, overworked and exhausted. It was the week of that six-car pileup, and I'd been pulling double shifts. Janie stopped by to give you something, and I thought she was you." He dropped to his knees by the bed and took her hand. "If I hadn't been so damn exhausted, I might have paid more attention. It wasn't until halfway through the kiss that I realized it might not be you. It just felt so good, and she was reciprocating, and before I knew it, we were—" His eyes fell to the floor in shame. "I hoped it was you. It felt different and strange, but I couldn't stop myself. I never wanted you so badly in all my life. Your sister is the one who aggressively kept it going. I'm sorry, Jess. I know this must hurt."

She watched the emotion sweep across his face. He seemed sincere. Still, she squeezed his hand hoping her flu germs would stick to his skin. "If you didn't know it was Janie, then you don't know me very well, Greg. There should be no way you could mistake her for me." That was all the proof she needed that he wasn't the man for her.

"I told you, I was exhausted. I wasn't thinking clearly. I know how you must feel, but—"

"You know how I must feel? You don't have a clue!" She pushed his hand away. "Keep telling me what happened. I want to hear the rest."

"It was a moment of weakness, and I was confused. It wasn't planned. I wanted it to be you."

"Yeah, you already said that." She wondered how long they'd been sleeping together behind her back. "What happened after the first time?"

"Well, we heard your car pulling into the garage, so Janie left quickly. She said, 'Please don't tell anything to Jessie, because it was an accident.' I was relieved to hear her say that. I thought maybe it was just the one mistake, and it would never happen again. I thought maybe she would move to California and—"

"And you could just sweep that little lie under the rug and move on and marry me? Wow, you're sick."

"I don't know what I thought, Jess." His voice trembled, but he continued. "The next day Janie called me at work, saying she had to see me. I didn't want to meet her, but she insisted, and truthfully, I was worried about her. She confessed to being madly in love with me, and she sounded desperate. I went to her apartment, and she was dressed in this very sexy little black—"

"Shut up, I don't need to hear that part!" She felt her nails digging into her fist. She was feeling more betrayed by her sister. She could imagine how Janie must've sounded to Greg on the phone, since she'd heard her sister like that many times before. It used to worry her when Janie would call late at night, frantic over losing their parents. She would hurry over to Janie's apartment to console her, worrying if she might hurt herself. Jessie understood why Greg went to meet her, but she wasn't about to admit that to him.

Greg rubbed his eyes. "She said she needed to know if I had

any feelings for her, and if so, we owed it to ourselves to find out if it was real. She said she couldn't go on with her life and move to California if there was even a small chance we were meant to be together. Maybe I simply chose the wrong sister, and it was her I was meant to be with. Jess, I was so confused. She manipulated me, confused me, and made me doubt our relationship. You were working a lot, and she kept telling me how she was able to give more love than you could."

"I've heard enough." It was killing her to think badly of Janie. It didn't sound like something her sister was capable of, but part of her had always suspected that Janie liked Greg more than she should. She looked into Greg's eyes and wondered what it was about him that would cause her sister to betray her. Greg was nice-looking, but he wasn't all that. He'd always been a bit too thin, and she was always trying to fatten him up. Perhaps it was his brilliant mind and the appeal of him being a doctor. Being a surgeon and saving lives was definitely sexy, but with that came a certain amount of arrogance. It bothered her that he was abrupt toward the elderly and lacked patience when it came to children. In fact, she wasn't sure he really wanted kids. Now that she allowed herself to think about the things she disliked about him, she realized she wasn't even feeling devastated. She would miss their medical talks, and how she could always turn to him for advice. She'd miss the energy he displayed after a successful complex surgery. There was a sense of security in their daily living, and that, she realized, she might miss more than the man himself— the comfort of just having someone to share her day with. But what else, more meaningful, would she miss?

"What are you thinking? Please say something." He got up and walked to the dresser, picked up his cell. "I'll call Janie right now and tell her you and I are getting married."

"No!" Jessica needed to get away from him now that her mind was made up. She pulled the covers back and stood up. "You and I are done. I'm moving out, and Janie can move in. You tell her she's the one you want to marry, Greg." She held the ring out to him.

"I'm never going to look at you the same, and I'm never going to let you break her heart." She took a deep breath. "And the truth is… I'm not really as upset about this as I should be. I think Janie's right, Greg. I don't love you as much as I should. I don't love you the way she does." She placed the ring in his hand because he wasn't taking it from her. "We're over." She turned and walked into the bathroom, locking the door behind her.

Chapter 4

Standing in the shower, Jessica enjoyed the warm water beating on her sore muscles. She was beginning to regain her strength, but even shampooing her hair was still exhausting work. She moved slowly, getting herself dressed. Surveying the bedroom, she realized there was little to pack beyond clothes, because everything else in the house belonged to Greg. She shared a small apartment with Janie when Greg asked her to move in years ago. The only things she'd brought were clothes and a few sentimental items from her parents. She'd never felt the need for a big, fancy house, and she rarely took time to shop and buy 'things.' Part of her was accustomed to his lifestyle, and perhaps she'd been spoiled living in his upscale home, but it was never something she really needed.

The house wasn't even her taste, and she'd often thought about changing the décor. Greg's house was modern, black and white, crisp, straight lines, clear glass. Cold. She preferred more traditional earth tones, soft, floral, repurposed. Warm. It was, however, a beautiful neighborhood, and would've been perfect for raising a family. Relief suddenly washed over her. She could've married Greg and made the biggest mistake of her life. Now that she thought about it, what kind of father would he be? All the reservations she'd tucked away in her subconscious came to light. If she were honest with herself, she wasn't even that surprised Greg had cheated. The surprise was her sister, and even that wasn't completely shocking. Greg was a charmer. He seemed to carry a sexual vibe Janie had probably felt from the beginning.

After she put on her work clothes, she headed to the kitchen.

Canned chicken noodle soup would be the final step in her recovery. As she searched the pantry, she heard her cell phone buzz. Greg had plugged it in the charger and left it on the counter. Every once in a while, he managed to do something thoughtful. She picked up the phone, seeing it was Mike calling.

"Hello?" Her voice still sounded hoarse.

"Jessica, it's me. Are you okay?"

"I'm better… flu's gone. I'm—"

"Jessie, listen to me. I'm at the hospital and they just brought in Janie. She's had an overdose of pills. They've pumped her stomach and she's stabilized."

Jessica's legs went weak, and she slumped to her knees. She couldn't imagine a world without her sister, and the tears came almost instantly. "Is she okay? Is Greg there? Does he know?"

"Greg's the one who found her. Look, stay put and I'll come get you. Don't leave, you hear me?" He knew she'd be too upset to drive safely.

"I'll be here. Please hurry." She choked on her sob. "Mike… is she going to be okay?"

"Just hang on kiddo, I'm on my way."

Mike didn't have to pull into the driveway. Jessica met him halfway down the street. Her eyes were dry, but he could see she was struggling to control her emotions. She jumped in the car, and he reached out for her hand. "You're freezing. You should have waited inside." He understood her relationship with Janie. Everyone knew how close they were, how much they'd been through together after losing their parents. The snow fell in tiny wisps, quickly melting on the ground, making it easy to drive fast.

Jessica kept her eyes on the road. In her mind she saw Janie pulling her shirt down, and the shamed look on her face when she said, "I'm so sorry." She replayed yesterday over and over, still hearing Janie's words. It wasn't until her vision blurred that she realized tears were streaming down her face, as Mike pulled into the hospital visitors' lot.

Once in the hospital, Mike led through the halls, intercepting mutual friends who might have questions. All he had to do was give a stern 'not now' look and wave them away.

Jessica wasn't prepared to see her sister lying in a hospital bed but was even less prepared to see Greg sitting beside her, affectionately stroking the side of her face. He quickly stood when Mike pulled back the curtain.

"She almost died, Jess, but I got to her in time." Greg wiped his eyes, then ran a hand through his mussed brown hair. "Whatever she took made her blood pressure drop so low we almost lost her."

Jessica took the chart Mike handed her and read the stats. There was always a risk of brain damage when a person O.D.'s. She felt tears prick her eyes again and pushed them back.

"She's not out of the woods yet," Mike noted, staring at Greg, feeling something wasn't quite right.

"I stopped by her apartment to talk." Greg glanced at Mike with a distraught look. "Mike, would you mind giving Jess and I a moment alone?" He was trying to be polite, but the truth was he never liked Mike. Greg hated Mike's constant grin, and his "this-couldn't-be-a-more-perfect-world" attitude. And all he did was brag about his wife and kids.

Mike gave Greg an apprehensive nod. "Sure, I'll be at the nurse's station if you need me, Jess."

Jessica's hands were shaking, so she carefully set the chart down and walked to the other side of the bed. She took her sister's hand, careful not to touch the IV. The double tape and slight bruise meant the IV had already been moved twice, because like hers, Janie's veins were hard to find. Jessica examined her sister's face and felt like she was looking in the mirror. Janie had been crying. Streaks of dried tears lined her cheeks. Jess looked up at Greg, feeling this was partly his fault. "What happened?"

"She called me crying, and I was worried about her. When I got to her apartment, she didn't answer the door. I found it unlocked, so I let myself in. I found her lying on the floor, and pills were spilled all over." He grasped Janie's hand again, and gently kissed her fingers.

The gesture was sincere and sweet, and Jessica couldn't help but feel relief in that small act. "You really do care for her." His betrayal, at least, was more than just sex. For Janie's sake, she was glad. If it were any other woman, it might have hurt more. "Did she do this because she thought you were leaving her?"

"I just told her I needed time to figure things out. That I'm confused right now." He let out a long sigh. "The truth is I'm a wreck, Jess. I don't want to lose you, and yet…" He looked down at Janie and felt his heart squeeze.

"Are you seriously in love with *both* of us?"

"God help me, I think I am."

"Then I'll make the decision for you. It has to be Janie. You stay with her, Greg." She moved around the bed ignoring the sounds of the busy ER around them. The curtain offered little privacy, so she tried to lower the tone of her voice. "Look at me, Greg." She stood a few inches from him. "You will *never* have me again. It's over. But Janie loves you and needs you. You will fix this, Greg." She leaned over to touch her sister's soft hand, instinctively resting her fingers on her sister's pulse. "You need to make it work with Janie and make her happy. I swear to God if you break her heart, I will never forgive you." The curtain pulled back, and she realized she hadn't been able to keep her voice down. Mike stood there with concern on his face. Without another word she stormed out of the ER. Greg looked after her with an anguished expression.

The cafeteria was clearing after the lunch rush. Only a few customers still sat at tables, eating and texting. Jessica took a chair by the large window in the corner. The cafeteria always smelled like canned peas and disinfectant, an odd scent she never cared for. She felt drained and defeated as Mike sat down across from her and gave her the "spill-it-all-right-now" look.

"I don't know if I can talk." She didn't want to start crying again.

"Okay, take a sip of this coffee." He handed her a cup and

spoke softly. "I'll tell you what I figured out." When he was done repeating what he'd learned he sat back in his chair. "You know I never liked him, Jess. My wife Maria has incredible intuition, and she doesn't like him either."

"That doesn't help, Mike." Maybe she'd made a mistake with Greg, but she didn't want to hear that everyone knew it. She wanted to believe there was some good in him, because he was going to be with her sister. Poor Janie.

"I'm sorry." Mike studied his friend's downcast face, feeling protective. She was obviously attractive, but he'd never thought of her romantically. His own beautiful wife filled every desire he had. Over the years, his friendship with Jessica became a valued one, without distracting sexual tension. He valued her work ethic, sense of humor, and most of all her ear for listening. His wife Maria was crazy about her, and never questioned their close working relationship. He had a great relationship with his wife, and their obvious love shone for the world to see. He'd never seen evidence of Jessica having that kind of soul-binding love for Greg. Even Maria suspected that if they married, they'd never share the kind of deep fulfillment that pulls people closer over the years, rather than drifting apart.

"I have an idea I think will help." Mike slowly offered a sympathetic smile. "You know I have that cabin in the Upper Peninsula. It's on Chicory Island in Lake Superior."

Jessica sat back in her chair, crossing her arms in front of her. "I know all about your cabin, Mike. Every summer Greg and I promise to come up, and we never do." Greg was always working, which is why they never went anywhere.

"You're emotionally distraught, Jess. You can't be a good doctor right now. I'd like you to visit the cabin for a few weeks. Give yourself some time alone to rest and grieve." The cabin was a special place. Often, the burden of an exhausting work schedule, kids and bills became too much for him. He'd need to decompress and relax. That's when they would leave the kids with Maria's parents, and head for the cabin. After a few days surrounded by nothing but nature and each other, he'd feel like a new man. "You can get there today. There are only about eighty people who stay on the island through the winter. I've got a buddy who lives there year-round and maintains the cabin for me. He'll be happy to pick you up at the ferry and make sure you get settled." His friend Seth was a good guy and would look out for her. Maria wanted Jessica to meet Seth years ago, but the opportunity never arose.

"I appreciate the offer, but I'm not sure—"

"Listen. I'm not taking no for answer. You can't work with this emotional disaster on your mind." He leaned forward, setting his hand on her arm. His tone turned serious. "You need time to sort things out. If I were you, I'd be looking to get away. Even if you don't go, I don't want you coming to work for at least a couple weeks."

She sighed, knowing he was serious. And maybe he was right. Her life was suddenly torn, and even as they spoke, she was pushing back tears. She had nowhere to live and would have to stay in hotels until she could find a place. She also didn't want to run into Greg. He needed time to accept the fact they were over, and he needed to focus on Janie. Perhaps a getaway to a remote island was exactly what she needed. She saw the concern in Mike's eyes and trusted that he knew what was best.

"Jess, I—"

"I'll do it," she interrupted. "I'll go to your cabin."

A look of satisfaction crossed his face, creasing the lines around his eyes. "It's settled then." He was pleased with himself for convincing her. "I don't think you should go home, and I don't like the idea of you being alone." He glanced down at his watch. "I've got to get to work, but I'll drop you at my house. Let Maria take care of you, and she can help you pack."

Moved by his concern, she set her hand over his. "I really appreciate your friendship, Mike." She didn't have many friends, and the few she did were also friends with Greg. They probably wouldn't be as helpful. "Thank you." She'd follow his advice and head to the island as soon as Janie awoke.

Chapter 5

Mike's wife was in fact a big help. Maria insisted on helping Jessica, including packing up her closet, which she and her daughters did after Mike dropped her off at their house. Maria was the kind of woman whose inner beauty poured from her heart, making her even more attractive. She was half Cuban and half Mexican, and liked to keep her lush, long black hair swept up in a clip. Just moments after Jessica arrived, she found herself sitting in a plush chair, eating the best lasagna she'd ever tasted, with a glass of red wine. The house smelled like cinnamon, the cheerful décor relaxed her, and Maria fussed over her. She made sure Jessica was warm enough, had enough to eat, and even pushed gourmet chocolate on her. Five minutes with Maria and it was easy to see why Mike was so happy. Heck, anyone would want to be married to Maria.

"This is all of it, Jess." Maria smiled and her teeth seemed to sparkle like her eyes.

Jessica was used to managing her own life, always doing everything for herself. For the first time since her parents died, she found herself being cared for. Maria and her daughters had packed all her belongings. Her boxes filled much of their three-car garage.

"I'm amazed." Jessica sat in the guest room, watching the girls carry out orders from their mom. All three had their mom's long black hair. It reminded her of a coven of witches, except they were all gorgeous. And for young teen girls, they seemed oddly respectful and obedient. "What's your secret, Maria?" Jessica wondered. "I'd like to know in case I ever have kids of my own. Are they real?"

Maria arched a brow, "Real?" She zipped the suitcase and turned toward Jessica. "What do you mean?"

"They're Stepford children, right?" Jessica teased. "Seriously," she winked at the 15-year-old. "Do you ever get mouthy or refuse to help?" She hadn't heard a single complaint from the girls, who'd done a tremendous amount of work.

"It's called bribery, Jess." Maria tossed a knowing look at her kids. "They want their curfews extended, and Mike said no. They know the only way to Dad's approval is if I work a little magic." Maria glanced at the suitcases on the floor and sat on the loveseat across from the bed. "I've also found that with teens, all needing money for various things, it's the easy chores they're happy to do." She smiled at her daughters. "We had fun packing up Jess's things, didn't we girls?"

"It was fun. You have a lot of shoes, Jess," Angie, the 17-year-old, remarked.

"Yes, well… when you become a doctor, you can own lots of shoes too." Jessica felt her spirits lift for the first time that day. She stood up, feeling relieved so much was accomplished so quickly. "I really can't tell you how much I appreciate your help. I don't know what I would've done without you." They'd cleared all her belongings from Greg's house. He was at work and would eventually arrive home to find no trace of her. She hoped it would help him see they were truly over.

Angie took the last pile of sweaters and set them inside a box. But first she held up a white fuzzy sweater with a low V-neck. "I think you should wear this to the island." She looked back at her mom.

"Seth is picking her up, right?"

"Yes," Maria smiled, and then repressed a laugh when her other two daughters chuckled. "It's a good choice."

"I thought I'd just wear jeans and a sweatshirt to be comfortable." Jessica wondered what the women found so humorous.

"No, trust me, you'll want to look good," Heather, the 15-year-old, commented.

"Who is Seth again?" Jessica noticed the wide smiles and looks being shared among the girls. "What am I missing?"

"Oh nothing," Maria shook her head.

"I'm not—" Jessica felt her phone vibrate in her pocket and quickly pulled it out. It was the hospital, and she prayed it would be good news.

"Come on girls," Maria stood up. "Let's give Jess some privacy." She knew Jessica was waiting for word on her sister. She crossed her fingers and held them up for Jess to see.

Jessica mouthed "thank you" to Maria as she and her daughters stepped out of the room. She clutched the phone at the sound of Janie's weak "Hello."

"Are you okay?"

"I'm good. No permanent damage done."

"Oh, thank God!" A weight lifted as Jessica collapsed with relief on the bed. "It's so good to hear your voice. You scared the hell out of me!"

"I know, and I'm sorry. I swear to you, I wasn't trying to kill myself." Janie paused and gave a small sniff. "It was a total accident, I swear. I just felt so sick and wanted to take something to make it go away. I forgot I'd already taken anxiety meds. I just wanted to sleep, so I was looking for those sleeping pills you gave me last year. That's why pills were on the floor. I was searching for the right ones. I wasn't thinking straight or paying attention to what I'd already taken. I told Greg it was an accident."

Jessica could sense the tears streaming down her sister's face. She could hear the pain and regret in her voice. "Your blood pressure dropped so low you almost died! You think you hurt me with Greg... what the hell do you think that would do to me?"

"I know Jess, I'm sorry. You have to believe me, it was an accident, and I promise I'll be more careful."

"Janie, I love you, and my love for you is unconditional. No matter how much you've hurt me, that will never change. I need to know that whatever happens between you and Greg, you're not ever going to hurt yourself." She listened to her sister sniffle and blow her nose.

"I can't sleep or eat knowing how much I've hurt you. It's tearing me up. I just want you to understand what he means to me. I can't help—"

"Janie, stop and listen to me for a minute, okay?" Jessica couldn't understand Janie when she was crying, and she knew her sister well enough to know the situation was truly killing her. "I need to say something important, and I need you to listen."

"I'm listening."

Jessica took a deep breath. "I want you and Greg to be together. You have my blessing and my support. I think you're right. I don't love him anywhere near as much as you do. I've had time to think about it, and the truth is we've always been more friends than lovers. I want you to stop torturing yourself. I've already moved out of Greg's house." She heard Janie getting ready to speak. "Don't interrupt. Please just let me finish what I need to say." When the phone was quiet, she continued. "Mike has a cabin on an island in the Upper Peninsula. I'm heading there first thing in the morning. I wasn't going to leave until I knew you were okay. Now that I know you're safe, I'm going away for a few weeks… maybe longer."

"But—"

"Sis, I haven't had a vacation in five years. I've done nothing but work and center my life around Greg. I need some time to myself, and more importantly, I think you and Greg need time alone. He's very confused right now, Janie. The dumbass thinks he's in love with both of us, but in time he'll see I'm not an option. I've already told him he needs to make you happy."

"But—"

"All I've ever wanted is for you to be happy." The loss of their parents was extremely hard for Jessica, but it almost destroyed Janie. Maybe Janie had a bigger heart or was just needier, but either way, she struggled with depression and anxiety. Jess believed herself the stronger one, the one Janie leaned on. "I'm going to be fine. I'm just asking for a little time away from both you and Greg. I need this."

"Can I talk now?"

"Sure."

"What about all the dead fish?"

"What?" That wasn't the reply she was expecting.

"I've got the hospital TV on. It's showing thousands of dead fish washing up on the shores of Lake Superior. Isn't that where Mike's cabin is?"

Jess shook her head. She couldn't care less about some dead fish. Her sister's voice sounded better, stronger. That's all that mattered. "I'll be fine. I won't eat any fish when I get there. Are you okay now, sis?" The relief that Janie was alive and recovering was overwhelming.

"I'm okay. But only if I know I haven't lost you."

"You haven't lost me. I just need some time."

"Promise you'll text and tell me how you're doing."

"I will." Jessica heard the relief in her sister's voice and felt surprisingly better herself. "I love you."

"I love you more."

Chapter 6

"We need more police tape to block off the beaches, and I want the main access roads closed," Seth Johnson told his deputy. He removed his black knit hat to scratch his scalp. He'd been wearing it all day since being called down to the beach. He glanced sideways as a man approached him. Seth noted the EPA badge on his coat.

"Hi there." The man offered his hand. "Are you the Sheriff in charge?"

"I am. Sheriff Johnson." Seth shook the man's hand before putting his gloves and hat back on.

"I know Chicory Island has only one Sheriff and one deputy. I've been told County authorities are going to investigate if there's been any illegal dumping. I'm wondering if I should contact you, or the mainland State Police?" The guy jammed his cold hands in his jacket pockets. "Not sure who's in charge."

"I'm in charge of Chicory Island, but I use the State troopers in Dell County when I need backup or help with cases outside my jurisdiction." Seth assumed the problem of dead fish and wildlife washing up on the island shores was his problem. But he had a buddy, Officer Kyle Steller, who worked with the State Police and helped Seth when needed. Kyle loved working around the clock and having state-wide authority to conduct criminal investigations. "You can call me," Seth told him. He wanted to know what was going on, and maybe this guy would have answers. He watched the guy dig in his pocket for a business card.

Deputy Dean was standing close, listening. He leaned in. "You guys think something was dumped in the water?"

The official shook his head. "I doubt this has anything to do with illegal dumping, and I didn't find any arsenic in my analysis, but it won't hurt to do a little digging. Ask around."

Dean glanced from Seth back to the man. "So, what do you think this is? Have you seen this before?"

The man shook his head again. "I'm sorry I can't tell you anything at this time. I'll conduct some studies of the wildlife I collected." He looked at the islanders taking pictures of the fish with their phones. "Until we know more, I'd keep people away from the carcasses. The fact that not just fish are dying indicates an unusual problem." He turned to the bags of dead wildlife he'd set on the sand. One bag contained a large turtle, another had birds and ducks. He'd be taking them back to the lab. A dozen more dead Seagulls were pushed up on shore by the waves.

"I'll be in touch with you." Seth tucked the man's card in his jacket pocket and folded his arms as the man turned away. He glanced around at the beach that stretched for a quarter mile. In the summer it would be filled with islanders and tourists. In a few days it might be covered in snow, with snowmobile tracks.

Seth noticed two more EPA officials and a handful of gawkers, all bundled like Eskimos, trying to ignore the bitter bite of the cold wind. Only a few men appeared immune to the cold, wearing long black trench coats with black pants and dress shoes. Seth figured they were either FBI agents or Men in Black looking for Aliens.

"This has been a crazy day, hasn't it?" Deputy Dean said, staring at the fish. "I'll have Carl and Chris patrol the streets around here too." He wanted to cover his nose from the stench. "How soon did the EPA say this would be cleaned up?"

Seth shook his head, reaching in his pocket for his cell. "They didn't. I'm not sure this gets cleaned up." He wasn't even sure if it was his problem. He glanced at the phone. "Damn."

"What?" Dean leaned over, looking at Seth's phone.

"I forgot, I promised Doctor Mike I'd pick up his friend at the ferry. I forgot she was coming today." He'd already missed two calls from her, and now she'd left him a voicemail. "Hang on a sec." He listened to the message, and a slow grin formed on his face. Doctor Bennett was angry, and yet clearly trying to keep her cool while politely letting him know she'd be heading home if he didn't reply within the next half-hour. He stared at his deputy. "The Ferry broke down again, so she has no way to get here unless you pick her up in the patrol boat." He pointed where the thirty-two-foot police boat bobbed beside the long dock that would soon be stored for the winter. Waves of silver smacked the sides of the boat, as the scales of dead fish reflected in the water.

"No way, man." Dean held his hands up. "She's not my problem. Look, I've got to get home. My shift ended hours ago, and Becky has to get to work."

Seth shook his head. All day he'd dealt with the EPA and concerned residents who wanted to stand around counting the hundreds of dead fish. The last thing he wanted to do was take the boat to pick up Jessica, but he'd promised Mike he'd help her. Mike stressed the need for him to be sensitive since she was going through a tough time. He didn't get the specifics, but he figured making the woman mad wasn't what Mike had in mind. "Fine." He'd already taken the patrol boat out when some other men from the EPA asked for help collecting underwater soil samples for testing.

Jessica was beyond irritated now. It was four in the afternoon, and she couldn't reach Mike's friend, Seth. Mike programmed the number into her phone, but it wasn't doing any good. The young ferry attendant, who looked as young as twelve but was probably older, said the ferry was having engine problems. It had broken down before, but usually repairs didn't take long. That information didn't help Jess, and she was beginning to feel she'd made a huge mistake. Perhaps visiting a remote island on a broken-down ferry in need of replacement wasn't the best idea after all. She'd been on the road since five a.m. and was tired and hungry. She'd wait a few more minutes for Mike's friend, and then she'd look for the nearest hotel. If

Mike and Maria hadn't been so wonderful and generous, she'd be tempted to call and tell them what a bad idea this was. But they'd gone out of their way for her, and she didn't want to disappoint or worry them.

At least the ride up to the U.P. had helped. It was good to have hours of peace and quiet, where she could focus on her thoughts and feelings. Normally the long hours of her high-paced job kept her mind off anything non-medical. Perhaps that's why she'd never really examined her true feelings about Greg. She was surprised when she'd reached the Zilwaukee Bridge, and tears were finally flowing. But they weren't tears from heartbreak. She'd been missing her parents and wondering what life would've been like had they not been taken so soon. Maybe her mother would've seen what was lacking in her relationship and given some solid advice. Janie had been the only person in her life until she met Greg, and he'd filled a certain emptiness she had. But that didn't mean it was love. Now she wanted to stand up and face her life. Face her fears and insecurities and find what would truly make her happy. There had to be more to life than just working sixty hours a week, going to dinner with Greg, and reading medical journals. There must be things she was missing out on, and love had to be more than just 'comfort.'

A car door slammed, and she quickly looked up to see a large black pickup with snowmobiles in the truck bed. Two men in full snowmobile gear got out of the truck and began walking to the ferry station. She thought about rolling her window down and telling them they'd be waiting awhile, but they were laughing and already headed to the teller window.

A strange feeling settled over her, as she thought about her life with Greg. How many times had she suggested they try snow activities to embrace the long, monotonous winters? Each time she'd suggested snowshoeing, snowmobiling, or even sledding, Greg would remind her of the dangers involved with each activity. "Doctors can't afford injuries like normal civilians can," he'd say. She remembered laughing, thinking it was funny the way he didn't consider himself a "normal civilian," just because he was a doctor. Now, watching the men walk back to their truck, she didn't find Greg's comment very funny.

A sudden thud against her window made her jump. All she could see was a thick black jacket, and a man's gloved hand tapping on the glass. Her heart raced from the surprise interruption. The man leaned down and stared at her through the glass.

"Are you Doctor Jessica Bennett?"

For a moment she just stared, before remembering the two snowmobilers standing by the tailgate of their truck. If there was trouble, she wasn't alone. She rolled her window down a crack, feeling a gust of cold wind across her face. "Yes."

"I'm Mike's friend, Seth."

"Oh." Part of her was relieved it wasn't some stranger approaching her, and another part was instantly annoyed. "Is there something wrong with your cell phone?" Why hadn't he called her back to let her know he was on his way? She opened her door and stood, expecting to confront him face to face. Except that when she stood, she was staring at his chest. She had to look up to meet his eyes. "Did you get my messages?"

"Yup, all three."

She was immediately intimidated by his size, but his body made an effective shield from the wind. "I was about to leave because I hadn't heard back." His dark, glowering eyes made her voice softer than she wanted it to be.

"I've got my boat over there." Seth pointed to her left, where he'd tied the patrol boat to the dock. He needed to get it back to the slip, and he needed something in his stomach besides coffee. "I'll grab your bags." He stepped around to peer in the back seat. "Is this all there is?"

"Yes." She watched as he opened the back door, pulling her two large suitcases out as if they were filled with helium. She was staring at him with her mouth slightly agape, before she caught herself and quickly reached for her cell phone charger, purse, and laptop bag on the front seat.

"I can take that as well," Seth offered and held his hand out.

Jessica recalled Mike lugging one of her suitcases with both hands and heaving it into the backseat with an audible grunt. His two teen boys both carried the second suitcase together, each holding an end as if it contained lead weights. She stared down at Seth's one hand that held both handles, with the thickness of the one suitcase overlapping the other. Obviously, the large bulk of his body wasn't just from his puffy black winter coat. "I've got this," she managed, watching in awe as he turned to walk toward the boat.

"Don't forget to lock your doors," he said over his shoulder casually. He walked quickly to the wooden dock, and then reached his hand out to help her board the boat. The wind was blowing her long hair, and a golden strand swept across her eyes, blocking her vision. "Do you own a hat?" he asked, offering his hand. She didn't see it or the large step onto the boat. He quickly grabbed her arm to keep her upright if she slipped.

"Oh," Jessica felt clumsy, trying to move her hair from her face with already-numb fingers. "Thank you." She stood on the open bow, glancing out at the rough, dark water. "How far is the island?" Apprehension filled her cold body, as she wondered what sane person would want to be on a boat in the freezing wind with large, angry waves.

"It's only a fifteen-minute ride. You're not dressed for this, so sit below. I'll turn the heat on for you. You'll need to hold on, the waves are kicking today."

She nodded and gladly walked the three steps down into the small cabin. One long bench behind a table stretched under a glass window, and a small sink and oak cabinet were beside a door she assumed was the bathroom. She heard Seth yell, "Hang on!" as the engine revved.

The water splashed across the glass, blurring her view of the lake. She held onto the small wooden table, which was securely fastened to the floor. It was the only thing that kept her from bouncing off the leather bench. Her red North Face Jacket kept her upper body warm, but she wished she'd taken the time to unpack her gloves and hat from the largest suitcase. Her phone vibrated in her pocket, and she quickly took it out. Just another text message from Greg:

Mike's cabin? Running away is not the answer! Call me back... please.

She sighed, putting the phone back. Janie obviously told him where she was going, and he wouldn't stop trying to call her. She wasn't interested in what he had to say. Maybe he was angry she'd moved out while he was at work. She honestly didn't care. She couldn't deal with his emotional confusion. The boat bounced again, pushing her into the table. She heard Seth yell, "Just hang on! We're almost there."

Seth Johnson wasn't what she'd expected. She tried to recall what Maria and her girls had said about him. She found a few days' worth of stubble on a man attractive. Seth's rugged appearance fit with his deep voice and rough attitude. He had the kind of face that made you take a second and third look. Perhaps with some improved manners, he might be handsome. He hadn't bothered to explain why he didn't return her calls, and he was nowhere near apologetic. His responses were short and clipped, as if he was annoyed. And if she had to guess, she'd say his full lips were permanently curved downward to reflect his perpetual bad mood.

The engine shut off, and Jessica rose to stand, feeling unsteady on her feet. She was ready to leave the boat and find a restaurant. The sky was darker when she exited the cabin. Seth was tying off the boat. Gray clouds swallowed whatever was left of the afternoon sun. A stench rose from the water, but that's not what made her gasp. "Why are there so many?" For some reason what first came to her mind was the expensive Fish Farm Restaurant Greg used to take her to. They served the most incredible pecan-encrusted perch for fifty dollars. Good fish was expensive, and somewhat hard to find. The smell here was strong and repugnant, but what disturbed her most were the white, lifeless eyes of the dead fish bobbing in the waves.

"The waves are rolling north, pushing all the fish here. The mainland and other islands are also covered with them." Seth carried her bags to the dock, then turned to help her. "Watch that board, this dock needs repairing." He noticed she'd tied her hair into a knot, and now only a few stray strands blew over her face.

"Have you ever seen anything like this before?" She followed him to his truck. Of course, he owned a black diesel F150. He was a big guy, and nothing would suit him better than a big, manly rig. He opened the passenger door for her before setting her luggage in the back seat.

He climbed in and turned the key. "There have been incidents where hundreds of dead fish washed up on lakeshores and rivers. Scientists believe lack of oxygen in the water causes the fish to die. This is totally different though. There are too many dead birds and turtles."

She waited for him to elaborate, but he instead began to drive. "So, how is this different? What do you think it is?"

He gave her a look that made her feel he wasn't interested in conversation.

"The EPA was here this morning removing the bodies of turtles and seagulls. So, it can't be lack of water oxygen, as that wouldn't kill the birds." Seth turned the heat up full blast, aiming the vents toward her. "There's clearly something more going on, but I didn't get a lot of answers today."

"Mike told me to only drink bottled water, and my sister mentioned seeing the fish on the news." Her phone vibrated in her pocket, and she jumped a little, feeling startled. She didn't need to look to know it was another text from Greg. "It's scary." She studied Seth's profile. "The water must be contaminated."

"I'm sure they'll discover some spill or environmental hazard." Seth hated pollution, and just thinking about it made him edgy and irritable.

The narrow road was lined with pine trees, reminding her of the drive up. Northern Michigan was rich with national forests, and Chicory Island appeared one solid wilderness with a two-lane road winding through it. Her stomach made a loud, embarrassing sound. She felt her cheeks flush as she caught Seth's slow grin.

"Sounds like your stomach might be as empty as mine. How would you like to stop for food before I take you to Mike's cabin?"

"I'd love that." Her phone vibrated again, and this time she covered her pocket with her hand, as if that would make it stop.

"It's okay if you want to answer your phone. I'm not one of those people who thinks it's rude. Phones seem to be a part of the human body these days." Like an extension of the hand that gives your fingers something to do, he thought. There were dozens of people on the beach texting and taking pictures. Chicory Island managed to get decent reception, thanks to the new cell towers that went up a few years ago. Most of the locals left for the winter, but there were a handful of teens whose parents ran little mom and pop shops in town. They catered to the snowmobilers and other winter enthusiasts, and this was no doubt the most excitement those teens had seen in years.

"I don't need to answer it."

They drove on in silence, and she caught herself glancing at him too much. It was hard not to. He was powerful and intimidating, yet she decided that his strong bone structure, smooth skin, and thick arched eyebrows did in fact make him quite attractive. If he wasn't Mike's friend, she might feel leerier of him. She assumed he was around her age. It was hard to tell from his five o'clock shadow. "For some reason I thought everyone on the island would be over sixty. I assumed only older retired people lived here."

"Your assumption was right. Most of the town is well over fifty and retired. But I'm the sheriff, and my deputy is even younger than me." He got the feeling she was fishing for his age. "How old do you think I am?"

"Oh no, I don't want to guess. I'm terrible at guessing." Mike didn't tell her Seth was the sheriff. She tried to remember if Maria said anything, but she'd been distracted with her worry over Janie.

"I'm thirty-four." He looked her up and down. "I expected

you to be older too."

"I'm thirty-two. I didn't realize you were the sheriff." She leaned forward to see if she could see a uniform. He caught her looking and moved one side of his jacket to reveal the gold star pinned to his sheriff's jacket.

He was surprised she came right out with her age. Most women didn't. He chose not to comment on it. "I wear my winter coat over my uniform jacket, because it's not warm enough alone when I'm outside all day." He also didn't keep siren lights on his truck, but he didn't feel the need to explain further. He slowed to a stop at a three-way intersection and glanced at the desolate road. "There's very little traffic here. Mike's cabin is straight ahead on Corpse Road." He turned right. "I'm going to show you the town before daylight's completely gone. Mike said you can drive his car, but if we get the big snow that's forecast, you're going to want to stay put."

So that explained the snowmobilers. "Do a lot of people ride sleds here?"

"Yes. The island is known for its fishing and the forest trails are great for ATV's and sleds. That's why I'm worried. We can't afford to lose our tourists. The perch are schooling fish and spend their time in deep water. For them to be affected like this…" He pinched the bridge between his eyes. His day was catching up to him. "There's something seriously wrong." He saw the concern on her face and thought scaring her maybe wasn't the best idea. "But they'll figure it out, and I'm sure it'll be okay. There were enough federal agents here today, and they seem to be on top of things. Mike tells me you're staying till after Christmas."

"Yes."

He pulled up to a gray brick building with "Al's Diner" painted on it. It looked like it could've been a small factory from the Industrial Revolution that somehow got dumped in the middle of a forest. With its square shape and seven massive windows overlooking a narrow stream, it looked more like a picture from a history book than a restaurant.

Jessica followed Seth inside as he opened the door for her. The interior had exposed brick, high ceilings, and a rustic appeal that made the restaurant a popular tourist attraction. It was also the only restaurant open late on weekdays.

"Wow. This looks amazing." She moved aside as Seth muttered something to the hostess. "What was this place?" She assumed it wasn't always a restaurant.

"Al built this himself. It's always been a restaurant though obviously you wouldn't think that." Seth noticed how her face lit up. It was the first time he'd seen her smile, and for some reason it seemed tremendous, changing her face from beautiful to stunning. "They make the best burgers."

The aroma from the crackling fire burning in the large stone fireplace filled the open room. While the restaurant was clearly able to accommodate large numbers of people, only three tables were full. Two had elderly couples and one was a family with a small child. "I'm so hungry. A burger sounds fabulous." Jessica took in the entire room, feeling like she'd truly just arrived on vacation. The enthusiasm of being somewhere new was instantly lifting her spirits.

Chapter 7

"You know, you're not at all what I expected." Seth sat back in his chair, placing his napkin over his cleared plate. They'd each just enjoyed a giant hamburger and fries. Conversation had been simple and light, both of them aware hunger needed to be satisfied before any real communication.

Both Jessica and Seth turned to the young child running toward their table with a giant grin on his chubby face. Seth rose from his seat as the boy practically dove into his legs. Laughing, Seth picked up the blonde-haired boy, tossing him gently in the air and then catching him. "Where's your dad, Zack?" Seth asked, smiling as the kid giggled.

"He's in the kitchen making *hummbiggers*. I want to go fishing!" Zack replied in a sweet, enthusiastic tone.

Jessica figured the boy couldn't be older than four, and he was obviously very fond of Seth. She listened in amazement as Seth's voice assumed a gentle, friendlier tone. His smile was amazing, with straight white teeth and dimples that seemed to completely transform him.

"Tell your dad that next time I want more pickles on my *humbigger*," Seth told the boy.

"No!" Zack giggled. "I'm going to eat all the pickles, Sheriff!"

Seth tipped the kid back and then grabbed him by his feet so he could hang him upside down.

The boy had the most charming giggle. "Oh no you're not," Seth laughed. "I'm not going to let you go."

Laughing and trying to reach for Seth's arm, Zack yelled out, "Okay, okay, you can have pickles, but you have to take me fishing!"

Zack ran off to the kitchen, and Seth sat back down. "Zack's a cool kid. His dad owns the restaurant. He's got an older brother named Eric. Sometimes I take the boys fishing for a break from the restaurant. They spend a lot of time here."

"That's nice of you," Jessica replied, noticing the sincerity in his smile. He was obviously very good with children, which was surprising, given his tough appearance. "You know… you're not at all what I expected either."

He watched her lean back slowly in her chair, placing a hand over her belly. She wore a white V-neck sweater and jeans. Her fingers were slender like the rest of her, and she wore no nail polish or rings. "What did you expect?"

"I don't know. Someone older maybe."

"For some reason I pictured you to look like Mike's mom."

Jessica laughed. It was nice the way he could soften his hard expression, while his voice sounded less forced and more congenial. "Mike's mom?" Now that she had a full stomach, she could easily slip into a food coma. She glanced down at her watch. It was six-thirty and already the December sun was gone.

"Yeah. She's the only female doctor I know who has that look about her, like she belongs in a white lab coat with a stethoscope around her neck." He caught her glancing at the time and assumed she was eager to get settled.

"Did you picture me with curly white hair?"

"I did."

She chuckled softly, then waited while the waitress cleared the table and said goodbye. Seth stood and thanked the waitress, patting her on the back. It was obvious he knew her well. Jessica hadn't expected to leave just yet, but Seth reached for her coat. "Don't we have to pay the bill?"

"I've taken care of it."

"Oh…" she glanced around the empty restaurant. "Well, I'd

like to pay for my dinner." She slipped her arms through the jacket he held for her and felt a small flutter when he stared at her a moment, his lips drawn in a hard line.

"No. You're all set." He walked toward the door.

"Okay, so that's not open for discussion," she whispered with a slight smile. She quickened her stride, catching up to him. "Thank you, Seth. That was nice of you."

He gave a slight nod while holding the door for her. The wind had died down, and thick large snowflakes slowly swirled and danced in the air. The forest was utterly silent, and when Jessica tipped her head back, she admired the layers of pink and lavender stretched clouds. She took a long deep breath, loving how the air held a distinct winter smell, with a touch of pine. "This is wonderful." Now it was hard to believe she'd spent five years never going anywhere or doing anything like this. Greg had plenty of money and not an ounce of desire to spend it vacationing.

As she climbed in the truck and fastened her seatbelt, she realized she was eager to see Mike's cabin and fall asleep. Because the sooner she slept, the sooner morning would come, and she could then explore. "Is there a place to rent snowmobiles here?" she asked Seth.

"Not on the island, but Mike has sleds in his garage."

"Oh." Of course, Mike would have sleds for his family. She knew he'd be fine with her riding one, as long as someone was with her. "Would you mind showing me how to ride some time?"

Seth noted the excitement that once again lit her face. "Sure. I know all the trails on this island. We'll hit the grocery store too. You'll need to stock the fridge."

Jessica's phone vibrated again in her pocket, and again she jumped slightly. She should turn the phone off, because the darn vibration would startle her just as her tension was rolling away. She frowned at her phone that showed six texts from Greg. For the first time in many years, she wasn't on call. There was no reason to keep her phone on. She wouldn't even be receiving patient notifications from the hospital. So, for the first time in her life, she turned her phone off.

"Mind if I ask who you're dodging?" Seth studied her as she exhaled an apparent sigh of relief after turning her phone off. "I noticed you jump every time that goes off."

"What?" She glanced at him quickly before staring at her phone again. Should she leave it on? What if there was an emergency and Janie was in trouble? "I need to let it go. It's not important." Why was turning off her phone so difficult? It was unnerving and felt wrong. "I—"

He slammed on his brakes, and his arm instinctively shot out across Jessica's chest.

The seat belt tightened across her shoulder and waist, as she grabbed the arm that was suddenly in front of her. A pack of dark gray and black dog-like animals ran in front of the truck. A few loud yelps, snarls with fangs, and yellow eyes staring at her briefly before disappearing quickly into the thick trees. "Were those wolves?" She could hardly believe what she'd just seen.

"Yup." Seth's eyebrows pulled together in concern. "Are you okay?"

"Yes, I'm fine." Her hands were still securely gripping his arm. "That was close."

"I've never had that happen before. With deer it's common, but never wolves. They live on the island, but they keep their distance." He slowly pulled his arm back and squeezed his hand around the steering wheel. "I'd feel horrible if I hit one." He drove a little slower the rest of the way to Mike's cabin. "We're supposed to get about two inches of snow tonight, with a storm coming sometime tomorrow. Roads will be bad." He glanced at her again as she let out a slow, deep breath. He suddenly had a hundred questions he wanted to ask, but it wasn't his business. He'd call Mike and tell him what a bad idea it was to send Jessica up here with snowstorms coming, and whatever strange things were happening with the Lake. He had enough on his plate and didn't want to worry about her. And yet, now he wanted to know what her story was.

The cabin was spectacular, and decorated with the same warm, welcoming feel that Mike's house had. It was clearly Maria's touch, and if Jessica ever got her own home, she'd ask Maria to help decorate it. The open floor plan centered on a large kitchen, which allowed her to see from room to room. The vaulted ceiling with detailed layers of crown molding seemed to compliment the thick rustic log walls. The wrought-iron spiral staircase added incredible charm to the loft above, which held three bedrooms.

"This is amazing." She felt a little of her trepidation dissolve.

Seth watched the smile light up her entire face. "Yeah, it's nice, but did you expect anything less from Maria? I've had a crush on that woman for years."

Jessica laughed. "Does Mike know?"

"Of course. I'm still single in case she decides to get rid of him."

"You know you'll be waiting forever. I'm not even sure death could separate those two."

"Yeah, they're kind of sickening, aren't they?" Seth was envious of any man with a relationship as good as Mike's. "I was married once, and boy, was that a disaster." He mumbled the last sentence as he tossed a large log into the fireplace.

Jessica heard the remark, then instantly thought of Greg and what a disaster their marriage would have been. Her eyes roamed over Seth as he bent over the fireplace. His jacket lifted, revealing a gun holstered on his side. The fire began to pop and crackle from the damp wood. "I love this place. I have a crush on Maria too," she joked, admiring the room. She felt more tension drain from her. She plopped down on the red plaid sofa, just close enough to feel the heat from the fire. An impressive built-in bookshelf filled the wall opposite the French doors, which led to the two-story deck that wrapped around the house.

The fire was burning brightly, and as he turned to study her, he decided he wouldn't pry into her personal life. He wanted to ask why she was here alone, but he'd ask Mike instead. He caught her yawning, placing her hand over her mouth. "I'll head out now. Let you get some rest."

"Okay."

"I only live a few miles away. So don't hesitate to call if you need help." For some reason he didn't like the thought of her being alone.

"Okay, I'm already familiar with your voicemail." She said it teasingly, but couldn't resist the little jab.

He liked her humor. "Next time you call, I'll pick up." He glanced at the fireplace. "You can let this fire burn down. I've got the temp set at seventy for you, so…" He started to walk to the door as she stood up.

"Thanks for picking me up today and taking me to dinner. Thanks for everything."

He paused at the door. "I'll come get you tomorrow morning and take you to the market. Mike's got a few staples here, but the refrigerator's empty. You'll need to fill it before the storm hits."

"Okay. Thank you."

Once she shut the door, she leaned against it and studied the room. Seth had carried her bags upstairs. She wasn't sure what to think of him, other than that she'd had a hard time not staring at him. He'd sounded a bit abrupt at times, and wasn't overly talkative, and yet he'd also done some very nice things for her. She closed her eyes and imagined Greg for a moment. He'd been texting her all day. Was the silent treatment the best approach? What more could she say to him? Her thoughts were exhausting. Tomorrow she'd sleep in for the first time in forever. Climbing the stairs, she could hardly wait to get in bed. But first, she would call Mike and Maria, as she'd promised to when she was safely settled in. She'd find out a few details about Seth, the Chicory Island Sheriff.

She took her phone from her pocket, pressing the power button. The phone lit up with a picture of Greg and her as her background screen. But when she saw it, she thought of Greg and Janie together at the hospital, and how he lovingly caressed her sister's hand. And Janie's voice also came back to her: 'He's everything to me.'

As she changed her background screen to a picture of a sunset, she realized she felt no pain at seeing Greg's face vanish from her screen. She paused a moment waiting for a flicker of heartache to come, but instead she felt relief. She thought about how drastically her life had changed in a matter of days. The fire crackled, breaking the absolute silence. For a moment she just leaned against the stair railing, the flicker of glowing firelight heat at her back. With her medical training, she was extremely knowledgeable about human emotions and behavior. She understood what she should be feeling, but it simply wasn't there. Somehow, the weight of her situation was not crushing her… at least not yet.

Chapter 8

Malek's father became a recluse years ago. The old man refused to leave his home in Santa Fe. As much as Malek disliked boarding planes just to cater to his father's eccentricities, he needed his signature for the final merger. Soon his father, Laurence Edgar Malek, would be signing over his legacy to his son. Steven Malek would receive full Power of Attorney, along with complete access to the wealth of his ailing father.

When the housekeeper opened the door, Malek didn't bother with pleasantries. "Where is he?" He asked the young woman impatiently.

"The patio."

The cigar Malek took from his portable humidor consisted of 19-year-old tobacco, soaked in a $3,000 bottle of Louis XIII de Remy Martin cognac. "Father, you're looking well." Malek barely glanced at his dad before taking the seat beside him and holding the cigar out to his father.

Laurence took the cigar from his son, a look of contempt crossing his wrinkled features. "Have you taken care of all the problems?"

Right down to business as usual, Malek thought. "I have." The lie came easy, because he had no doubt that soon everything would be exactly as it should. He pulled some papers from his briefcase. "I have the final merger. We have now monopolized the entire bottled water industry."

"Don't look so smug."

Malek *was* smug. His father had no idea the magnitude of what he'd created. The sheer brilliance of his idea, his plan that had not only taken root, but was working better than he'd imagined. This wasn't just about money, or greed. This was about power and proving to his father that he was ten times more brilliant, creative, and competent. His father had once called him a failure, a worthless child who'd never achieve anything great in life. Well, he'd surpassed greatness. He'd impacted the world and created a new life form that wouldn't exist if not for him. After all, he was the one who found Mark Williams and coaxed him into doing what was needed.

He leaned back, refusing to drop the smug smile he'd earned with every genius bone in his body. He watched his decrepit father's hands shake as he tried to light his cigar. "Here." He took the lighter from his father and pressed the button. He noticed the weight loss. His father was smaller, thinner in the face, with an almost skeletal appearance. "When the world turns to safe drinking water, IM H2O is what they'll turn to."

It wasn't just pride Laurence heard in his son's voice, but steel arrogance. He smiled at the younger version of himself in the neatly tailored suit. It was his son who took his small Irish Mountain Water (IMH2O) and built it into a multi-million-dollar corporation, but the pride he felt was in himself. It was after all his own teaching and discipline that shaped his son into the man Laurence expected him to be. "The media is just now starting to dramatize the dead fish. Within days the news has created widespread fear. My housekeeper said her family in Ohio has already begun to stockpile bottled water. I'm enjoying watching our stocks skyrocket."

Soon Malek would be the wealthiest man in the world. As long as no one feared drinking tap water, the demand for "pure" bottled water was limited. "Soon no one will trust tap water. All the small, bottled water companies sourced from municipal drinking water will go out of business. The rest belong to me." He glanced at his father's sunken eyes. "I mean us." The organism was released a month ago, and already the affects were becoming catastrophic.

Laurence took a long pull on his cigar, choking as some of the smoke accidently filled his lungs. It was hard to resist the urge to inhale, as the taste filled his mouth. He brushed his son's hand away as he cleared his throat. "Tell me about the organism." He was fascinated by it.

Between the pounding on the door and the sunlight filling the room, Jessica woke, forcing an eye open to view her watch. She was shocked to see it was eleven o'clock. The curtains were open, revealing a sparkling layer of snow that'd fallen through the night. There was more pounding, and she could imagine Seth getting ready to break the door down. "Hang on," she muttered, walking over to let him in.

"I've called you three times this morning." Seth brushed past her into the house as she opened the door. "I was getting worried." His cop eyes quickly scanned the house. The cushions were hanging almost off the couch, throw pillows on the floor, and one pillow scrunched where her head must have lain. Cookbooks were stacked on the coffee table with one open and a pen and paper beside it. Her laptop was open, probably in sleep mode. The TV was on CNN, but muted. Finally, his eyes settled on her. Her long blond hair was tossed, not a stitch of makeup on her almond shaped eyes, and her face was sleep flushed.

"My phone's plugged-in upstairs. I came down here in the middle of the night and finally fell asleep on the couch." She noticed the brown paper bag he held and the paper coffee cup with a brown plastic lid. "Is that for me?" She ignored his frown and took the cup. "God bless you!" She immediately took the lid off to view the coffee. "It's got cream in it? How did you know I like cream?" She took a sip.

He knew how she took her coffee because he'd called Mike and asked him. He'd gotten enough information on Jessica to satisfy any would-be stalker. And what he hadn't liked learning was that she'd just had her heart broken. He'd asked Mike if there was any chance Jessica could be suicidal like her sister. Mike assured him Jessica was strong and nothing like her twin. But everything that Mike told him just made him more concerned. He thought it was a terrible idea for her to be alone. He hadn't expected to find her in— "are those pajamas?" The very short pink shorts and matching tank top were decorated with, "Is that Tinker Bell?" He ran a hand through his hair.

"I haven't slept this late in years," she laughed. She liked his hair. Yesterday he'd worn a hat the entire time. She assumed his hair was short, but it was long enough to run fingers through, and the color matched his dark brown eyebrows. He looked more like a sheriff today. His belt held a radio, his gun, handcuffs, and a small flashlight. He wore jeans, but his brown button-down shirt had a sheriff patch and his badge. She glanced down at her pajamas, wondering if he had something against Tinker Bell. "What's wrong with my pajamas?"

He glanced away from her. "Did you have trouble sleeping?" He shook his head when she offered him a bagel from the bag. "No thanks, I already ate… been up for hours." He'd spent two of them on the phone drilling Mike.

"Salted bagels are my favorite." She broke off a piece and stuck it in her mouth.

"I know… I talked to Mike."

She glanced up at him in surprise. "Oh?" She felt her cheeks warm. "What did he tell you?"

"Enough. You couldn't sleep?"

She took another sip of her coffee, before sitting on the couch. "No. I felt tired, but when I laid down my mind wouldn't shut off." She glanced at him with a wide smile. "Did you know Mike's son has a Pac-Man machine in his bedroom? I'd never played it before, but last night I got to level 5. And Maria has these cookbooks with pictures, and I've found about a hundred recipes I can't wait to try. And Greg called me last night, and I got so worked up I could practically feel my brain's left hemisphere stimulate as my arterial tension and testosterone increased, making my autonomous nervous system go nuts."

"O… kay…" Seth sat on the edge of the coffee table watching her closely. "So, you're slightly sleep deprived, maybe a little slap-happy, and I can't take you to the grocery store dressed like that. I'll come back in an hour and get you."

"No!" Jessica stood up. "I'll be ready in five minutes. Please just give me five minutes." She ran up the stairs. She was wide awake now and eager to start the day.

Chicory Town was on the east side of the island, nestled between plush forest and scenic rocky shoreline. Viewing the quaint little town in winter had to be an entirely different experience than in the summer. Jessica could imagine the tourists walking along the cobblestone sidewalk, eating ice cream, and browsing the few shops that displayed souvenirs and antiques. The brown brick buildings with wooden roof peaks gave it an old, historic feel.

There was an ice cream parlor, Chester's Post Office, the Popcorn Theatre Express, Katie's' Card Shop, and even a Starbucks.

"How do these little businesses survive during the winter?" Jessica noticed very few cars, and only one or two pedestrians.

Seth slowed the truck as he turned the corner. "Most of the businesses are run by third-generation retirees. The stores are paid for, and the summer tourism profits usually cover the winter months. Since there isn't much to do in the winter, most locals take in a weekly show. The restaurants survive the same way all the B&B's and cottage rentals do." Seth pulled his truck into the parking lot and cut the engine. "The snowmobilers and cross-country skiers show up to eat, party and play in the snow. It keeps us busy."

The grocery store definitely fell under "mom and pop" heading, and appeared as if it was opened in the 1800's. The shelves were old wood planks that matched the dated wood floor. The place was no bigger than the historic schoolhouse Seth pointed out on the way, but luckily it sold all the ingredients on Jessica's list.

She was pleasantly surprised at how fresh and inexpensive their poultry selection was. However, having seen the dead fish on the coast, she avoided the seafood section altogether. She reviewed her list. She'd filled one half of the page with the recipe ingredients she'd collected from Maria's book, and the other half of the page with the comfort food she decided she wanted. Greg was a health nut, never keeping any form of junk food in his house.

"Are you ready?" Seth asked, noticing her shopping cart, wondering if she was secretly planning to live at Mike's forever.

"I just need ice cream." She glanced at the bag of potato chips and Doritos she'd just set in her cart. "And maybe some Oreo's."

"They've got double-stuffed in the next aisle over. And the best ice cream here is the Caramel Swirl with nuts."

She met his eyes as a huge grin crossed her face. "Sounds perfect." She followed him down the aisle. As they walked, an elderly woman with thin white hair down to her chin was trying to reach for a box of cereal on the top shelf.

"Hey Claire, let me get that for you," Seth said, quickly reaching for the box and placing it in her cart. "Are you here alone?"

"Yes. Bill wasn't feeling well today. He worked too hard cleaning out the garage so we can park our cars in it for the winter." Claire was so much shorter than Seth, she leaned backward to stare up at him.

"Well, let me help you get your groceries to the car." He turned to Jessica. "Claire, I'd like you to meet Doctor Jessica Bennett. She's Mike Brown's partner, and she's staying on the island a couple weeks."

"It's very nice to meet you, Doctor Bennett," Claire said. The wrinkles around her eyes deepened as she smiled, and she had that serene sincerity that Jessica often appreciated in the elderly.

"Please, it's just Jessica." She never felt the need to be addressed as doctor, the way Greg did, unless she was at work.

"We just adore Mike. We look forward to when he and his kids spend the summers here. Such a nice family."

"Yes," Jessica agreed. After a few minutes of small talk, Seth showed Jessica where the ice cream was, and pointed out his favorites. She found herself watching Seth as he helped Claire place her purchases on the counter, then bagged them for her. When he spoke to Claire about her husband Bill, it was obvious he was friends with them, and genuinely cared about the condition of their health.

As they all walked outside together, Seth set stern eyes on her. "Go sit in my truck and stay warm. I'm going to help Claire, then I'll put your groceries away."

"Oh, that's nice, but I can put the bags in the car myself."

"No." Seth's voice held authority, as he handed her the truck keys, and took hold of her cart. "You stay warm. I'll do it."

She wasn't sure how to reply, because she didn't know yet if he was someone you could argue with. She nodded and left the cart with him.

As she sat in the truck, she couldn't help but watch him. He loaded all of Claire's bags in her car, then gave her a smile and a hug. There was a true tenderness in his actions, and sincere warmth in his eyes. It made her curious about him, and she wondered if perhaps his hard, stony exterior was simply a façade.

"I just got a call from the station," Seth said as he got in the truck. "If you don't mind, Mrs. Connor's house is on the way. I need to stop by there and see what's wrong. It's cold enough, the food will keep."

"That's totally fine. I hope everything's okay. Who is Mrs. Connor?" She wondered if Seth knew all the residents on the island personally.

"Linda Connor is a retired schoolteacher. She and her husband Jack moved here years ago. They have a handicapped son they care for." Seth's radio crackled, and Jessica sat quietly while he answered. He told the station dispatch to make sure the veterinarian and animal control were sent to the Connor's home. When he set his radio in his lap, he turned on the emergency strobe light attached magnetically to the truck's top. "Guess we need to hurry. Mrs. Connor claims someone shot five wolves and they're all dying in her backyard."

The roads were slick from the snow that continued falling since morning. Jessica gripped the roof handle nervously, glancing at the speedometer. His eyes were focused on the road, but that didn't ease the anxiety suddenly clenching her stomach. "Um… Seth."

He glanced at her quickly, then back at the speedometer. He eased off the gas a bit. "I don't mean to scare you. I just happen to love wolves."

"Who would have shot them?"

"No one." He kept his eyes on the road. "Doesn't make sense."

She was so focused on his eyes and the steel look on his face that she hadn't realized they were already pulling up to a small white house. The mailbox at the end of the driveway was a giant imitation bass fish. The mouth pulled down to open it. A snow blower was left in the half-cleared driveway.

"Listen, Jess. I need you to stay right here."

"Nope. Sorry." She was already getting out of the truck. The minute she opened the door, she could hear the cries and yelps echoing from the backyard. The sound made her stomach flip. She followed Seth around to the back of the house, grateful she'd worn her winter boots and gloves.

A short woman bundled up like an Olympic skier bolted from the back door. "Seth, it's awful! Something is hurting those poor dogs, and I don't have any idea what to do for them!"

Seth gave a curt nod before heading toward the pack, lying on their sides in the snow. Their cries of pain matched the glazed look in their eyes. It was heart-wrenching to see the animals in pain. "Get back, Jess."

"The Vet's off the island till after Christmas," Jack said, as he reached his hand out to shake Seth's. "I was snow-blowing the drive when Linda saw them walk into the yard and collapse. They just sorta' plopped down and haven't moved. When they started yelping and howling, we called the station." He swiped his hand across his face. "Christ, Seth, I think they're dying." His eyes moved to Jessica.

Seth tilted his head toward her. "This is Doctor Jessica Bennett." She said hello, accepting Jack's hand in greeting. Then she moved closer to the wolves. "Jess, don't. They could attack." He reached for her arm.

"They aren't going to attack, Seth. Look at them." She glanced up from the wolves to Seth. She was moved by the look of concern in his eyes. Not just for her, but real concern for the animals. "Let me take a look at them. I want to feel their sides." Some of the dogs were twitching and whimpering, while two had already closed their eyes and were lying still.

Seth moved in front of her. "I don't want that pretty face of yours too close to their teeth." He bent his knees down in the snow, gently setting his hand on the neck of the wolf. "Let me just see if he's going to cooperate first." He was ready to grab the dog if it tried to bite. It helped knowing Jack had his slug gun aimed and ready to shoot. "Easy now, boy." He rubbed the top of the wolf's head between the ears.

The wolf whimpered a pitiful sound as Jessica slowly knelt beside Seth, reaching her hands out to feel the coarse fur. "They're dying," she whispered, glancing at its eyes. She sunk her fingers down into the thick, cool fur and started at the wolf's back, gently feeling and rubbing. "Easy now…" she pushed the fur apart to look for wounds. "You can rule out gunshots. There's no blood or any visible flesh wounds, Seth." The animal flinched again, and Seth was ready to hold it down. "It's too weak now. Maybe they've been poisoned. Whatever's happening to them is internal." Her hands trailed down the forearms of the wolf. "Nothing feels out of place. I'd like to look at the flews."

"What?" Jack asked.

"The hanging part of the wolf's upper lips. I'd like to see what color the inside mouth is. There isn't any foam around the teeth, and I don't think this behavior is typical for rabies." She paused when Seth set his hand over hers. She looked up to see him watching her carefully. "It's okay."

"Try looking in this one's mouth," Jack said, pointing his gun at another lighter-colored gray and white wolf. "I think this one's already dead."

Jessica sighed, noting the still body, and realized that the one she was currently examining was also no longer breathing. "I don't know, Seth." She looked at him helplessly. "This is very strange."

Seth's sullen eyes swept over the other four wolves. It was silent now, except the wind that whipped, and seemed to echo their earlier cries. Or perhaps it was the sound of distant animal cries he was hearing. It would take a long time to get that sound out of his head.

"Animal control's here," Linda said, drawing everyone's attention to the side of the house.

"We'll know more after the autopsy." Seth stood, helping Jessica to her feet. As the men approached holding a cage, Seth drew in a long deep breath. "You're not going to need those cages."

"I've never seen anything like that," Linda said, leaning into her husband as he wrapped his arms around her.

Chapter 9

Jessica waited in the truck until Animal Control left, and Seth spoke with Linda and Jack briefly. When Seth climbed back in the truck, his shoulders slumped, as he rested his head against the steering wheel.

"I'm sorry." It was the only thing she could think to say. For a long moment he just stared at her.

"Did you also learn about animals in med school?"

"My dad was a veterinarian, and my mom was a nurse. I tried my hand at vet school, but decided I preferred working with humans more. I love animals, but I found their inability to speak frustrating. They can't tell you how they're feeling and what's wrong." She preferred conversations with her patients and liked the ability to solve human problems.

"Makes sense." He set his hand on top of hers for a quick moment. "Let's get you home."

Seth talked on his radio during the ride back to Mike's cabin. He gave some orders on the follow-up care of the wolves and stressed the need to have complete autopsies done on each wolf. From what Jessica could gather from the other end, it sounded like an environmentalist wanted to speak to Seth.

He'd taken in all her groceries except the few she insisted on carrying. She began putting away the milk and eggs. He pulled some produce out of the bags and handed it to her. Was he the type of man who insisted on doing chivalrous things all the time, or was he just being nice because Mike had probably lectured him?

"I'm planning to make a chicken pasta dish for dinner tonight."

She closed the refrigerator and found him staring at her again. "I'd like it if you could join me. You've been a huge help, and I'd like to say thanks with a nice dinner."

"You don't have to thank me, Jess. I'm happy to help."

She knew he was upset over the wolves. She was too. "I'd like it if you would come."

He moved closer to her. "What time?"

She swallowed. "What time works for you?"

He stepped a little closer. "Is seven too late?"

She shook her head.

"I'll see you then." His phone buzzed, and he reached in his pocket to answer it. He kept his eyes on her. "News travels fast here. What did you expect? Yeah, I asked Linda not to say anything, but—"

With her mouth suddenly dry, Jessica opened the refrigerator and reached for two bottled waters. She handed one to Seth, as he continued his conversation, and then took a seat on the bar stool. She peeled the label off her water bottle, needing to do something with her hands. She tore the letters, IM H2O. It occurred to her that she'd never noticed that IM H2O stood for Irish Mountain Water. She wondered if the water came from a spring in Ireland or if it was just glorified tap water. The fine print read "manufactured by IM Enterprises, in Northern Ireland." Perhaps she'd place a giant order and have it shipped to Mike's house.

"I have to go, Jess. I'll be back tonight."

The moment she showed him out, she picked up her cell phone. There were three more missed calls from Greg that she ignored. She paused a moment, waiting to see if the emotions she was lacking would finally come. She should be missing him. She should feel more heartbroken, more devastated. But then the sound of the wolves filled her mind, and she pictured Seth, and the way he called her Jess.

Chapter 10

The snow was falling in heavy sheets by the time Seth arrived at the station. A good four inches already covered the ground, and it was safe to say the big snowstorm everyone anxiously anticipated was finally making its winter welcome hoorah.

He found the normally quiet, diminutive brick building bustling with people. As the Sheriff in charge, he needed to focus on what the hell was going on with the island. As he put the truck in park, his phone rang again. All he heard was the word "dead body," as he entered the station full of teenagers, all talking and shouting over each other. Deputy Dean approached Seth with his serious, you're-not-going-to-like-this look. It wasn't a look Dean had very often, so Seth knew something major was up. He put his phone back in his pocket, as everyone approached him at once.

"A bunch of teens were hiking Old Man's Trail. When they got to the water, one of the girls found a dead body. The kids didn't touch it, but of course every kid has a picture of the body on their cell phones, and no doubt the news is spreading across all their social media."

Seth surveyed the kids. They all looked like they could pose for a winter GAP commercial, with an abundance of bright hats matching striped or solid-colored scarves, and thick colorful parkas. A few of the girls clung to their boyfriends as if a serial killer was on the loose and they feared for their lives. The sound of snowmobile engines rumbled sounded outside, and Seth shook his head as Connie walked up. Connie was the first female dispatch they'd hired since

Lou died from a heart attack two years ago. He'd been the dispatch ever since Seth took the Sheriff position. It took Seth awhile to get used to Connie's young, shy demeanor. He hadn't thought she was right for the job, but she'd proved herself good at handling people, and answering distress calls. She was already clearing out the station house with gentle words of reassurance to the kids.

"I've got a coroner from the mainland coming in on the eight o'clock ferry. And I've called all our volunteer firemen to help out tonight." Connie handed Seth a business card. "This guy, Shawn Sharconnon, asked me to call him if anything strange happens here. I think a dead body might count. I gave him a call."

Seth glanced at the name. The words "Environmental Protection Agency" and a phone number was the only other information on the card. It didn't look like the other cards he'd been given by the other EPA workers. He handed the card back to Connie. "This guy doesn't need to come here." He didn't want the island turning into media frenzy. People were already anxious and concerned over the dead fish. News of a dead body wouldn't help.

"He's already here," Connie replied. She looked down at the card and smiled. The only reason she'd called the guy was because she thought he was handsome, and he'd seemed to think she was very pretty. He'd complimented her a dozen times, and he'd made her laugh. He'd asked her if she liked playing pool, and for a moment she thought maybe he was going to ask her out. He was a few years older than her, but he appeared to have money. An attractive older man flirting with her gave her self-esteem a much-needed boost. He'd been interested in the dying fish, and specifically stated that if anything else dead washed up, he wanted to know. "The news says we can expect another foot by nightfall. The blizzard is coming," she told Seth, and then turned back to a few teens who were listening to her conversation.

Dean pulled his dark blue parka on over his uniform jacket. "We need to get to the body before the snow covers everything. I'm not sure we have enough time to wait for the M.E. I'll go attach the trailer."

Chris and Carl from the firehouse walked in, and Seth began giving them orders. He needed statements from the kids, and then he needed someone to wait at the ferry for the coroner. They would need to take snowmobiles on the trails, as there was already too much snow. For a brief moment he thought of Jessica again, and how she'd seemed excited to try out Mike's snowmobile. It was going to be a long day, and he'd be lucky if he even had time to see her for the dinner invite. He walked past a few kids who were commenting on how disgusting the dead man looked and made his way to Connie's desk. "Have you heard anything about the wolves yet?"

She shook her head as the phone rang. "No, but I've got reports of more dead animals. I put the notes on your desk." She answered the phone.

Jessica strolled around the kitchen getting familiar with where things were. It was a fully stocked kitchen, probably every amateur chef's dream. She couldn't know for sure since she'd never spent much time in Greg's kitchen. Greg preferred to eat out, and when they were too tired to leave the house, he'd order in. The extent of her cooking was usually a box meal with a three-step process.

Now she was eagerly preparing a meal with more than four ingredients. It was something she'd long wanted to do, and she hoped to impress Seth.

When the prep work was done, she needed to kill a little time so it would be fresh when he arrived. She also prepared the Pillsbury dinner rolls that would bake in the oven 15 minutes before dinner, so they'd be warm, and the house would smell wonderful. She missed the smell of home-cooked meals, which reminded her of when her mom was alive and often baked in the evening.

There was time for her to catch up on her emails and check in with Janie and Mike. She'd tell them about the wolves, and how seeing all the dead fish was disturbing. She hadn't been able to talk to Mike last night because he'd been asleep when she called. But Maria was unusually gossipy in giving plenty of details on Seth. She practically made him sound like a saint. Poor Seth married a woman he'd met in college. They'd moved to the island because Seth was offered the sheriff job. Apparently, his wife hated living on Chicory Island, and began cheating on him with some lawyer from the mainland. Seth tried to make it work, but she'd basically told him he wasn't wealthy or ambitious enough for her. Several times, Maria made a point of noting how Seth had treated his wife with total respect and loyalty to the end.

The television was muted, but when she glanced at the TV and saw a newscaster standing on a shore surrounded by dead fish, she turned the volume up. Then her phone rang, and she was going to ignore it until she saw it was Janie.

"Hello?" She could ignore Greg, but she didn't want to ignore her sister.

"This fish thing is crazy." Janie didn't need formalities with her. She was watching the news and freaking out. "They're not saying what it is. They're saying it's an organism of unknown origin. What does *that* mean?"

Jessica walked over to the couch and sat in front of the TV. She pressed mute so she could talk. "I guess it means they don't know where it came from. It's creepy."

"It's not just fish. Wildlife is being affected too because they're drinking the water."

"I know. You won't believe what happened today. Seth and I were heading home from the store when…"

"Who is Seth?"

Jessica smiled. "He's the sheriff on the island, who happens to be good friends with Mike and Maria. He picked me up from the ferry yesterday, and he took me to the grocery store today."

"Oh. What does he look like?"

There it was. The inevitable inquiry, and Jessica knew her sister would enjoy hearing this. "He's *tall!*" That was all she'd need to say to her sister. "He's like really tall, maybe six-four or six-five, and he's incredibly built."

"Single?"

"Yes, divorced, and Mike and Maria love him." Jessica leaned back on the couch. "But he's kind of intimidating. He's got this deep voice, and most of the time he looks angry or irritated." She found it fascinating the way his rough/tough demeanor could change and soften so drastically, as if flipping a switch. She thought about how intriguing his smile was, knowing he only used it sparingly.

"I knew you were never really in love with Greg. You're not even miserable over him, are you?"

Jessica sighed. What Janie did was wrong, and there was part of her that didn't want to let her sister off the hook that easily, even though she already had. But admitting Janie was right would give her the validation she clearly needed.

Janie instantly regretted her words. "I'm sorry. I shouldn't have said that." She felt uneasy with the sudden silence. "I guess I shouldn't assume you're fine. Are you? Do you miss him?"

What the hell. Lying was something that didn't come easy, but the truth did. "I keep waiting to feel sad that we're over. I keep thinking I should be more devastated, but you're right. I know you want to hear this, and truthfully, I don't like that I'm giving you this satisfaction, but I think you did me a favor." There… she admitted it. "Deep down, I guess I didn't really want to marry Greg. The truth is, I had tons of reservations that I was ignoring." And if it wasn't for Janie, maybe she would have kept ignoring those feelings, and made the biggest mistake of her life. "I do care for him. I think he has a lot of special qualities, but—"

"You're not really in love with him." Janie sounded relieved. "I never saw the passion and crazy love you're supposed to have." Janie knew Greg was in love with Jessica right from the beginning, but it wasn't that way for Jessica. "I think you preferred him more as a friend."

"That's kind of what Mike said too."

"Mike's a smart man. Look how happily married he is."

"It's going to be weird, though… seeing you with Greg. It feels strange."

"I know. I'm afraid he might always love you too, but I know he loves me. I can't worry about it, because I think we belong together."

Jessica closed her eyes. "Maybe you do."

"You were going to tell me about Seth. What happened today?"

And just like that, the subject was changed. Jessica wanted to tell Janie about the wolves, and about the island. She wanted to talk about how nicely decorated Mike's cabin was, and how she got to sleep in till eleven o'clock. Janie was always the person Jessica shared everything with. She was closer with her sister than anyone, even Greg. She couldn't stay upset with Janie, and the fact was, she wasn't.

Chapter 11

A foot of snow already blanketed the body. The tide had pushed it far enough onto the shore that only the victim's feet were now splashed with water. The beach was narrow there, the grass close to the lake, and underbrush grew heavy but now bore more bare branches. The victim's head was pushed against a log, and snow-covered seaweed draped over the left eye.

Snow whipped Seth's face as he carefully photographed the body. He had to shield the lens with his hands. There were strict protocols for handling scenes where bodies were found. Normally the body would stay put until the Medical Examiner arrived. But the blizzard shut down the ferry, and Seth didn't know when the M.E. would arrive. There were too many snowmobile tourists to leave the body unattended, and no way Seth or anyone could stay there to watch it. Seth had little experience with crime scenes but knew what steps to take, though securing a crime scene in the middle of a blizzard made the job far more difficult. The fact the victim had a clear bullet hole through his frozen shirt meant Seth needed to be extra careful in handling potential evidence. So, when Dean noticed what appeared to be a zip-lock bag sticking out of the man's jeans, Seth took a ton of pictures before carefully retrieving it.

"It's got paper in it." Seth held the bag at the corner, noticing no water had leaked inside. "Evidence." He handed the bag to Dean, who carefully sealed it inside another bag.

"There's too much snow coming down. We need to get going before we get stuck out here." Dean's boots were waterproof, but they were sinking in the wet sand as cold waves lapped his ankles. His gloves were soaked, and his fingers were going numb. He felt they had secured the scene as best they could.

Once they arrived at the station house, Seth carefully opened the evidence bag. Keeping his gloves on, he removed the papers. It wasn't proper procedure, but he'd seen some words that aroused his curiosity. There were six pages that would leave with the victim when the M.E. was able to take the body and evidence away. Most of the paperwork appeared to be chicken scratch, written in scribble. A couple pages had some detailed charts, and a few scientific equations with medical terms. Seth immediately thought of Jessica and glanced at the clock. It was six forty-five. He swore silently under his breath and walked over to Connie's desk.

"Connie, can you put some gloves on? I'd like you to copy these papers for me, but I need you to be really careful with them. Handle them with gloves and touch them only in the corner."

He pulled his cell out and swore again. His battery was dead, and he didn't have Jessica's number memorized. Without his contacts he had no one he could call. He didn't want to disappoint her, but handling the body was his first priority. He had to make sure someone was on guard at all times. He only had Connie, Dean, Chris, and Carl. Carl didn't count. He wasn't really an officer, just a volunteer firefighter who happened to be friends with Chris, making him an extra hand to help when needed. Chris was a retired officer who volunteered part-time. He and a few of the volunteer firefighters would normally help with lost snowmobilers or naive tourists whose cars might break down trying to find restaurants. The island usually ran smoothly with little trouble, so there wasn't a need for more than one Sheriff and a deputy. Connie was on the night shift, but he wasn't sure about leaving her in charge. He sighed as he glanced around the quiet station, noticing Dean vigorously rubbing his cold hands together, Connie like she was in a daze.

Jessica checked the clock and decided she was done waiting on Seth. Once again, he didn't have the decency to return her call. If he were going to be late or cancel, he could at least call to tell her. As she carefully poured the marinated chicken pasta into a container, she realized she was more disappointed over his not showing up than she was to find Greg banging her sister.

A knock sounded at the door and her pulse quickened. Okay, so he wasn't a complete no-show.

"Hi." Seth stepped inside and removed his shoes and coat. "I'm starving and it smells incredible in here."

"I just put it away."

Seth glanced at his watch. "I'm an hour late. My phone died." He left Connie in charge at the station and raced to the house in a crazy blizzard. He'd be lucky if he could get his truck back home. Halfway there, he realized he should've taken the snowmobile. "I can't stay long. I've got to babysit a dead body."

"What?" She followed him to the kitchen. "You found a dead body?"

"Some kids did." He saw the food in a container on the counter. "Can I heat this up?" He didn't wait for her answer and began putting the food on a plate. "Did you eat?"

"I did. You told me you'd answer your phone if I called you. When you didn't reply, I figured you couldn't be trusted." Frankly, she had expected to hear the words, "I'm sorry." But she was beginning to think those two words weren't part of his vocabulary.

"Well, my battery died. The cold kills it a lot faster." Seth took the plate from the microwave, and immediately began eating. "What's in this? It tastes amazing. Is it basil?"

Jessica nodded, pulling up the stool next to him. Dealing with a body was a pretty good excuse.

"Damn, this is good!"

When he gave a compliment, it seemed important. "I'm glad you like it. It has a ton of fresh basil in it." She gathered he liked basil as much as she did. "So how did the person die?" She wanted to hear more about the body.

"Looks like he was shot, and his body washed up on shore.

I won't know anything until the M.E. comes." Seth carried his dish to the sink and washed it. "I found some documents on the body. Normally I'd never show them to anyone because it's potential evidence. But I'm curious about this." He pulled the papers from his back pocket and unfolded them. "I was wondering if you knew how to read chicken-scratch?"

"Seth, I'm a doctor. We invented chicken-scratch."

He handed her the papers. "So can you tell me what these papers say?"

She took them from him, quietly looking them over. After a few long moments she looked up to find his eyes on her. "I can't understand some of the formulas here, but I think this is some kind of biological manipulation data."

"Huh. What makes you say that?"

She held up the paper and pointed to the sentence at the top of the page. "It says, 'biological manipulation data.'"

Seth smiled and leaned against the counter to watch her.

"I find this one sentence very disturbing." She focused again on the paper and began to read, "*The organism resembles a maggot, but some have grown larger in size. It's an invasive species, marine life. I'm starting to think it could live outside the water. Tests will begin shortly for life sustainability and duration. Organism attaches itself to living tissue, and then slowly eats its way through. Hard outer shell protects it. An accident of genetic coding, but very real.*"

"Jesus." Seth leaned over and took the paper from her hand. "It says that?" He was amazed she could read such sloppy cursive.

"Listen to this." She held up another sheet. "*This organism is unlike anything. Capable of eating all marine life, but growth is minimal. Should be immediately destroyed.*"

Seth pointed to an underlined sentence in the left corner of the page. "*Destroyer of Human Life*. This is the only thing I could read that caught my attention." He picked up another sheet that had a chart on it. "I have no idea what this is." He handed it to her.

"It's a standard hypothesis chart." She took a deep breath. "See here," she pointed to the chart. "He gives the data entry for each test he did on the different forms of Cyanobacteria and Phaeophyta."

"What the hell is that and how do you know how to pronounce it?"

She smiled. "It's different families of seaweed. Cyanobacteria is blue-green algae, and the other is brown algae. The person who wrote this was trying to see what the organism he calls 'the entity' will do." She trailed her finger along the chart. "These are his controlled variables, and these are the—"

"Jess, I was never good at science. Can you just tell me in layman's terms what it means?"

She continued to read the chart. "The hypothesis was to test whether the entity would feed on any living form of marine life." She paused studying the paper, and then quickly picked up the last sheet. "Seth, according to this, it eats everything and anything. He made reference to the Zebra Mussels that have taken over the Lakes. I'm wondering if this organism was designed to kill the Zebra Mussels."

"There's more."

Jessica flipped the paper over and continued to read. "It looks like he was trying to see what kills it." She mumbled the words, "sodium hypochlorite, antisepsis, bactericide, sporicide." She ran her hand along the sloppy words. "These are all things used to kill organisms. But…" she looked puzzled.

"What?"

"There's a formula here I don't recognize. I'm guessing maybe that's what killed it, because down here," she held the paper up for Seth to see. "He drew stars and exclamation marks by the formula. And this says, 'growth decline' and 'destroyed'." She dropped the paper on the table. "This seems really important. I wish I knew what it was."

"I'm impressed as hell." He met her eyes with a serious face. "I think you'll know more than anyone else who looks at this." The papers would need to be studied by the right kind of scientist.

"I really liked biology and chemistry in school. I thought about becoming a biologist before I entered med school." She was consciously aware of how his simple praise, stated without a trace of a smile or humor, made her feel really good. And since he was staring at her so intently, she forced her eyes back to the paper. "I can't make out this word. It starts with 'B' and the end of the word looks like 'ST.'" She wrinkled her nose trying to figure it out. "B…something… ST H2O breeding." The sentence was underlined three times, so she assumed it was something important. "I don't know."

Seth had an appreciation for smart people. In law enforcement he often came across people lacking common sense and basic intelligence. When he'd first met his wife, he found her ditzy behavior cute and endearing. He'd thought she maybe behaved that way to appear innocent and specious. But over time he grew tired of her silly ways and lack of sense. Seth walked to the refrigerator and pulled out a beer. "Want one?" When she shook her head, he popped the cap off, and downed half the bottle in one gulp.

Jessica folded the papers, feeling a bit uneasy about their content. "Do you think this could have anything to do with the dead fish?"

"I think it's possible. The original copies are with the body. When the forensic team takes it, they can investigate further. I'm putting my buddy Kyle in charge of the investigation. Mainland authorities will be able to do more. If there wasn't a raging blizzard right now, the body would already be headed to the mainland."

"This could be huge. If this is what's responsible for killing all the fish and the… oh my gosh, what about the wolves? Could they have eaten the fish?"

Seth watched how her eyes widened, and the way her soft lips parted. "It's possible the pack I almost hit was coming from the beach. They probably did eat the fish."

"And the next morning they were dead." Jessica glanced down at the papers again. "This is crazy."

"The guy protected these papers in a zip-lock bag and shoved them down his pants. My guess is he knew he was going in the water and wanted these papers to be safe." That was another reason Seth didn't wait to find out what the papers said. "What are you doing?"

"I'm hiding these. This is important evidence. I feel like it shouldn't even be sitting on the counter right now. I'm glad you made a copy." She walked over to the cookbook open on the counter and pulled out the roll of scotch tape she'd seen in the utensil drawer. She stuck one side of the tape to the papers and slipped them under the paper cover of the cookbook. If anyone picked the book up, the papers wouldn't fall out.

Seth laughed. "You watch a lot of movies, Jess?" He wanted to tell her it wasn't necessary to hide the papers, but she seemed so pleased with herself, he didn't bother. The original papers were safe at the station. He noticed her black pants. She'd changed her outfit from the earlier jeans and sweater to a pair of black pants and a white blouse.

"You don't seem very alarmed. Do you not think this is important? I think this is a big deal."

He took a step closer to her. "I think it's a big deal."

She leaned against the counter and looked up at him. "You do?"

He took a step closer to her. "I do."

She swallowed and held her breath, unable to read his stoic face.

"Thanks for dinner."

She blinked. "Are you leaving?"

"Yeah. It's coming down in sheets out there. I don't want my truck getting stuck, and I can't leave that body unattended." It wasn't right to leave Connie in charge. "You're a pretty damn good cook."

She followed him to the door and put her hands in her pockets while he put his boots back on.

He opened the door and looked back toward her. "Make sure you lock up behind me. Thanks again for dinner."

And just like that he was gone. Jessica once again leaned against the door and let out a long breath. "Hate to eat and run," she said quietly. She wasn't sure what she had expected, but she was learning that Seth was a man of few words.

Chapter 12

It felt like Deja vu when Jess again opened her eyes to pounding. "Hang on!" she yelled, as she stumbled half-asleep to the front door.

"You have to answer your phone when I call. I get worried." Seth walked in, and once again scanned the cabin. "Another sleepless night?" He could see she'd slept on the couch again. There were no cookbooks this time, but her laptop was still on, and a bed pillow was on the floor.

"Yes, I'm having trouble sleeping."

He looked her up and down. She was wearing baggy sweat-pants and a t-shirt with the words 'I DON'T NEED NO EDUCAS-HUN' on it. "Nice shirt."

"Thanks. My sister got it for me when I complained about med school being too much work. I'd reached a point of feeling overwhelmed and burnt out. She has a great sense of humor."

He handed her the travel-cup coffee he had brought for her and laughed when she gave him a look that said, thank you God! He enjoyed watching her hold the cup like it was the Holy Grail, and moan with that first sip. She clearly loved her coffee. "I'm going to the mainland today. The vet called, sounding stressed. He wants to talk to me about the dead wolves, but insists I have to be there in person."

"Really?" She set her coffee down, rubbing the sleep from her eyes.

"I'd like you to come."

"Really?"

He found her humorous. "Get dressed, Jess. I'll wait. Oh, and dress warm. We're taking the Sheriff boat instead of the ferry, and it's going to be freezing."

When Seth docked the boat at the ferry, he planned to use Jessica's Land Rover. Her four-wheel drive would handle well on the ice and snow, and since she'd parked at the Ferry station, it was convenient. It was heavily covered with snow but he cleaned it off as she sat in the passenger seat to keep warm. Seth insisted on driving and that was fine with her. He'd been on his phone all morning, and she was hoping the drive would give them a chance to talk. When her phone vibrated in her pocket, she glanced at the screen to see it was Greg calling. She was hesitant to take the call, but she'd texted Janie last night and had not heard back. There was always a fear that something could be wrong.

"What?" She refused to be friendly.

"I'm calling about Janie."

"What's wrong?" Fear instantly gripped her, and she couldn't hide the worry on her face when Seth entered the car shaking snow from his boots. "Is she okay?"

"She has the flu," Greg stated casually. "She's been up puking since last night. You must've given it to her."

Jessica leaned back feeling slightly relieved. "Are you taking care of her?"

"I'm doing what I can, but you know I have to work. It would be better if you were here."

So that's why he was calling. He'd use Janie being sick as a way to get her to come home. "I'm eight hours away. The roads are really bad so it would probably take twelve or more to get home, even if I wanted to… which I don't." She pressed her fingers over her eyes, absorbing her situation. "I'm saying the word home, but it just dawned on me I don't actually have a home. I have nowhere there to live."

"How long do you think you can stay there? Running away and hiding isn't doing any good. Your sister needs you."

She gave a fake chuckle. "Actually, being here is doing me a lot of good. I've got to go now." She wasn't going to continue a conversation with him now that Seth was driving. "Text me if there are any *real* problems. Janie will survive the flu just like I did. Just take care of her. It's your job now."

"Damn it, Jess. This whole situation is killing me. You can't tell me you don't miss me. You can't tell me you're not in love with me anymore."

That was Greg. So damn conceited. "Greg, do you even know how lucky you are that Janie is so in love with you? She loves you more than I ever could, and since she's great, and looks just like me, you should appreciate that. You need to accept this. Trust me, she *does* love you more. You made this situation what it is, so man up and do the right thing. Love her and take care of her. I've got to go. I'm being rude to my friend."

"Yeah, Janie told me you met some new guy. I guess this is your way of getting revenge."

Jessica rolled her eyes. "Goodbye." She pressed the end button. He had a way of really irritating her. It was probably a good thing because it only made her dislike him more. Any respect she had for him was slowly dissolving. And she was very much aware of the fact she wasn't yet missing him.

Seth looked at her briefly and wondered if he should keep quiet. Mike had told him about her messy and somewhat strange situation. He wasn't interested in getting to know a woman who would be leaving the island.

"I'm sorry." She glanced at Seth. "I guess Mike probably told you what's going on with me."

"Yeah, he did."

They drove in silence for a few minutes. He wasn't going to pry, and she didn't have a need to talk about it. She'd made peace with her sister, and that was all that mattered to her.

Her phone dinged, and she glanced down at the text from Greg:

I'm sorry. Please don't sleep with him just to get even with me.

Jessica groaned. "Gosh, he's so annoying. What in the world did I ever see in him?"

"You're not in love with him anymore?" *So much for not getting personal.*

Her Land Rover had four-wheel drive, and while the streets were plowed from yesterday's storm, they were still slick. Seth drove slower through spots where wind blew snow drifts on the road. She assumed they wouldn't be driving at all unless it was important. She turned to face him. "The first time Greg met my sister I remember noting how well they hit it off. I didn't think my sister was necessarily flirting with him, but there was some obvious chemistry. My sister laughed at all his jokes and seemed to admire everything about him. She saw things I didn't always see. It's hard to explain, but I knew Janie really liked him. I'd see the way she'd look at him, and I guess part of me knew I didn't look at him quite the same way."

"If you're comparing your feelings to hers, I'm not sure that's a good indication of whether or not you're in love with him. Everyone shows and feels love differently." Seth studied her briefly before setting his eyes back on the road. He shouldn't be digging, but he wasn't yet satisfied with her answer. "You could still be in love with him."

"I'm not. I do care for him, but I think I love him more like a friend. Before he proposed, I had actually considered breaking up with him. I was feeling things weren't… right." She shrugged her shoulders. "I think I accepted his proposal more out of obligation, and maybe fear of making a mistake. I mean, how do you know if you're really in love?"

Seth smiled. "I think the fact you have to ask that means you weren't really in love. When it happens, you just know. I know I just met you, but you don't appear very sad to me." The car slid a little as he came to a stop outside a blue house with a big white wraparound porch. The driveway wasn't plowed, so he'd have to park in the street.

"Is this it?" There was a large wooden sign between two light posts that read "Emergency Veterinarian" and "Boarding House."

The porch was slightly slanted, probably from sinking over the years. She checked her watch. It was 12:30, and she felt hungry.

Seth saw her check her watch. "We can get lunch after this." He opened the door and got out, but waited for her. If she fell or had trouble walking through the snow, he'd help her. He set his hand on the small of her back to guide her to the front door.

Doctor A.J., who met them at the door, was the spitting image of Clark Kent. Not the newer, younger Superman, but the actor Christopher Reeves who'd starred in the older movies. He was tall, straight postured, wore the same glasses, and even sounded a bit like him. "Hurry inside. Leave your boots on. I haven't had time to shovel or anything," he told Seth and Jessica after quickly introducing himself.

"Has anyone ever told you—"

"I could be Superman's twin?" Doctor A.J. interrupted Seth. "All the time. My wife was a huge fan of the movies, and she admits that's why she married me." Normally he would laugh at his own joke, but he wasn't in the mood today. He was eager to show the sheriff what he'd found, and very glad the sheriff brought a doctor.

Seth and Jessica followed the doctor down a set of wooden stairs. Seth noticed every detail of the house. It was obvious the doctor lived there and made his home his office. There was a musty smell when Seth first walked in, but the basement smelled like bleach. "Nice place you've got here," Seth told Doctor A.J.

"Thanks. We just remodeled. The clinic is down here, and I use my foyer for the waiting room. I appreciate you making a special trip here today. I know the roads are bad, but what I have to show you is..." He stopped at the bottom of the stairs when his daughter approached him and said, "Dad, your one o'clock cancelled because of the roads."

"Good. That's good," Dr. A.J. replied. He was frazzled and wasn't really up for working but hadn't wanted to cancel the day's only appointment.

Jessica studied the petite teenager who had her father's square jaw and felt a little twist in her stomach. Her dad had also been a Vet, and she'd been about that girl's age when she lost him. Clearly Doctor A.J. ran a family practice, and it hit close to home for Jess.

Dr. A.J. opened a door to what looked like a typical exam room. Jessica hadn't been prepared to see a wolf sliced open and lying on the metal table, its bloody insides displayed like an open cadaver. The stench suddenly rose and caught her under the nose. She turned her head into her arm.

"Sorry, I should have warned you. I've got the bleach to try and keep the odor down, and it won't be like this for long, but I was videotaping my findings." Dr. A.J. ran a shaky hand over his face. "What I've found is extremely disturbing. I wasn't sure who to call, and truthfully, I'm a little worried about this falling into the wrong hands. I called you because your dispatcher, Connie, kept calling me. She said you wanted to know the results."

Seth continued to survey the exam room, which had a small sink and counter. "Let's hear it."

Doctor A.J. picked up a glass jar and looked from Jessica to Seth. His hand trembled, and the worry lines on his forehead and around his eyes suddenly deepened. "I'm really not much of a Pathologist, but I've studied animal bodies in investigations of illnesses. I dissected this wolf and looked for all the things that typically kill them. I found his heart to be in relatively healthy condition. But when I examined the intestines, I found… holes."

Jessica glanced at Seth, as a slight chill ran up her spine. "What do you mean, holes?"

"I mean tunnels. I mean…"

"Eaten flesh?"

Tipping his head, Dr. A.J. gave Jessica a quizzical look. "Yes. Yes, the flesh was eaten. What do you know?"

"Finish telling us what you found, doc." Seth rested his hand on Jessica's shoulder. He wanted to hear what the doc had to say first. He knew what she was thinking.

"I found this." The doctor held the jar out to Seth. "I don't know what it is. I've never seen or heard of anything like it. It's not characteristic of heartworms or any other parasites I know. Most parasites like roundworms and tapeworms absorb nutrients and don't normally injure an animal's intestines. They certainly don't eat their way through the body." He placed his hands on his head. "This… this… thing… actually eats flesh, and not just soft flesh, but layers of epithelial tissue. I first noticed a gastrointestinal perforation in the stomach."

Jessica glanced at Seth. "That explains why they were whimpering. They had severe stomach pain."

"Yes, and this wolf also had internal bleeding, because whatever this thing is, it eats right through blood vessels. This thing travels." His voice raised a few notches on the last word.

"Easy there, Superman. Stay calm." Seth held the jar up to look at the pea-sized shell.

"Maybe you're not understanding!" Doctor A.J. looked at Jessica now. "This thing… it actually eats through flesh. It has teeth for God's sake!" He handed Seth a magnifying glass. "It's like a snail, protected by a hard shell, but when it emerges from the shell its body resembles a worm. I counted about ten teeth. It's hard to see, but I've been looking at this thing all morning. Now watch this." Doctor A.J. picked up his scalpel, cut out a small piece of the dog's lung, and rinsed it off in a glass of bleach. Taking the jar from Seth, he dropped the piece of lung tissue into it. "Just watch."

Seth and Jessica moved closer to the jar. The small snail slowly slithered over to the piece of tissue. A small worm-like body emerged from the shell; its rounded front began to poke through the tissue. It continued to move until the snail disappeared.

"It's inside the tissue. Watch, and see how it comes out the other end. It's eating a hole now."

"This is crazy." Jessica took the jar from the doctor and held it up for a closer look. "It eats dead tissue dipped in bleach?" She was utterly amazed. "If this thing came from the lake and is responsible for all the dead fish, then I wonder how many of these things there are." Her eyes moved to Seth. "The EPA or other scientists must be finding this. Doctor A.J. can't be the only one to have discovered this so far. Why isn't this all over the news?"

"My God," Dr. A.J. laced his hands atop his head again, feeling more distraught. "I hadn't thought of the fish or even the possibility of there being more parasites! This is…" He had no words. His mind was racing with terror. "Who do we call? The EPA? The FBI? The news? We've got to warn people. This creature needs to be in a lab being examined by experts. I'm actually afraid to examine the other wolves."

Seth didn't look away from Jessica as he replied to the doctor. "I'll make some calls." Jessica had said too much and alarmed the doctor more than he would have liked. He took the jar from her and set it on the counter. "You did good, Superman. This isn't your problem though, and I think until the experts are informed, we all just need to keep calm and not say anything. We don't need to create a panic." He was ready to leave.

"That's it?" Jessica couldn't believe how calm Seth was. Didn't anything ever ruffle him? "You'll make some calls, but let's just remain calm?" She was ready to start calling everyone herself. "Look, this is a flesh-eating creature that is killing wildlife, and will also kill humans if it gets inside one. This thing is deadly!"

Seth sighed. Jessica was as worked up as Doctor A.J., who Seth just couldn't take seriously with Superman's face.

"I've got a good friend who works at the Salk Institute for Biological Studies. I'm going to record this and send it to him. What do I do with the other wolves? I haven't finished examining the other four. I'm assuming I'll find more of these." Dr. A.J. looked grimly at the jar. "You're joking around calling me Superman, and to be honest I wish I was, because maybe then I wouldn't feel so terrified right now."

"With good reason," Jessica added, patting his arm in agreement.

"Do you have a freezer?" Seth asked.

"I have a deep freezer, yes."

"Put the wolves in bags and put them in the freezer."

Jessica looked from Seth to the doctor. "That's a good idea. I don't think you should handle the creature further, and I definitely agree about not cutting the other wolves open."

Chapter 13

Back in the car, Jessica waited for Seth to buckle his seatbelt before turning to him. "Okay, I'm officially freaking out, and you seem totally fine. Please tell me what you're thinking."

Starting up the car, Seth leaned back comfortably. "I'm thinking that I've got a dead body, evidence that apparently relates to this thing, and a buddy on the mainland I'm going to call in just a few minutes." He wanted to scold her for saying too much in front of the doctor. He wouldn't have brought her if he'd known she was going to fuel the doctor's already-frightened emotions. But he could see the concern and fear in her eyes and softened his tone. "Look… this whole thing may be way bigger than we thought. If it's linked to a murder, we can't just start telling everyone about it. I've got to get back to the station and make sure the body was taken by the M.E. I need to make sure the evidence gets into the right hands." He was also hungry, and knew Jessica was too.

"Seth, I have to tell my sister about this."

"The sister that betrayed you by sleeping with your fiancé?" He regretted the words immediately. It wasn't his place to comment. When Mike told him Jessica's twin stole her fiancé away, he was surprised Jessica was still talking to her. But he was beginning to feel he'd made a mistake getting Jessica involved in the case. He shouldn't have had her review the evidence, as she was now aware of a disturbing situation. He couldn't trust her to keep quiet. "I'm asking you not to say anything. I've got a case to handle, and I can't have gossip spreading. You shouldn't even be involved in this."

She recoiled at the edge in his tone. "First off, I don't expect you to understand my situation with my sister and ex-fiancé, no matter what Mike may have told you. You really know nothing about it. Just because Mike told you his version—"

"Stop." He didn't like that her eyes were suddenly watery, and her voice quavering. He was afraid she might break down. "I shouldn't have said that about your sister. It was out of line. But I do need you to not say anything to anyone for at least a few days." He rested his hand on her shoulder. "I know this is a lot to process, and you're scared. Hell, I don't even trust Superman not to start a panic, but I need you to trust me."

She restrained her emotions. She hadn't been sleeping well, and fatigue made it easy for her to cry. Seth was right. He was trying to do his job, and she probably wasn't helping. "I won't say anything. I'm really scared though, and I'm trusting you to get this information to the right people."

He nodded and began to drive. The sun was shining, making the snowbanks glisten like tiny diamonds. The bright sun and blue sky felt deceiving, knowing it was cold and windy outside. The blizzard had turned everything white as far as Jess could see.

They didn't speak further on the way back to the boat, and occasionally Jessica would glance at Seth. She noticed the set of his jaw that added to his hard expression. Her pulse raced as her mind replayed the visit with the Vet. Part of her wanted to keep discussing it, another part wanted to lighten the mood. But Seth was already pulling up to the ferry.

"Oh good, it's running again." That meant the M.E. should already be on the island, and he needed to get back to the station.

Seth helped Jessica onto the boat, and this time they both stood on the bow and gazed at the dead fish in the water.

Jessica's stomach clenched, and goosebumps crept along her arms and down her spine. She imagined each fish with a tiny snail-like creature eating its way through inside. How many could there be, and how would they be stopped? Where would the organism go?

Were they just floating through the water, waiting for another host? "Thank God it's not swimming weather," she whispered.

"Hey," he set his hand on her arm. "We don't know anything yet. We don't know if that thing is causing this." His eyes roamed over the lifeless fish with blank eyes floating above the waves. He dropped his hand and turned to untie the boat from the dock.

Jessica didn't go down below to stay warm. She pulled her hat down over her ears and used her scarf to shield her face. Her fingers were freezing on the railing of the boat, but she needed to hold on. The lake was calmer, but the boat still bounced. Jessica didn't pay attention to the cold, the spray, or the boat's speed. Instead, she kept her eyes on the dark water. It appeared black even as the sun shone down. Lake Superior was deep and ominous, and she'd never look at a lake the same way again.

Many seagulls lay dead near the scattered fish along the shore. Some had mangled feathers, and some had wings bent outward as if the bird had fallen from the sky while gliding. An elderly couple with matching black parkas stood on the dry sand holding hands. Seth shook his head. The beaches were closed, and no one was supposed to be there, but he knew them. It was Sam and Kristen, who ran the town bank. They were a nice couple, clearly disturbed by the eerie scene. Half the town had probably ignored the police tape and wandered down to stare at the dead sea life. He decided not to rebuke them as he and Jessica walked to the truck.

"I know I said we could grab lunch, but would you mind if I took you home instead? I've got to get back to the station."

She shook her head. "I wasn't even thinking about food. I lost my appetite." As they began driving back to Mike's cabin, she turned to study Seth's profile. He was not an easy man to read, and she wondered if he was still upset with her. "I'm sorry you regret getting me involved, Seth. I promise I won't say anything, and I'm glad you brought me along." When he didn't say anything, but offered a nod and a small smile, she continued. "You said earlier I don't appear very sad. I'm actually not sad at all. I'm relieved. Deep down, I didn't want to marry Greg. I've been feeling more concerned about my future and how I need to start living life more for me now. I think being with Greg was holding me back. He's one of the top surgeons at U of M Hospital. He works insane hours and can never do anything. Until now, my life has completely centered on our work. But now I want to start living."

Seth listened as she opened up, and for some reason her words were easing the concern he'd been feeling. Why her confession suddenly made him feel lighter and better, he didn't know. He could see her from the corner of his eye as he drove. "Mike said you lived with him for a few years."

"Yeah. And all the time I lived with him, I knew Janie was jealous. She's gone through horrible relationships and had her heart broken way more than I ever have. I think she and Greg are good together. I want her to be happy. And I'd like to find out what makes me happy. Being here, and seeing the things I finally have time for, I'm realizing I've been missing out on a few things."

"Like what?"

"I started a bucket list last night. There are so many things I want to see and do. I've been so career-focused that I've missed out on simple enjoyments." She lifted her hand to the window. "This island… I like it. I never knew how much I'd enjoy the silence, the tranquility."

"What's on your bucket list?"

She smiled as she thought about it. "I'd like to cook more. I'd like to try painting or sewing. I'd love to climb a mountain, and backpack through the Appalachians. I'd like to try whitewater rafting, kayaking and snorkeling. I've never been anywhere, so seeing some waterfalls or traveling to Europe is first on my list." She could go on forever with the things she wanted to experience in life. "The point is, I'd like to do many things besides just being a doctor."

Seth was surprised that she would enjoy backpacking. His ex-wife would never go anywhere that didn't include a five-star hotel and spa. But looking at Jess, he could see she was a no-fuss kind of woman. She wore little makeup and didn't bother with jewelry or nail polish. Her hair was naturally long and shiny, requiring little effort. She didn't need time to get ready in the morning, and yet she appeared gorgeous. Seth pulled up to Mike's house. "I'm going to come back later and clear the driveway."

Jessica suddenly felt silly for sharing her private thoughts with Seth. She probably spoke too much, and why would he care about her bucket-list? He was a busy sheriff with a lot on his mind. "Thanks." She opened her door abruptly and jumped out.

Seth also got out. "Hey," he strode over to her. "Are you going to be okay? I know you're upset from the vet."

"I'm okay."

The way she looked down at the ground, he didn't believe her. He felt maybe he'd upset her more. "Look, I'm glad you're here, Jess. I don't regret sharing this case with you, and I think your sister *did* in fact do you a favor. You don't belong with that guy." He folded his arms. "I'm going to come back, take care of this driveway, and then show you how much fun snowmobiling is." He started back to the car. "Get some rest."

As she watched him back out the drive, she felt a chill as the organism's image again arose in her mind.

Chapter 14

A cloud of smoke caught Seth's eye just before he heard the fire engine's blaring horn behind him. He slowed and moved to the shoulder so the engine and ambulance could pass. His radio crackled, and Dean's urgent voice came through.

"The station's on fire!"

Seth sped up. He'd wondered where the smoke was coming from when he'd seen it billowing over the trees. "What happened?"

"I'm guessing it was torched deliberately. I came back from a false alarm and found Connie unconscious in the snow. The building is toast, it's already collapsing."

Pulling up behind the fire engine, Seth stared as the massive flames devoured the small building to charred wood and ash. "I'm here." He turned off his radio and climbed out of the cab. The heat was immediate against the cold wind, and the scent of smoke filled the air. Connie was being placed on a medic board. Dean approached him rapidly.

"The back of her head is bleeding. They're taking her to the clinic now." Dean glanced at the burning building. "What the hell is going on?"

A loud cracking suddenly echoed as the roof split and crashed to the ground. The firemen continued to aim their hoses, raining water on the fierce flames. Somehow, Seth knew all the unusual recent events were in some way connected. "Did you contact the mainland?"

"I did. Kyle and his men are already on their way. I had them transfer the station phone to my cell phone. I figured people need to reach someone when they call the station."

Pleased with Dean's thinking, he gave a nod of approval. "You can forward calls to me. We'll have to use the firehouse for now."

"Kyle said the State Police will provide a temporary trailer if we need it, and they're sending more deputies. If someone knocked Connie out and started this fire, we need to find him." Dean rested weary eyes on Seth. "You know the body was in there. It's ashes now."

Seth folded his arms across his chest. "I'm thinking that was the plan."

"You think this was about the dead body?"

"Yeah." There was a lot he could tell Dean. He was still thinking about the organism the vet found, and how important those papers might be. He suddenly realized how great it was that he'd made a copy. Otherwise, all that evidence would now be ash. He felt relieved, knowing it was safely hidden in Maria's cookbook.

One of the firefighters approached Seth and shook his hand. "Dean told us there was a body inside. We're sticking around until forensics arrives. They're on their way now. I'm sorry this happened." He shook his head. "We don't expect this sort of thing here." The island was normally quiet, with only occasional trouble from ornery drunks.

"I don't expect this sort of thing anywhere, Matt," Dean replied. "Who the hell has the chestnuts to torch a police station?"

"I guess it's easier to accomplish here," Matt said. He rubbed the stubble on his chin. "I don't like the idea we've got an arsonist running around. This is a peaceful place. We never needed a big police force, but now we don't even have a station."

Matt was only voicing the likely concern of all island residents. There was already worry over the dead sea-life, and Linda had managed to freak out half the island blabbing about the wolves. Seth assumed they'd fully panic if they had any idea what was causing the deaths. Maybe there was reason to panic. Things were happening that didn't make any sense. He thought about Jessica and Superman, and the way they'd reacted to the organism. He'd been careful to keep his own concerns to himself. They were worked up enough that he didn't want to share his thought: the organism reminded him of the old horror film, "The Blob."

"Hello?"

"What?" Seth focused again on Dean. He hadn't been paying attention.

"The mainlanders are here." Dean pointed to the State Police SUV's pulling up. "We've got work to do. I'll start with my report. Connie got a call that gunshots were fired at Tom's hardware shop. But when I got there, nothing was amiss. When I reported back to Connie, I got the machine, and she wasn't answering the radio. She didn't answer her cell either. That's when I came back here and found her unconscious, and the building in flames."

The forensics team would be a big help. If someone deliberately burned down the station to destroy the body and any related evidence, this was a serious crime. Seth needed to get the copies he'd made to his buddy Kyle. Kyle could drive the papers anywhere they needed to go, which was first priority now. Seth couldn't leave the island himself given the growing chaos. And now, he had a manhunt to lead.

The thermostat in Mike's cabin was set at 69, but Jessica felt much colder. Like a door had been left open. She put her coat and hat on, then slipped on her boots. She'd left her gloves on the stairs, and when she walked over to get them, she noticed dirt on the steps. She'd have to be sure to sweep it. Keeping Mike's house clean was important to her.

She stepped out the front door, heading toward the side, where wood was stacked high along the entire length of the house. She'd gotten used to the smell and crackle of the fireplace. Greg had an electric fireplace, and rarely used it. A real fire was so much better, she thought, as she placed logs over her arm. The sound of a branch snapping made her look up quickly. The forest was only a few feet away, so maybe she'd see a deer. Her eyes swept the leafless trees with ice-covered branches, and the hills of snow that swept up and down over the forest terrain. The air held the clean pine scent of winter, and now only distant bird chirping filled her ears. Mike's place was wonderful. She couldn't be more content and happier, but she needed to start looking for a place of her own. As she turned to gather more logs, she noticed footprints in the snow. They led from the back of the house to the deck. She knew Seth had gathered wood earlier but wasn't sure he'd gone on the deck. She looked closer, noticing the footprints led up the stairs to the patio door. She'd ask Seth about that later. The wood felt heavy in her arms, and her nose was cold. She hurried back inside the house.

She carefully placed the logs in the fireplace with newspaper under them, as Seth had. Then she turned to reach for the lighter. From the corner of her eye, she suddenly saw a quick shadow, and then was yanked back by her hair, her body slammed to the floor. The wind was knocked from her, and a piercing pain shot across her chest. Before her breath could return, a man was suddenly on her. She saw a blur of black, and then brown eyes staring as a hunting knife was waved in her face.

"Stay still or I'll cut your throat."

When the cold blade touched the flesh below her left ear, she froze. Her heart hammered, and a whimper escaped her throat.

"I won't hurt you if you cooperate."

The words penetrated her mind past the loud pounding in her ears. If cooperating kept the knife outside her body, she was open to it. "Okay," she managed.

He moved the blade to the front of her face, holding the steel inches from her nose. "Where are the papers the Sheriff copied? If you get them for me, I won't hurt you."

Jessica could barely catch her breath, and her chest ached from her pounding heart. "I'll get them." Her response was immediate. She didn't think about what giving him those papers would mean.

She didn't care. No evidence was worth her life.

The man moved off her carefully, and then grabbed a handful of her hair, pulling her up. "Don't try anything. Don't piss me off."

His voice was so eerily calm that the words were more frightening than if he'd screamed them. She gasped at the pain when he tugged her closer to his body. "It's in the kitchen."

"Move."

He wasn't releasing her, and his grip on her hair was painful. "Please let go so I can get them." When he released her hair, she stumbled to the counter. She picked up Maria's cookbook and handed it to him.

She couldn't see his face, because he wore a ski mask, but his dark eyes glared at her. "Is this a joke? He held the knife out toward her. "I will cut every inch of you off one piece at a time."

"It's inside the paper cover. I… it's taped to the book." Her eyes darted around for a weapon. There was nothing but the cutting board. She quickly reached for it and swung the cutting board hard at the knife that was rapidly coming toward her. The knife went flying, and she ran around the island. He came up behind her and grabbed her hair again. She screamed out and kicked him in the shin. The recoil made her stumble back, and she turned to run to the door.

He tackled her from behind, and her shoulder smashed into the coffee table. She twisted forward, so she could kick him again.

He was very fast and suddenly on top of her, his strong hands circling her neck.

Eight years ago, she and Janie had taken a self-defense class. Janie was having panic attacks, and suffering anxiety. Her psychiatrist suggested she study martial arts as an exercise/meditation outlet, while also making her feel empowered. She'd taken the class with Janie to be supportive. The things she learned was what to do if someone comes up behind you, what to do if someone grabs you from the front, and what to do if someone straddles you. She was being straddled, and her hands were free. She remembered "RRG." Ridge them up, roll them over, get away. She pressed her pelvis up and to the right. It threw him forward enough that she could then grab his arm with both hands and pull to roll him off. The technique worked in the class she'd taken. But it wasn't working now. Her heart sank when he pushed her back down. His hands wrapped tighter around her throat again. Panic shot through her body, and her vision blurred from the rush of blood to her head. She tried to gouge his eyes with her nails, but ended up moving the ski mask, blinding him. That helped because he released her throat to straighten his mask. She had one more chance to try the pelvic lift. With all her strength she did it the way she'd done it in class and this time it worked. He fell off her enough that she could roll away and kick at him.

He was still fumbling with his mask as she got to her feet and ran. With her pulse pounding, she almost lost her balance, and stumbled to the front door. He was right behind her and grabbing for her jacket. She screamed as she turned, kicking her leg out, landing a very lucky strike to his groin. The man doubled over with a groan, and Jessica didn't hesitate. She opened the door and ran as fast as she could through the deep snow that covered the driveway. She glanced back and saw the man bent over at the front door. Adrenaline and fear surged through her, forcing her onward. She reached the plowed road. Her feet were suddenly free of snow, and she could run much faster. When she looked back, the man wasn't chasing after her. Maybe he was going to get a car. Horror film memories coursed through her mind, where the woman runs and runs, and yet suddenly the killer is right in front of her. She spun around, searching the woods for him. She didn't know where the closest neighbor was, but she wanted to keep running. Then suddenly her phone vibrated in her pocket, reminding her that she had it. She stopped a moment and tried to pull her phone from the side pocket of her jacket. Her hands were shaking so badly, she couldn't make them work. Her fingers were numb, and tears pricked her eyes as she tried to swipe the screen. She missed the call. It was Janie. She looked up again, half-expecting the man to appear. She was standing in the middle of a narrowly plowed road. Snowbanks lined the sides, and quiet empty forest. She willed herself to slow her breathing and calm down. Then she slid her fingers across the screen and tapped her screen till the phone dialed Seth.

Seth was pulling into the clinic to check on Connie. His friend Chris had called to tell him Connie was awake. She had a concussion, and seven stitches in the back of her head, but was okay. He'd just spent two hours with the mainland police and forensics team. They'd found footprints behind the station that led to the woods. He'd filled Kyle in on everything he'd learned from the vet, the papers Jessica read, and the organism. When he saw Jess's name on his cell phone, he considered not answering. But then he remembered how he'd promised to start taking her calls. "Hello?"

"Seth, I need help! I was attacked! He wanted the papers! I'm running from him!"

Seth could hear the fear and heaviness in her ragged voice and didn't hesitate for even a second. "Where are you?" He slammed into reverse in the clinic parking lot, spinning toward the exit. Dean was just entering the lot when Seth gunned his gas petal and skidded next to him, leaning his head out the window. Dean rolled his window down, noting the fury in Seth's eyes.

"Follow me! Jess was attacked!" Seth didn't waste time explaining more. He held the phone to his cheek with his shoulder, putting both hands on the wheel. "I'm on my way, Jessica. Keep running. Stay on the phone with me."

He could barely understand her as she cried, breathing heavily. "I'm so scared! He was going to kill me!" She choked on a giant sob. "Seth, he got the papers!"

"Jess, listen to me. I'm five minutes away. Do you see anyone? Can you see him?"

"No!" She couldn't run anymore. Her chest and throat were burning, and her heart was racing so fast she couldn't catch her breath. She stopped a moment holding the phone to her chest. She turned around, scanning the woods. Her vision was blurry, and she wiped her cold hand over her wet eyes. Her rapid breathing was making her lightheaded.

It felt like an eternity. She wanted to slow her breathing but couldn't stop crying. Then she heard the tires crunching over the snow, and turned to see Seth's black truck, followed by a navy-blue SUV. A single red light flashed on his cab, and she sank to the ground as her knees gave out in relief.

Seth stopped the truck in front of her in the middle of the road. "Jess!" He glanced around as he ran to her. She wrapped her arms around his waist and buried her head in his chest. She was sobbing so hard he couldn't understand what she was saying. "Are you hurt?" He wanted to look at her, but she held him tight.

Dean ran up, gun in hand, also studying the thick woods lining the narrow road. "Is she okay?" Dean asked, looking concerned.

Seth gently rubbed her back. He knew she would need a minute to calm down but wanted to know what happened so he could know how to proceed. He bent his head, and put his lips close to her face, whispering, "You're safe now."

Jessica took a deep breath, and then leaned back. "I didn't know he was in the house. I was making lunch, talking to Mike on the phone, and I think the whole time he was in the house." He'd probably been watching her for over an hour. "I went outside to get firewood, and when I came back in to…" She was talking too fast and paused a moment to catch her breath. "I was making a fire, and he came up behind me. He was on top of me so fast…." Fresh tears spilled again, and her breathing increased. "He had a knife."

"It's okay." Seth glanced at Dean and gave him a nod. Dean had heard what she said and would know what to do.

"I'm on it. I'll call Chris for backup." Dean was already pulling his phone from his pocket. "You take her to the clinic."

"I will."

Jessica gripped him tighter. She wasn't ready for him to let her go yet. "He wanted the papers. He knew I had them. I had to give them to him, Seth. I had to." She sobbed harder, heaving between the words. "He was going to kill me."

"It's okay." He squeezed her closer, trying to control his anger. Not at her, but at himself for putting her in danger. He'd shared important evidence with her, and her life could have ended as a result. He felt his chest ache at the sound of terror in her voice and held her tighter as her body trembled. After a few moments, he helped her to stand and guided her to the truck.

He reached in the back seat for a blanket and draped it over her when she sat down. Then he grabbed an unopened bottled water from the back seat of his truck. "Here, take a drink." He held the water up to her lips. Her eyes were a brilliant aqua greenish blue with black mascara now smeared around them, and she hiccupped as she exhaled deep heavy breaths. She took the bottle and sipped a little. Seth brushed her hair away from her face, and she grimaced at the pain.

"He pulled my hair." She softly tucked it behind her ears.

Seth instantly saw the red bruise marks on her throat. "Son of a…" He stared into her eyes, and for a moment he wondered if she was distraught from a sexual assault. "Jess, did he…"

She shook her head. She could see from his sudden change in expression what he was thinking. "He only put the knife to my throat and tried to strangle me." As if that wasn't much. The words sounded silly, but she knew it could have been much worse. Seth nodded and then closed her door.

Chapter 15

As Seth turned his truck around, Jessica raised her head. "Where are you taking me?"

"The island doesn't have a hospital, but we've got a small clinic that can handle emergency injuries. I want you looked at."

She reached out and squeezed his arm. "No. Please, Seth. There's nothing to be done. I don't want to be examined." Her head was pounding now, and she felt bile fighting to be released. "I just want to lie down and rest. I can go back to Mike's house, I'm sure it's safe now."

He shook his head, knowing he wasn't taking her back there. Dean's voice came across the radio. "What have you got?" Seth asked.

"Door wall lock and handle are busted. That's how he got in. Footprints lead to the woods, and my guess is he stayed there awhile watching her. There're a few drawers thrown open, some scattered papers on the floor. Looks like he may have been looking for something. I called Kyle, filled him in. He's meeting me here after he finishes up with the station fire."

Kyle was going to have his hands full. He already knew about the wolves, the organism, the body and evidence being burned with the station, and now this. Seth was teaming up with Kyle, but Kyle and his taskforce were handling the murder investigation. "I'm going to have Chris stay with Jess." Seth replied, as he eyed her carefully. "I don't want her alone. And I want someone to watch Connie too. Not sure if she's in danger, but let's not take any chances. I'll meet you at Mike's." He wanted to see things for himself. "I'll probably be there when Kyle arrives."

Dean checked his watch and then held the radio to his mouth. "I've got the camera in my jeep. I'm going to secure the core areas and start the documentation. I'm thinking those footprints might match the ones behind the station. Did you get her statement?"

"Not yet." Seth watched her closely as she tried to pull herself together. "I'll get back to you shortly." He needed pictures of the bruising around her neck.

She shook her head. "I'm not going to the clinic. I don't need a babysitter." The idea was upsetting her again. "Is there a hotel nearby?" She had no idea where she could stay if he wouldn't let her go back to Mike's.

Seth sighed and lowered his eyes to her neck. The road was deserted, so he didn't bother to pull over. He simply stopped the truck and put it in park. "I need to take a picture of your neck." He used his phone to take a few shots. "I'm sorry, I have to do this." He ran his hand gently over her collar, so he could push her blond hair aside. "Can you take your jacket off?" He hated having to bother her when she was still distraught, but collecting evidence was important, and he had to handle her the way he would any victim.

She winced when she pulled her right shoulder from her jacket. "I hit myself on the coffee table."

He pressed his lips together hard. "I'll have to take more pictures later." He'd need her to undress.

She waited for him to finish, and then she rested her trembling hand over his. When he met her eyes, she said, "Seth, please, don't take me to the clinic."

"Okay." At that moment he'd do anything she asked. "I'll take you someplace safe. Can you tell me what happened? Don't leave out any details." He set his phone on record.

By the time Seth pulled into his driveway, Jessica was near hysterical again. She'd managed to explain most of the ordeal before she lost it and began sobbing again. Her body was shaking, and he knew she was coming down from an adrenaline rush. When she said she was going to be sick, he quickly walked her into the house.

She didn't take any time to view Seth's home. She wasn't even sure how she ended up with her head near the toilet, but she was grateful she got there before being sick. Seth handed her a glass of water and a towel.

"You're in shock, and your adrenaline held you together. Now your body is reacting. Don't feel bad."

She looked up to find his face held that angry look she'd seen before. His lips were compressed tightly, and the tick in his jaw made her wonder if he was grinding his teeth. She understood now he wasn't angry at her, but at the situation. This was his demeanor, but it wasn't him. Under the tough exterior, he was a kind man with a good heart. But there was no question that right then she appreciated his strong toughness. Because being with him, she felt completely safe. She didn't know what to say and looked down at the bathroom floor. She had enough awareness to recognize that the tile was very nice. It had swirls of grays and beige. It looked like slate, and the stones were set in different geometric patterns, rather than lined neatly in a row. And it was clean, as was the rest of the bathroom.

Seth knelt down beside her. "Can you pull your sweater up enough for me to take a picture of your shoulder? If you're uncomfortable, I can wait and get a female officer from the mainland to come."

"Seth, I'm a doctor. I probably make people uncomfortable all the time. You're doing your job. I'll have a lot of bruises for pics. I might have a mild concussion."

"I should have taken you to the damn clinic. Doctors are stubborn."

"Cops are more stubborn." She smiled and pulled her shirt up further.

When the pain shot through her arm, he helped her. He carefully held her sweater out of the way as he took a few pictures with his phone. She glanced over her shoulder at the round bruise that formed just below her shoulder blade and reached just below her bra strap. "It'll be sore, but it's just bruised." She knew nothing was broken and was grateful. The attack could have been worse. She could be dead.

"Let me see your hands." Seth carefully examined her fingers. "Did you scratch him?" He'd need to clean under her nails for possible DNA evidence.

"No. I didn't feel skin because his ski mask got in the way."

"Can you stand?"

Slowly, she tried to, and felt a rush of blood race to her head, making her sway back. Strong arms circled her waist, and she leaned into Seth for support. He led her to a soft, beige microfiber couch, and she sunk back into the couch pillow.

"I've got an alarm system. My doors are reinforced steel with triple locks. You're safe here." He walked into his kitchen and opened his freezer door. All he had for an icepack was a package of frozen peas. He walked back and knelt beside her, softly placing the bag of peas on her bruised shoulder.

She noticed how gentle he was with her. He held the bag of ice for her while she slowly turned her head, admiring his beautiful home. It didn't fit his outward appearance at all, and she immediately wondered if he'd hired an interior decorator. She wasn't sure what she expected his house to look like, but more rustic/plain is what she would have guessed. Instead, it was exquisitely decorated in Old World English, with deep orange walls crowned with thick three-tiered dark walnut molding that matched the distressed hard wood floor.

Rough-hewn beams lined the ceiling. Every piece of furniture had an antique or distressed charm to it with intricate etchings. She glanced down at the yellow, orange, and forest green striped throw pillows. The soft yellow, burgundy, and deep orange colors and dark wood stains blended together beautifully. His fireplace was cased with walnut-stained pillars, and on the mantel was a vintage gold mirror with tapestry candles on either side. "You have throw pillows," she muttered to herself. "Did your ex-wife do all the decorating?"

Although the home had a masculine touch to it, she would have never imagined it to be HIS style. She couldn't believe he lived in such a house. Her eyes continued to scan the arched doorways and windows, the fantastic, small, colorful rugs, and the wrought iron and ceramic sculptures and accent pieces. The house was probably no larger than Janie's two-bedroom apartment, but very impressive. "This is the most beautiful house I've ever seen."

Seth glanced around his home. "That's quite a compliment, considering you've been in both of Mike's homes." He shrugged his shoulders. "It's small."

"It's perfect. Did you do this?"

Seth felt a pleased satisfaction at her praise. She seemed genuinely in awe of the room, which seemed to lift the gloom and despair from her face. "My Ex and I had a three-week honeymoon in Europe about seven years ago. I liked the old cottages we stayed in that had that comfortable broken-in look with warm colors. I decided I wanted that in my own home. My wife hated it. She hated the cottages we stayed in because they were old and small. She wanted a mansion with modern high polished furniture and surfaces that held reflections." But her taste suited her personality, he thought.

"That's Greg," Jessica whispered.

"I guess repurposing furniture is a bit of a hobby of mine, and I like working with wood. I did all of the molding and woodwork myself."

"You do good work." Her eyes held his a moment.

"Thanks." He lowered the bag and sat down on the couch beside her. "Jess, I have to leave. I need to meet Kyle at the house and find the man who hurt you." He didn't want to leave her, but he had a job to do. "I'm going to have my buddy either sit outside or come in if you want. Either way, you won't be alone. You can stay here and rest, and I'll be back later to check on you."

She stared at him a moment, trying to gather her thoughts, but she couldn't seem to think straight, so she nodded. When he went to stand, she grabbed his arm. "Wait. I…" Now that she'd had time to calm down, she wanted to talk about what happened. "I'm sorry I gave up your evidence. He took the papers."

Seth rubbed his thumb gently along the side of her cheek. "I don't want you to worry about those papers. All that matters to me is that you're okay."

"But how did he know? I mean, how did he know the papers were at Mike's house?"

"I plan to find that out. My guess is he was following me, and perhaps watching us from the woods. Dean said there were a lot of footprints behind the house." No one else knew about the papers other than Connie. "I think the guy that attacked you set fire to the sheriff station. It completely burned to the ground."

"Oh my gosh." She set her hand over her mouth. "Seth… the papers. I shouldn't… I wish…"

"Hey," He took her hand. "You did the right thing. You did everything right, and you're alive because of it. We'll find this guy. Chicory Island isn't big, and he'll need to leave it soon. We've got the ferry covered and extra deputies patrolling. Connie, my dispatcher, was the only other person who knew I had the papers, and she's in the hospital. I need to talk with her, and I need to check out Mike's house. Make sure the papers aren't still there."

"They won't be. I think he didn't run after me because he went back to get the evidence. That's what he wanted. I can't believe what this guy has done to…" Her eyes grew wide. "Seth, is all the evidence gone? Are we the only two who know what was written on those papers?"

She was getting worked up again, and Seth didn't want to leave her upset. "Jess, this isn't your problem. You can't worry about it. You're alive and I'm going to keep it that way." He needed to go. There was a lot of work to do, and he wanted answers. He stood up and sighed when he saw tears forming in her eyes again.

"I'm fine. I'll be fine," she waved him off.

"Go take a bath. Make yourself at home, and if you need anything at all, call me."

Chapter 16

It was a perfect evening for snowmobiling. The island looked like any normal winter's day, except that things were far from normal. The sun was setting, with brilliant orange and lavender clouds stretched like taffy across a deep turquoise sky. Many sleds glided across the thick snow, with tails of white kicked up behind them. Two SUVs were parked in front of Mike's house. Seth hadn't yet been able to shovel the driveway. He'd promised he'd look out for Jessica and help her. He wasn't doing a very good job. She'd told Seth what happened to her in detail, and he kept playing it over in his mind. He was picturing her on the floor with a knife held to her throat. The more he imagined the scenario, the more worked up he got. Seth opened the door to Mike's house to find Kyle and Dean talking. "Hey." He jammed his hands in his pockets.

"How's she doing?" Dean asked, pulling his knit hat out from his jacket pocket.

"She's pretty shaken up. The psycho almost strangled her to death."

"How'd she get away?" Kyle asked.

"She's taken self-defense classes." He glanced around the house, his eyes already seeing the struggle that took place in front of the fireplace. "She got lucky."

"We swept for prints and photo'd everything. Just need her statement now." Kyle looked at Seth, thinking his buddy looked tired and in need of a shave. "I've got some extra patrol units searching the island. If he's still here, we'll find him. Not too many places he can hide, and the temps are dropping."

Seth had already radioed Dean earlier that the assailant was wearing a ski mask and gloves. They weren't able to get a positive ID from Jess. The attack happened so fast she wasn't even sure how tall or heavy the man was. Only that he wasn't really muscular, and his eyes were dark brown.

"I'm headed to the clinic now to be with Connie. Carl's been watching her, and he needs to get home for dinner. I'll get a deputy to guard her for tonight. I'll be available," Dean said. "We need to find this bastard."

Seth nodded and stepped aside as Dean opened the door to leave. He glanced at Kyle before heading to the kitchen. Jessica told him she gave the papers to her attacker when he threatened to kill her. He didn't expect to find the papers in the house but wanted to check anyway.

"What are you doing?" Kyle asked, watching his friend walking around.

"The son of bitch burned down the station to destroy the body and the evidence. Then he comes here and takes the only other copy I had. He knew it was here. This means he was either watching me, or someone told him." He looked up at his friend's brown eyes. "The only person who knew everything was Connie. The papers aren't here, so I'm headed to the clinic now. I'll find out who Connie's been talking to."

"Let's go."

The sound of a thump followed by a loud bang came from somewhere close. Both men looked at each other, then quickly pulled their guns from behind their backs.

"Garage." Seth pointed to the garage door and followed behind Kyle. Kyle pushed the door open first, as Seth aimed his gun. The side door to the garage was open, allowing daylight to beam over Mike's Hummer.

"That door was shut." There was nowhere to hide in Mike's clean-kept garage, so Kyle looked under the cars.

Seth noticed a shovel on the ground and figured whoever was inside had knocked the shovel over, hitting the car. That would make the same sound they heard. "If that was the perp, he's got a lot of balls." He walked over to the door, noticing the trim was split. He'd used a crowbar or something to pry the door open. Footprints filled the snow.

Kyle gave Seth a questioning look, and when Seth nodded, they both stepped outside back-to-back, their guns drawn. The tracks led through thicker snow piles where the drifts were easily three feet deep. Seth was the first to pick up the pace, thinking there was a good chance the guy was still nearby, and they could find him.

"Listen." Kyle stopped and tried to quiet his ragged breath. "It's too quiet."

"Doesn't mean he's not out here."

"No, but it means he's too far away for us to hear him running. It means we probably won't catch up to him on foot."

Seth was pumped. He wanted the bastard that hurt Jessica. "Want to get the sleds?" They could easily run back to the house and start up Mike's snowmobiles.

"No." Kyle wasn't prepared to go on a manhunt. He wasn't dressed for snowmobiling, and his cheap black boots were already chafing against his heel. He ran his hand over his buzzed head and glanced around again. "Maybe I'll call the K-9 unit and have their team do a run through the woods. He's got to end up somewhere."

The man's scent would be on Jessica's clothes. "Do it."

Mike's locks would need replacing, and even then, Seth didn't trust that Jessica would be safe there. Not until the assailant was caught. Kyle called an extra deputy to come stake out the house in case the perp decided to return. And Seth felt better not leaving Mike's house unattended. He'd have to call him and explain everything that happened, and it wasn't a call he was looking forward to.

Jessica splashed cold water on her face, glancing at herself in the mirror. Her mascara was streaked clear down to her chin, and black smudges were smeared all around her eyes. Her neck was badly bruised, and painful to the touch. Her hair was tangled at the nape of her neck and combing through it with her fingers wasn't helping. She opened the drawer in the vanity and found a man's brush. After she fixed her hair, she used the soap and hand towel to clean her face.

The shower looked inviting, but aside from not having any clean clothes to change into, she felt drained. Heading back to the family room, she walked slowly through the small kitchen. She couldn't help but become more curious about Seth. What kind of man was he? Did he paint the white cabinets, and distress them himself? Did he pick out the red rooster cookie jar and the striped, yellow hand towels sitting on the granite counter? It seemed so different from what he personified. She peered out the window, seeing nothing but darkness. A chill ran down her spine, and her thoughts went back to the home invasion. She heard her phone ring, and quickly pulled it from her pocket. "Hi."

After spending an hour with Connie, Seth was finally leaving the clinic. "I'm headed home and was wondering if you'd like me to stop at Mike's and pick up your suitcase. Maybe I can grab your toothbrush for you."

How thoughtful. "Yes, thanks. My clothes are still in the suitcase. If you can just grab the toiletry bags on the bathroom counter, that would be great. And my toothbrush is beside the sink. It's yellow."

He didn't like the hoarse sound of her voice. "Are you okay?"

"I will be. Did you find out anything else?" She wanted the man caught ASAP.

"We can talk about it later." He had an idea who attacked Jessica. He'd learned from Connie she'd been talking to that supposed environmental agent named Shawn Sharconnon. Kyle ran a check and found that no man by his name worked for the EPA. The guy was a fraud. They weren't even sure if he'd given Connie his real name. But Connie gave a description to a sketch artist, and deputies were searching for a male Caucasian with brown eyes, short blond side-swiped hair, and a medium build. The island had its own public website which noted store closings, if the ferry was shut down, and what time snowplows were running. Residents could also use it for live chat if they had comments or concerns. Dean posted the sketch there and warned residents to keep their homes locked and be wary of strangers. Seth felt confident the guy would soon be apprehended. At the moment, his concern was for Jessica. "I'll be home in about half an hour."

Chapter 17

Seth walked in his house, immediately calling out Jessica's name so he wouldn't startle her. She didn't answer, or turn around, and he found her sitting on the couch right where he'd left her. He set her suitcases down by his bedroom door, and slowly walked toward her, concern knitting his eyebrows together. "Jess…"

He knelt in front of her, studying her eyes. She seemed removed… lost. He wondered if she was in a state of shock. "Hey," he reached his hand up and raised her chin until her eyes met his. "Are you okay? You haven't checked out mentally, have you?"

"What?" She was happy to see him, though no smile formed on her face.

"What are you thinking about, Jess?"

Her mind was focused on a memory, her eyes seeing a glimpse from the past as she lowered them to Seth's chest. "There is so much I can't remember. My childhood… vacations we took, events…." She paused a moment. "I can't remember taking drivers ed. I barely remember how I felt the first time behind the wheel of a car. I can't remember the day I passed my test, or what I did when I got my license. I barely remember senior prom. I know what I wore, and that I hated my up do, but I can't even think of my date's last name." Her eyes stayed fixed, barely blinking, as an image of her father blurred in her memory. "I was remembering what my dad used to tell me. Whenever I'd have a bad day or a bad experience, he'd sit me down and say, 'Jess, in ten years you won't remember this. Nothing bad that happens to you really matters at your age, because in ten years you won't even remember it.'" She gave a sad smile. "I never really thought that advice helped. I didn't get the point of saying it. But now I know. I see how truly right he was, because I can't remember any of the bad days growing up. The day my parents died, it's a blur. Like high school is a blur. But what I do remember is Janie throwing up in the bathroom and sobbing. I remember thinking, 'thank God I still have my sister.' My parents were on their way to pick Janie up from a friend's house. The accident could easily have happened on the way back. I could have lost my parents *and* Janie, but...." She swallowed the lump forming in her throat.

Offering comfort was never something that came easy to Seth, so he was very much aware of his overwhelming desire to comfort her. He wanted to say something but had the feeling she needed to say whatever was clouding her mind. He assumed she was getting to something, so he sat quietly on the floor in front of her and waited for her to continue.

"It was only 13 years ago, and yet I can't remember the faces of the officers who came to our home. I can't remember the wake, or the relatives, friends, and neighbors who brought us tons of food. But I remember Janie opening the refrigerator and saying, 'we'll be fat as hell if we eat all this.' I remember she pulled out a banana cream pie, and we both ate the entire thing." She drew her eyes to Seth's. His face was soft. The hard lines that normally made him look tough and intimidating were gone. His concern melted a small piece of her. "My dad was right. The bad events that happened in my past...I can't remember them well. Only bits and pieces. So, what happened today doesn't really matter. In ten years, I won't remember this. I won't remember how I'm feeling right now. I might not remember that I could have died. I'll just know that it happened. I'll know that I lived because I took a self-defense class with Janie." She glanced down when Seth set his hand over hers. It was warm and big, and not something she'd expect from him. "I don't even remember taking that class, but I remember the moves I learned. I feel so sick to my stomach. I keep replaying it over and over in my head, and honestly, Seth, I don't even know how I got away. It was pure luck. But it doesn't matter, because in ten years I won't remember this. It's already a blur now…" Tears swam in her eyes again. "I have to keep telling myself that in ten years I won't remember. That what happened doesn't matter because I won't remember."

"Come here." He pulled her onto his lap and wrapped his arms around her. He hushed her softly, and rubbed her arm with one hand, and used his other to press the side of her face gently to his neck. He understood what she was saying. She'd been traumatized by a scary event. Probably the most traumatic event of her life since losing her parents, and she wanted to make sense of it, or put it in perspective. "Honey, is there someone I can call for you?"

She took note of the word 'honey,' and the way his tone changed. He'd never used an endearment before with her. She knew this was a glimpse of an entirely different side of him.

"Do you want me to call your sister or Mike? Maybe it would help to speak with them." He'd already called Mike to tell him about his house, and what happened to Jess. Mike wasn't going to come to the island, but he trusted Seth to handle the house for him. And he all but insisted he take care of Jess.

"No." Normally she would need her sister. Normally Janie would have been the first person on her mind, but being cradled on the floor by a strong man with a big gun strapped to his waist was all she needed. The tumbling in her stomach subsided. "This is good."

Seth thought about how at ease with each other they'd become and was glad it wasn't awkward.

"Seth? Will you tell me about your house?"

He was happy to take her mind off things and pleased that she was interested in his home.

Shawn's boss was never unsatisfied with his work. He did the jobs that needed doing, in any way that worked. Pouring gasoline over the dead body and inside the police station was easy. He'd gotten lucky that the blonde gave him the copies. And he'd overheard the two cops saying there was no more evidence. That was the confirmation he'd needed. He'd knocked over a shovel in the garage and practically pulled every muscle in his legs running in the forest, but he'd made it to his snowmobile and escaped in time. He successfully destroyed any and all trails that could lead the police to IMH20. Now his only dilemma was whether or not to finish the job of killing the blond. She was the only one who saw the papers and may have understood what they meant. Malek didn't like loose ends, and Shawn wasn't completely satisfied that the blond wouldn't turn out to be a loose end.

Chapter 18

The smell of coffee permeated the air as Jessica rolled over, opening her eyes. It took her a moment to remember where she was. The window to her right was darkened by hunter-green curtains, allowing a crack of daylight to pour through. Jessica reached for her phone charging on the nightstand beside Seth's bed. It was 10:30 a.m. She winced at the pain in her shoulder when she tried to sit up. Her arm was stiff, the joint extremely tender. She reached her hand up to her neck to feel the tender, swollen flesh, and yesterday's events immediately flooded her mind. She needed to stop thinking about it.

She climbed out of bed, feeling every sore muscle in her body. She'd need Motrin right away and headed for the bathroom. She made sure she looked halfway decent before making her way to the coffee pot.

"Good morning." Seth had been debating whether he should go in his bedroom and wake her. He figured the sleep was good for her, but also thought she might want to see what was happening on the news. He walked over to the kitchen counter, handing her a coffee cup.

"Thank you." She noticed he was dressed casually in a white t-shirt— that did wonders for the definition of his built body— and faded blue jeans that sat low on his hips. She'd seen nice bodies before, but usually on shorter men. Seth's height was already a thrill, and to have a build like his thrown in was somewhat rare.

"Nice shirt." Seth looked down at her baby blue t-shirt that read: PEOPLE LIKE YOU ARE THE REASON PEOPLE LIKE

ME GIVE OUT MEDICATION. The blue matched the stripes on her cotton pajamas bottoms.

"My sister got this for me. I was having trouble with this guy in college who wouldn't stop asking me out. It got a little creepy, and I finally had to get a restraining order against him. I'd been upset that week, worried the guy was going to go nuts. That's when Janie tried to cheer me up with these pajamas." She took her first sip of coffee and moaned. "I haven't had to make my own coffee once up here. I could get spoiled by this."

"Come watch the news." He turned from her, heading into the family room to grab the remote control. He hit the sound button and sat down. She took a seat beside him on the sofa, pulling up her legs, and he tried not to look at her. She was surprisingly beautiful in the morning. "They've been playing clips of this all morning."

Jessica stared at the TV. The screen showed long lines of people at the store, standing with grocery carts filled to the top with bottled water. Some people were fighting over the last cases on the shelves. Other clips showed people dressed in winter gear, picking dead turtles and birds up from the shore. Some locals who lived along Lake Superior were having bonfires in their yards and burning the fish and wildlife. "This is crazy." There were pictures of ships with equipment dropping large nets into the water. Arial views continued to show dead fish floating on the surface of the dark lake. "What are the nets for?"

"They aren't saying. The media can't seem to get any real answers. The EPA's response to all interviews is that they are looking into it, or they have no comment at this time." Seth had heard that fifty times already. "They've closed all the beaches, and there's talk of the military patrolling it. People become more scared and alarmed when they can't get answers. It's just not natural for fish and wildlife to die like this, especially during the winter."

Both of them sat quietly for a time watching the news. The media tried to calm peoples' fears by explaining in detail where tap water comes from. Most people don't know where their water comes from, and according to the news, many people believe it comes from lakes. However, sixty-five percent of drinking water comes from rivers and streams. In the Upper Peninsula, many people got their water from private wells. The EPA said water-treatment centers were being tested, to ensure the municipal drinking water was still safe. It was further stressed that reverse osmosis would kill any potential threats to the water system. However, people were still panicking. People were still stockpiling food and water.

"I'll admit that when I turned the water on to brush my teeth this morning, I stared at it a few minutes. I was still nervous to use it, simply because we don't know what's happening."

"Seth, *we* know what it is." Jessica let out a long sigh. She pointed to the TV. They know there's something in the water. But they might not know exactly what it is."

"We don't know exactly what it is either, Jess." He could see she was getting worked up.

"We have to tell someone!" She remembered how adamant Dr. A.J. had been about contacting people. He'd mentioned he was sending a video to his friend who was a scientist.

"I've told people." Seth felt as frustrated over the situation as Jessica. But what more could he do? "I suppose I should tell you Superman is missing."

She froze. "What? Dr. A.J.... the vet is missing?"

"My partner Kyle went to the vet clinic last night and again this morning. He's gone. His entire house is locked up tight and no one can find him or his family."

Moving too fast to set it down, she almost spilled her coffee. "Seth, this is crazy! We know what's happening. We know those papers are connected to this. If those papers had the formula for how to stop it, or, or... I saw the formula, Seth!" She set her hands on her head, anxiety surging through her. "It's not some bacterial infection! It's a creepy little snail that eats flesh!" She could picture in her mind the one sentence that she knew was important, but she couldn't read the key word. B s*omething ST H20*. "The right scientists need to know what was written on those papers." She stood up from the couch and began to pace the floor. Her mind was racing. "I was almost killed for those papers, and your station was burned to the ground because of them." She wrapped her arms around her stomach, flinching at the pain in her shoulder. "They must know what it is." She couldn't believe that she, Seth, and Dr. A.J. were the only ones to discover it. Surely the EPA would have found the organism when studying the other dead wildlife. "But they might not know how to stop it. What if those papers had the answers? Seth, we should've taken photos of it. We should have made more copies."

He'd already told himself that but wasn't going to beat himself up over it. He was lucky he'd even made one copy and had the chance to learn a little about it from Jessica. It wasn't procedure for him to make evidence copies before Forensics could see it. He'd shared all he'd learned with Kyle, and Kyle was contacting the FBI. Seth was more concerned with finding the man who attacked Jessica and torched his station. "We don't know for sure that the organism Dr. A.J. found is connected to those papers. And we don't have proof yet that the organism is what's killing the fish."

She put her hands on her hips. "I think we should call the news stations. I think we should explain what Dr. A.J. found. Where the heck did he go?"

"No." Seth eyed her carefully. "Jessica, I've followed procedure. We don't have proof of anything. You go telling the media, and it causes more panic. Don't you see what's happening already? People are stockpiling food and water. IMH2O is the largest bottled water company, and they're on backorder. There isn't anything we can do right now I haven't already done. My concern right now is keeping you safe." He glanced at his watch. It was already almost eleven. He needed to get to work.

"I don't feel right sitting here. I feel like I need to be doing something." She paused a moment to regard Seth. He sat there with his typical expression that she was now accustomed to. "You're always so calm. You just sit there with a pissed-off face. Are you mad at me?" She didn't say the words with anger, she just said them matter-of-factly. She was thinking out loud and the words accidently came out.

Seth stood up. "You think I look pissed off?"

"Yes." It was too late to take the words back, and she realized she wasn't at all afraid of him. "You're always scowling. Except when you smile. Like now you're smiling, and it totally changes your face." She took a step back when he moved toward her.

"You think I'm mad at you?" He took another step forward.

She nodded, and her stomach flipped. Her heart rate jumped.

"I've never once been mad at you. I don't think there's anything you could say or do to really anger me. If you want to know how I'm feeling, just ask." He stepped closer. "I feel the same way about all this as you do, but it's my job to stay calm. It's my job to make sure procedures are followed, and that you stay safe." He leaned closer to her face. "I'm thinking you need to trust me and do what I say." His voice dropped low. "Do you trust me, Jessica?"

She swallowed. "Yes." She did trust him. Completely.

"Are you hungry?" He leaned back, stepping away from her.

She looked up at him with her mind going blank and gave a small nod.

"I make a killer omelet." He turned and headed toward the kitchen.

Another winter storm was headed to the Upper Peninsula. Four to six inches of snow was possible by Tuesday. In the last few years, the winters had been worse than ever. It looked as if this winter would be no different. The snow was coming down but wasn't sticking. It was small, wispy flakes that seemed to melt before they landed. Seth was headed to the firehouse. The island was equipped with one fire engine, housed in a two-thousand square-foot brick building. It had three beds, a small kitchen, and five firefighters who took turns staying on call. The firehouse and ambulance normally saw about as much action as the police. Road accidents were fairly common. Too many tourists enjoyed speeding along the winding two-lane roads, where deer were known to frequently cross. Occasionally campers or teens hiking through the woods would accidently start forest fires. The island had its share of burnt trees. Now the firehouse was also going to be the temporary police station, until a new one could be built in the spring.

Seth knew all four of the retained firemen. Thursday-night poker was a weekly tradition that all the men enjoyed. Normally the games were held at Dean's house, but with his pregnant wife now complaining about the cigar smoke, poker night was held at the station. Dean was taking Connie home from the clinic so she could pack. She was leaving the island for a few days to stay with family. It made things easier, because Seth would otherwise have to assign someone to keep an eye on her. Kyle had agreed that the perpetrator may have intended to kill her. If he found out she was still alive, he might try to finish the job. Connie was the only one who could positively ID the man they suspected of attacking Jessica and burning down the station. Dean was going to escort her to her family, where a rookie from the mainland was assigned to protect her.

Chris was one of the first people to befriend Seth when he first moved to the island seven years ago. An older gentleman, almost thirty years Seth's senior, he had been working as a volunteer for the sheriff's office. Chris was retired from law enforcement, but you'd never know he was sixty-five, because he didn't look a day over forty. The man was in excellent health and in better shape than most teenage boys. If Seth needed extra manpower for any trouble happening on the island, he'd call Chris. Chris didn't mind babysitting Jessica. The man could watch the woods for hours and never view it as a burden. Seth felt confident Jessica would be safe inside his home with Chris sitting guard out front. He'd given her strict instructions not to leave the house, and if she needed to go out, to call him first.

The TV's volume was cranked up, broadcasting the news as Seth entered the firehouse. He found Rick, the firehouse Chief, standing with Matt and Carl in front of the flat screen on the wall. Even

Chipster the mutt, who may or may not have had some wolfhound in him, sat with his ears back, facing the television. Seth shook hands with Rick first. He glanced at the TV, and fist-bumped his other two buddies. The other men were extra mainland deputies Kyle sent over to help with the manhunt. Seth didn't know them as well. "They can't seem to come up with anything new," Seth commented, as he noticed the same news clips from earlier.

Rick folded his arms. "They don't have any answers, but it seems to me this media hype isn't putting anyone's fears at ease. There's some rioting going on in Canada. Apparently, they don't have as much bottled water as the U.S." Too bad he didn't own stock in bottled water. The stockholders of IMH20 were now extremely wealthy men. "And they're blaming the U.S. for whatever's killing the fish. Canada says the U.S. is negligent with pollution."

"Give me a break," Matt huffed. "They sure don't mind giving us all their damn garbage. Don't they know we're the "Great Lakes State," not the "Great Waste State?" He'd read that in an article a couple years ago.

"Well, soon we might be the "Deadly Lakes State," Carl added.

Seth turned and noticed the plastic-wrapped pallet of IMH20 water sitting in the corner of the room. "Looks like you guys are prepared. When did that arrive?"

"We pulled it from the storage room. It's all we have, but we've ordered more, even though we won't get it for a while." Rick turned the TV volume down.

"The mayor wants to call a town meeting," Matt told Seth. Matt was in his thirties and joined the Chicory Fire Department when he moved to the island five years ago to care for his elderly father. He'd helped put the fire out at the station yesterday. "It might not be a bad idea. Everyone is freaking out."

"The water's contaminated," Dean said, walking into the room and quickly joining the conversation. "My wife has every pot we own on the stove boiling water. We've got a criminal running around who attacked two women and torched our station, and another six inches of snow is expected by nightfall. Seems like good reasons to freak out."

"You've got a well, don't you?" Seth asked.

"Yes, and I tried to tell my wife that. But she got on the internet today, and someone posted that the government is secretly spraying chemicals into the atmosphere in an attempt to change the climate. People are saying those deadly chemicals are falling to the earth in rain and snow, and that's what's killing everything. My wife thinks that if the land and soil are contaminated, it will seep into our well. She's convinced all the water will be arsenic."

Rick rolled his eyes. "Your wife saw the famous Chemtrail Conspiracy Theory. My wife was suckered by that theory years ago."

One of the deputies from the mainland rubbed the stubble on his chin thoughtfully and spoke up. "Yeah, I remember that theory. Wasn't it believed that high-flying aircraft were dumping harmful biological agents in the atmosphere? And that's why the contrails that normally dissipate in the sky could be seen as white lines stretching for miles that didn't go away? It was supposedly chemicals being dumped."

"It doesn't matter where the water comes from, the point is something is killing fish and wildlife, and no one knows what it is. So, I'm not taking any chances," Carl said, jamming his hands in his pockets.

Seth heard enough. "Look people, we need to stop watching the news and get down to business. We've got a criminal to catch, and that needs to be our focus for the day." He was pleased when Rick shut the TV off. "Here." He handed Dean a folder. "Did Connie leave the island safely?"

"Yup, no trouble." Dean opened the folder. "What's this?"

"There are a hundred and twenty-three houses on this island. Fifty-two are tourist rentals. Most are currently booked. Forty-eight homes have full-time residents living in them, and that leaves twenty-three that are winterized and empty from the snowbirds. "

Dean glanced around the men in the room. "That means our

guy is probably hiding in one of the twenty-three empty homes. It's not a bad number. We need to break up into teams of two and start driving by."

Seth nodded. "The snow is our friend. If you see footprints leading to empty houses, remember not many locals are out walking around." The island was small enough they could visit all the homes to check for broken locks. "I've posted the sketch IDs at Al's diner and the grocery store. The man's got to eat. We'll find him."

Seth pulled the door open as the men stood up to leave. There was a lot of work to do. And he planned to follow-up with Kyle, who was still investigating the disappearance of Dr. A.J. Seth really hoped nothing bad had happened to the Superman look-alike. He also needed to speak with one of the FBI agents Kyle was working with about the dead body. It was starting to eat at him, knowing that he and Jessica were the only two people who saw the formulas. He couldn't remember them, but he'd bet that Jessica could. And he wasn't sure how involved he wanted to make her.

Chapter 19

There was no need for a shower this morning, as Jessica had had a bath last night. She'd lit some candles she'd found under the sink and tied her hair up in a bun. It felt wonderful to soak in a large tub with the stress of the recent past slowly easing from her mind. The knot in her stomach had started to relax. Seth's house was a safe, comfortable place to be, and as she enjoyed her hot bath, she realized how accustomed she'd become to his clean, small home. If she were to find a place to live, she'd like something similar. Seth insisted she sleep in his bed, while he took the couch. She heard him throughout the night, and figured he was checking on every little noise. Sometimes she'd hear the crack of a twig in the woods just outside her window. She could imagine a raccoon or deer wandering over to where the light shone through the window from Seth's family room. The wind howled and tree branches scraped along the roof. Seth's house nestled in the woods provided all sorts of pleasant nature sounds, but she knew he was on his guard. She felt safe and comfortable knowing he was out there.

As she brushed her teeth and splashed cold water on her face, she thought about calling her sister. Janie was sick with the flu and Greg said she'd spent all day yesterday in bed sleeping. A lot had happened to Jessica since arriving on the island, and she was trying to put yesterday's nightmare behind her. Telling Janie about the attack would only make her anguish resurface. She wasn't supposed to talk about the organism, and that too would only cause further upset. She sighed as she walked back into the kitchen and glanced out the window. Another cold winter's day, with the sun trying to peek from the thick cloud cover. Seth's friend Chris was sitting outside, and it seemed odd to her that he should have to sit in a car, running the heat to stay warm. She opened the refrigerator, feeling a stir of humor. There was a rather large pile of lunch meats, two jars of mayo and two loaves of bread. When the time came for her to eat, a sandwich was the obvious choice.

A cooked steak sat on a black plate with cellophane wrap over it. Her mind immediately recalled the piece of flesh Dr. A.J. had taken from the wolf. She felt her stomach twist as she remembered the small worm that extended itself from its shell and disappeared inside the flesh. Her appetite vanished at the thought of the organism's tiny razor-sharp teeth eating its way through flesh. She closed the refrigerator and quickly threw her jacket and boots on.

Chris sat in his car, pulling long drags from his cigar. When he saw Seth's front door open, he quickly put the cigar out and hopped from his car. From a few feet away all he saw was shimmery gold hair whipping up at all angles in the wind. "Hello," he called out.

"I'm Jessica." She offered Chris her hand. Seth had given her an excellent description of what Chris looked like. He'd told her Chris was sixty-five but appeared much younger. And that he wore his hair long, hanging just above his shoulders, with the most obvious feature being his unruly curls. Chris did in fact have very curly, salt and pepper locks framing his face. He also had piercing blue eyes, which Seth hadn't mentioned. "I feel silly with you being out here. I'd like it if you could come in."

"Are you sure?"

"Yes, please. If you're going to be watching out for me, I don't see why you can't sit and watch TV and stay warm inside." She thought she had wanted to be alone, but it turned out she didn't.

Chris followed her inside the house. After five minutes, he had the television on, his feet propped on the coffee table, and a beer in his hand. It appeared to Jess this wasn't the first time he'd made himself at home in Seth's house. She felt better as she sat down at the kitchen table with her laptop. It was time to focus on her future, and where she was going to live.

Searching for apartments and condos was about as pleasant to her as riding on Seth's patrol boat in the freezing wind. Her eyes grew heavy, and she glanced away from the laptop screen to view the oval clock on the kitchen wall. It was already four o'clock in the afternoon. She'd spent two hours just replying to emails, and the other hour and half searching for places to live. Chris had only gotten up once to use the bathroom, and the television had remained on some network that played old reruns of the show M*A*S*H. Apparently Chris wasn't interested in the news. He also wasn't interested in conversation, which suited her just fine. She rose from the table and decided to make a few sandwiches.

Her shoulder and back throbbed, providing a constant reminder of the attack. The images kept creeping into her mind, and her heart rate would increase, making her stomach flip and roll. She purposely thought of Seth instead. Funny how he was the only thing she could think of that didn't depress her.

"That looks good."

Jessica jumped a little as she glanced up to meet Chris's cheerful blue eyes. She'd been so focused on her thoughts she hadn't seen him approach the counter. "I hope you like ham and salami."

"I like everything." He stared at her up and down. "Nice pajamas."

She still wore her blue t-shirt, and again explained why Janie had gotten it for her.

A light chuckle escaped from Chris as he grabbed another beer from the refrigerator, offering her one. "I've got a similar story except I can guarantee that my stalker chick was way crazier. She broke into my house and stole all my underwear and socks."

Jessica laughed, and instantly felt a comfortable camaraderie with Chris. His friendly tone and easy laugh put her at ease. "So how long have you known Seth?"

"Oh, we go back a few years now. Seth's a hell of a good guy."

She fixed her eyes on him with curiosity. "He seems a little…" What was the word she was looking for? "Severe."

He nodded with an easy laugh. "Yeah, that's a good word for him. He comes off as being unfriendly sometimes, and it doesn't help he's built like a brick house, and has that harsh look in his eyes, but that's not who he is at all."

"All bark and no bite?"

"Exactly." Chris took a swig of his beer and continued. "Seth's the kind of guy who would do anything for you, and hates it when you say thanks, or try to return the favor. He's considerate to a fault and thinks nothing of it. He makes an excellent Sheriff because he's very fair and reasonable. He wears a hard outer shell, but the guy has a heart of gold. Don't let him intimidate you."

The microwave beeped, reminding Jessica that her coffee was ready. She walked over to retrieve her mug. "I was intimidated at first. He appears angry a lot, but now I know he isn't."

Again Chris chuckled. "It's kinda cool actually. All he really has to do is look at people and they straighten right out. The local teens fear him, and when tourists get out of line, all Seth has to do is lean in close. They stop whatever they're doing and forget to breathe."

"Oh my gosh!" Jessica set wide eyes on Chris. "I know exactly what you mean." Seth had done that to her twice. Both times, she'd frozen and held her breath. Of course, she also had thought he was going to kiss her. But now she knew that was just his way of settling her down. When she'd been on the verge of a panic attack, he'd managed to turn her brain to mush by just leaning close.

Chris finished his last bite of sandwich. "Seth's ex-wife… she was a real piece of work. She never saw all the good in him. I used to hate when she'd rip on him behind his back. She'd complain that he was never talkative, never ambitious. She'd comment that a thundercloud always hung over his head. Looking back, I'm pretty sure that thundercloud was her."

"He doesn't talk about her much. My friend Mike and his wife also told me a few things."

"She really messed with his head. Between you and me, I think she was verbally abusive. She was a very critical person in general. Seth's a tough guy, so you wouldn't think he would stand for any kind of abuse. But he'd never hurt a woman, and it's just not in his nature to criticize. He never said one bad thing about her in return. I think when you're getting verbally knocked around by someone you love, it has to hurt. If you hear things enough you start to believe them." He took a long, slow swallow of beer. "We threw Seth a party after his divorce. No one liked her."

When Seth walked in at six o'clock, he found Jess laughing on the couch beside Chris. He was showing her pictures on his phone, his head close to hers. Seth had never heard Jessica giggle before, and the fact she and Chris looked like best buds on the couch didn't help the somber mood he'd been feeling all day.

"Hey," Chris said, turning to Seth.

"I could have been a damn intruder walking through the door. You're supposed to be on guard duty." Seth noted the gun holstered at Chris's side, and the way he'd given Jessica a look that conveyed some secret they both knew and shared.

Chris kept his smile in place. "So, any luck today?"

"No."

Jessica stood up next to Chris, turning to Seth. "There's a sandwich for you in the fridge."

"Big guy's home, so I'm going to take off." Chris held his hand out to Jessica.

"I really enjoyed your company today. Thanks for making me feel safe." She ignored his hand and gave him a hug instead. "I'll see you tomorrow."

After Chris left and Seth locked the front door, he strolled over to the refrigerator and pulled out an impressive-looking sandwich. It had a little of everything piled high on it. He didn't look up, as Jessica leaned against the counter. "So, you and Chris hit it off, I see. I thought you wanted to be alone."

"Oh, he's wonderful. I like him a lot."

He raised his eyes quickly to her smiling face. "Why are you still in your pajamas?"

His tone was brusque, but it didn't bother her at all. "I haven't stayed in my pajamas all day ever in my life. I'm trying new things." She shrugged her shoulders, and immediately regretted it when pain coursed down her arm.

Seth's eyebrows drew together. "Are you still in pain?" He set his plate aside and moved to her. "I should have told you where I keep my pain meds."

"It hurts when I use it, but I'm okay."

He stared at her in concern. "What did you do today?"

"I found some apartments for rent, and a really nice condo overlooking a pond. Did you find out who attacked me? Do you know if he's still on the island?"

He felt his stomach tighten at her words. She was looking for a place to live, which reminded him she'd soon be leaving. He answered her question with a simple "no" and proceeded to eat his sandwich. A moment later he was looking in the refrigerator for something to drink. He tossed an incredulous look over his shoulder. "You let Chris drink up all my beer?"

"He only had three."

Seth growled.

"Did you really just growl?" She laughed, watching as he hovered in front of the refrigerator, and then was surprised when he turned to her with a grin. When his lips curved up, he looked much different. Younger. "Did you have a bad day?"

He had a bad day, because nothing was accomplished. The mainland deputies and local volunteers hadn't found a single home with forced entry. They hadn't a single lead on where the attacker might be hiding. Seth was starting to think the man may have managed to get off the island. Kyle called to say Dr. A.J. was still missing, and there were no leads there either. "I don't like not having answers. I don't like not knowing where that son of a bitch is hiding, and I'm not sure Kyle's getting anywhere with anything. I half-expected the

EPA or FBI to be calling me for information about those papers. But Kyle says no one seems interested."

The theme song from the movie "Shrek" sounded, and Jessica reached for her phone. "It's my sister." She hesitated a moment. She still hadn't talked to her yet. "I'll take this in the bedroom."

Chapter 20

Only a mere four inches of snow fell. That was nothing for Upper Peninsula residents. A slight inconvenience to shovel, and that's about it. Seth would have used the snow-blower, but with the sun shining, and the temperature right around thirty, he welcomed the exercise.

It was ten a.m., and Jessica was still in bed. Seth tossed a pile of snow onto an already-large pile of snow and thought about how she'd seemed withdrawn and quiet after her call with her sister last night. She'd been on the phone for hours, and when she finally emerged from the bedroom, it was to say goodnight. She'd asked if she could take a bath, and Seth hadn't seen her since.

When his cell buzzed, he set his shovel down to answer it. It was Kyle.

"You know how you were complaining about not having answers or leads and you didn't think I was doing a good job?" Kyle's voice sounded cheerful.

"I didn't say you weren't doing a good job."

"Well, you were grumpy, and you showed it."

"I'm always grumpy. What do you have for me, Kyle?"

"The forensics dental consultant was able to obtain DNA samples from the teeth they found on the burnt body, and we now have a name. Doctor Mark Williams, who also happens to have a missing person's report filed on him. Apparently, this scientist has an old Aunt he used to contact faithfully every three months. She hasn't heard from him in eight months." Kyle took a sip of coffee, and then cursed when the heat burned his tongue. "And get this… he was working on some scientific organism stuff."

"Any leads on where the Vet may have gone?"

Kyle shook his head while holding the phone to his ear. "No. We've got nothing on that yet, but the identification of that body is promising. We'll dig around on where the guy was working."

So, progress was being made. He still had no leads on Jessica's attacker but identifying the body could lead to something. "I'll be available all day."

"How's Dr. Bennett doing?" Kyle knew she was staying at Seth's.

"She's better." He hoped.

Jessica was pouring coffee when Seth walked in the door, stomping snow from his boots on the rug. He tossed his jacket on the bench by the door and took his boots off.

"Want a cup?" she asked, before pouring him some coffee.

He nodded, walking toward her. "Nice Pajamas." She was wearing black cotton pants with a white drawstring and a white t-shirt with letters that read, IF YOU'RE NOT FEELING WELL AND NEED A DOCTOR, HEAD TO THE NEAREST GOLF COURSE. "Let me guess… your sister got that for you."

Handing him his coffee, a warm smile curved her lips. "She sure did. I was going on a big golf outing with about seventy-five doctors. I kept complaining that I didn't want to go because I'm not good at golfing. I was worried I'd look bad. So, when she gave me this shirt, she said, 'don't worry, everyone will be looking at your shirt and laughing instead of your awful swing.'"

"Did it work?"

"It did. I told you my sister has a great sense of humor."

She seems to like t-shirts, Seth thought, but didn't say anything. He moved about the kitchen in comfortable silence, noticing the way she enjoyed her coffee. It was only her fifth day on the island, and already he knew that she liked to close her eyes after that first sip, and she'd hold the cup with two hands, as if she was holding the

Holy Grail.

"What time's Chris arriving?" Jessica thought she should probably put some clothes on today. She wouldn't mind taking a walk in the woods if Seth would let her outside.

"I told him not to come. I'm staying home today."

She turned to him. "Don't you have a lot of work to do?"

"Nothing I can't do from home, and Dean is handling a lot of things for me."

"Oh. Hey, I have something for you." She quickly walked into the bedroom, and then returned holding a pad of paper out to him.

Seth took it and glanced down. "What's this?"

"I couldn't sleep last night, so I decided to write down everything I could remember about those papers. I've already forgotten a lot, and I don't think the formulas are right, but I wrote down everything I could think of."

The words "Destroyer of Human Life" were written in the top corner the same way it had been on the originals. The hypothesis chart looked exactly the same to Seth. Her writing was sloppy, but he could read it. "This is really good work." It actually *was* good, because now he had something tangible he could give Kyle.

"I googled some of the formula that I didn't know. I think the CuSO4 was part of something else with more numbers. I wish I could remember because I feel like that was important. I think part of the formula was salt. After doing some research trying to remember the numbers, and given that NaCl is sodium chloride, I think maybe the organism might not be able to survive in salt water. That gives me a little hope." She stepped closer to him and pointed at the paper. "I remember seeing this 1:1, and I think that means ratio of sodium and chloride ions. And this Enterobacter Sakazakii is a type of bacteria that is found naturally in the environment, and sometimes in wastewater. I remember the sequence Type 4 was written on the paper." She lifted the page and pointed to the other side. "And this: 15-23 MYA. A good microbiologist will know more. I'm not positive this is right, but I hope it is." She hadn't been able to stop thinking about the papers, and how they must be connected to the dead fish. "I wish I knew what that one word that started with a B and ended with St could be. It was underlined, so I think it was important. I'm hoping it'll come to me."

He looked at her appreciatively. "I've got a feeling you might just be the one to save the planet." He tore off the three sheets of paper from the pad and folded them so they'd fit in his jeans pocket.

She scoffed. "Let's just hope the planet isn't going to need saving."

"Well just in case, it might not hurt to have a little fun before the world ends." A humorous grin stretched across his face. "I thought if you're feeling up for it, we could maybe go for a ride on my sled. My snowmobile seats two people. We can ride over to Mike's house, and you can then use one of his sleds." He studied her a moment. "If you're feeling up to it."

She didn't like being caustic about the possible end of the world because the organism was in fact real and terrifying. But Seth was right. If the shit was going to hit the fan soon, she wanted to experience snowmobiling first. "I'd like that."

He felt an immediate jolt, which he recognized as a thrill. Something he hadn't felt in a very long time. His facial expression gave nothing away as he told her, "Dress warm."

Chapter 21

The Touring Snowmobile had plush, heated seats, and was plenty big for two people. Seth made a point of going over all the parts and explaining how to use the clutch and brakes. Jess had to run back in to get an extra pair of socks. She joked that his long explanation made her toes freeze. When she came back out the front door, she found him waiting on the sled with his typical vexed expression. She couldn't resist picking up snow and forming a perfect snowball. She threw it at him, not expecting to hit him above his shoulder, and laughed when the snow broke apart, hitting him in the face.

Seth quickly turned, startled at first, but then smiled at the way she was laughing. "Oh, you want to throw snowballs, huh?" He got off the sled, bending over to sweep up as much snow as his big hands could hold.

"No!" Jessica held her hands up, and then squealed when she realized he was almost done packing his projectile. "I just couldn't resist, but…" The snowball landed on her chest, barely breaking apart. "Oh, you threw that so wimpy!"

"Wimpy?" Seth picked up more snow, smiling as she circled around the tree in his front yard. He took a few steps toward the tree, his feet sinking in the foot of snow that covered his lawn. He threw another snowball but hit the tree.

"You missed me!" She jumped out throwing another snowball at his head.

He laughed. "You've got nice aim, woman." He threw another one at her back as she bent over collecting more snow.

The snow was perfect for packing, and she couldn't remember the last time she had a fun snowball fight. "For a big strong guy, you throw like a girl," she teased, dodging his next snowball.

Seth couldn't remember the last time he really enjoyed himself. Her laughter and smile were infectious, and when she started kicking snow up at him, he dove on top of her. "I could give you an old-fashioned whitewash. You should be nice, and not antagonize me." He picked up a chunk of snow in his gloved hand and held it close to her face.

"No, don't!" she yelled out while laughing. "I'm sorry. I don't want a whitewash." She didn't feel cold, though she was breathing heavily, and her breath made a little cloud against the crisp air. She was aware that Seth was purposely trying not to crush her, as he leaned over to his side. "You know, you don't look so tough and scary when you smile." She loved his smile and was aware that her pulse was racing from more than exertion. She stared into his eyes, and realization struck her. This was the feeling she'd never felt with Greg. There was never a deep yearning. Perhaps because Greg pursued her so fast, she never had time to want or need. Without meaning to or trying, Seth was far sexier than any man she had ever known, and for the first time ever, she felt an incredibly strong desire. She reached her hand up and wiped the snow from his cheek.

Seth thought she looked radiant. Her eyes were a beautiful aqua green, and her cheeks were flushed red. He dropped his eyes to her smooth lips. It'd been almost a year since he and the guys had gone to the mainland city bars. He'd met a woman around last Christmas, and she'd invited him to her house for the night. She'd been nice, easy on the eyes, and eager to date him, but not someone he'd chosen to pursue. Staring down at Jessica, he realized she was very much a woman he would want to see again. But he'd learned the hard way that most women didn't want to live on a small, wooded island, and long-distance relationships were too hard. If he wasn't extremely careful, he could find himself thoroughly depressed when it was time for her to leave.

Staring into his eyes with anticipation, Jessica felt her stomach flutter. She held his stare, waiting for him to do what she hoped he was going to. But then he drew his brows together, clearly changing his mind, and rolled away from her.

"Let's go ride, before you get too cold." He helped her to her feet.

A moment ago, she'd been burning up, and now that he was heading to the sled she could feel the cool air creep along her skin, along with disappointment. She tried to brush off the awkward moment, by laughing. "I've got snow down my shirt now." She took the helmet he offered her and felt a little relief when he smiled.

A buck stood between two trees. A bare branch glittering with snow blocked the view of his thick neck, and his antlers seemed too big for his head. Jessica marveled at the big brown eyes staring right at her. She'd never been close to a deer before and felt a thrill at the simple pleasure of seeing him. Seth stopped in the middle of the trail to point him out. She'd been holding tight around his waist, and now leaned back slightly as she noticed a stunning doe step up beside the buck. Her career had taken her away from nature for far too long, and she knew this was something she wanted to keep in her life. She vowed to take long walks in the woods on her days off and make time for this type of pleasure that brought her so much joy.

Seth turned in his seat, catching the look of admiration on her face. The helmet she wore had a clear plastic shield, but he still knew the moment he caught her eye that she loved the ride. It couldn't have been a more perfect day for gliding through the forest. The snow was deep, and the sun shone brilliantly, causing the tiny snow crystals to glitter. They sat for a moment, admiring the beauty of the forest and the white-tailed deer as they leapt away, blending into the woods.

Just as Seth turned his head, he caught the flicker of light that reflected off a scope. He knew immediately what he was seeing, and quickly moved in front of Jessica. A loud shot cracked through the woods, and Seth felt a hot, stabbing pressure in his leg as he pushed Jessica to the ground, landing on top of her. He glanced up and saw the scope, and the muzzle aimed at them. Seth quickly rolled with her behind the sled. "Stay down!" The next bullet just missed them.

He pulled the sled in front of them for a shield and unzipped his jacket to reach for his gun holster. "It's him!" Another bang sounded, followed by a metal ping as the bullet hit the side of the snowmobile. Seth raised his gun, taking aim in the direction of the shooter.

When Jess heard the loud crack of Seth's gun, she was thankful her helmet and hat offered protection for her ears. She tried to lift her head to see what was happening. Seth's weight was pressing her into the ground, his body shielding hers. The exposed flesh on her neck was against the ice-cold snow. She couldn't move.

"Crawl over to that tree and get behind it. Stay as low as possible!" He rolled off her and began shooting.

She did as he said. Her shoulder sent a jolt of pain down her arm when she pushed up quickly and got to her knees. She moved as fast as she could and placed her back flush against the bark of a wide tree trunk. More shots sounded as she raised her face shield so she could see. Her breathing was so heavy it steamed up the plastic. "Seth!" she called out when she saw him lying face-down in the snow.

Lifting his head slightly, Seth pulled his helmet off. "Stay there!" he told her. A bullet hit the snow mere inches from his shoulder, and he quickly rolled away. Then he aimed his gun and pulled the trigger twice. He rolled again toward the tree that shielded Jessica.

She'd seen Seth's frequent look of indignation many times since she'd met him, but she now saw something different in his eyes. She knew immediately this was his true look of rage, and the difference was alarming. It was a look she'd never want to be on the receiving end of. But at the moment, it eased her fear. It assured her Seth was completely competent, skilled, and tough. If he got his hands on the shooter, that man wouldn't stand a chance.

He leaned in close to her, his back against the tree, as his stiff fingers quickly pushed rounds into the cartridge of his Glock 17. He pulled his cell out and swiped the screen. He was pleased when Dean answered on the second ring. "I need backup. I've got Jess with me on the trail, and we're being shot at. We're between my house and Mike's, a quarter-mile from Chick Cold Creek, and maybe a few yards from the road."

"Keep your phone on, I'll use your GPS to track you. I've got Kyle with me. We'll be there soon." Dean headed for his car.

"Oh, and call the Ambo. I've been shot." Seth ended the call placing his phone back in his pocket. He could hear a snowmobile in the distance start up. The guy was probably trying to get away now. He quickly peered around the tree and shot another round. He watched the man fly forward on the sled. "I think I got him!" The sled kept moving, and Seth's gun was out of range. "I hope I got the son of a bitch. He won't get far now."

"Seth, where were you hit?" Jessica was already pulling his jacket open, searching for blood. She couldn't believe how he'd just off-handedly stated he'd been shot.

"My leg. I'm fine." Although his vision was slightly off.

The red snow showed her which leg was bleeding. "Seth…." There was a lot of blood. She saw the hole in his black snow pants and pulled at the material until it tore a nice-sized hole in the nylon.

"Damn, Jess. These are expensive snow pants." He'd have kept wearing them with a little hole, but she'd just torn them apart.

She tried to tear his jeans also but couldn't. "I need a knife to cut through your jeans. I want to see the damage."

Seth tore the material for her. "I'm fine." His breathing was shallow as he leaned his head back against the tree.

The bullet wound oozed too much blood, and judging from where it was, Jessica feared a main artery could be hit. "This isn't okay. You're losing a lot of blood." She raised her head and met Seth's eyes. His features were soft, his face relaxed, and for the first time she was struck by how incredibly handsome he was. She quickly returned her attention to the three-inch gash in his upper leg. Needing to make a tourniquet, she pulled her snow pants down her hips, and quickly yanked her brown belt out from the loops in her jeans.

She worked fast, focusing on tightening the belt as hard as she could just above his wound.

"I'd like to go after the son of a bitch," he said, his voice sounding softer than normal.

Jess ignored him and pressed her fingers to Seth's pulse. "We can't stay here and wait. If the bullet went through your femoral artery, you'll bleed to death." Fear made her voice pitch. "Your pulse is weak."

He felt the change in his body, and knew she was right. His stomach felt queasy, and he sensed a decrease in alertness. He reached his hand up to set it on her face, but she moved too fast. She was on her feet, grabbing his helmet, and shaking the snow from it. She pushed it on his head and tried to pull him up. He felt a rush of blood weaken him and fell back against the tree.

Panic surged through her. "Seth!" she called out, trying to hold him up. "Oh my gosh, please, please try to get on the sled." He was simply too large and heavy for her to move.

He caught the look of distress on her flushed face, his vision blurred. He forced himself to stand and managed to stumble to the sled. It took all his energy to swing his leg over the seat.

"I'm driving!" She sat in front of him, practically on his lap, until he scooted back, and began telling her what to do. He used his clipped, bossy tone with her, which didn't faze her in the least.

Tightly gripping the handlebars of the sled, she gave it plenty of gas. It took a few moments for her to get the feel of it, her legs pressing hard against the seat for balance. The trail was wide, and she was thankful she didn't have to turn the sled too much in order to avoid hitting trees. Relief eased the knot in her stomach when the sled dipped down onto the smooth plowed road. She heard the siren and turned her head to see the lights of the ambulance coming toward her. Seth's heavy body leaned into hers, and she pushed him back enough to look at his face. His dark brown eyes were heavy, his mouth drawn down in that perpetual scornful pout of his. She knew he was close to passing out.

Chapter 22

A faint beeping repeated in Seth's ear. His eyes opened to bright florescent lights, the beveled square glass coming into focus.

"Hey buddy," Dean said, leaning over Seth. Dean turned to Carl. "Go tell the nurse he's awake."

Seth glanced around the room. "Where is she?"

"She's safe. She's right outside. Chris is with her. I've got a couple deputies guarding the entrances. Jessica said you shot the guy, so if he comes here for help, we'll be ready."

The beeping was from a machine that was pushing air into a bag strapped to his calf. Seth raised his hand and stared at the IV taped to his hand. "So, I take it I survived?"

"No. This is heaven. The bullet hit a main artery and you died."

Seth narrowed his eyes at Dean. "That's really not funny."

Dean laughed. "Yeah, my bad. The truth is you *would* have died if Jessica hadn't tied off the artery once they got you in the ambo. Once she had access to tools that lady did serious work on you." Dean had been extremely impressed. "She was also able to remove the bullet and thinks she may not have damaged too much muscle in the process. It didn't hit any bone. The docs here said Jess saved your life." Dean rolled his long black sleeve up and showed Seth the crease of his elbow. "We all gave our blood for you. Turns out Jessica has your exact blood type too." Dean lifted his eyebrows a few times and smiled.

"Great." A frown creased Seth's brow as he tried to sit up slightly. It felt like lead weights were pressing against his body.

"I know it's going to kill you to have to stay put, but you can't leave here until your blood count's back to normal. Kyle has everything under control. He's got his entire unit swarming the island. The K-9's will find this guy. He took a real chance shooting at you today." Dean handed Seth the cup of water beside the bed.

"Go get her!" Seth demanded, setting the water on the tray beside his bed. He didn't like that Jessica was somewhere in the clinic with Chris. Probably giggling with him.

"You're awake, and already barking out orders," Jessica said as she entered the room, feeling instant relief at his scowl.

Feeling his tension ease, Seth let his eyes roam over her. She was still wearing her white snow pants, but her jacket was off, and she wore a fuzzy, tight-fitting red sweater. The color looked great with her messy blond hair that fell in tangles around her shoulders. He knew the blood spots on her clothes were from him.

Chris entered the room. "There are two FBI agents here who want to speak with you. Are you up for it?"

"They've been here for hours. I told them to come back later, or go join the manhunt, but they insisted on waiting," Dean said, his tone ambiguous.

"It's okay." Seth turned his eyes on Jessica. "You stay here."

A minute later, two men wearing black pants and white dress shirts entered the room. Seth took in their appearance and offered a frank gaze, while feeling a sense of unease. He felt like he'd seen the men before.

"I'm agent John Rife and this is my partner, agent John Vaunt." They each nodded at Seth rather than offering a hand. They looked at Jessica. "Ms. Doctor Bennett." Rife gave a look to both Dean and Chris which clearly said "you-may-leave-now."

Dean cleared his throat. "We'll be in the hall if you need us." He followed Chris out the door.

Seth noticed both men stood about the same height, their body language similar in their rigid stance, and the way agent Rife put his hands in his pocket. Both men appeared to be in their late thirties.

"We're here about the papers you found on the dead body. We believe they contained—" John Rife gave a thoughtful glance to his partner— "sensitive information. We'd like to know exactly what you saw and what you think was on them."

Something about the way agent Rife spoke put unease in Seth's gut. "Does the EPA or FBI have any idea what's causing the fish to die?"

"We aren't at liberty to say."

"Have you found Dr. A.J. yet? Did he ever contact you?"

"No. We aren't here to answer questions, Sheriff. We're here for you to answer ours. And we're going to need Ms. Bennett to come with us."

"Well, you're a little late with your inquiry. Those papers disappeared days ago, and I can't for the life of me remember what was on them."

"Seth." Jessica gave him a confused look. "I—"

"Dr. Bennett, I know you think those papers may have had something to do with the fish, because there were notes about an organism that eats various algae, but I don't think that's enough to go on," Seth said, staring at her with steely eyes. "And since we don't remember exactly what was written, and you yourself said you can't remember the formulas, I don't think we should waste the agents' time."

Jessica didn't understand why Seth was lying, but she trusted him. She noticed the way he'd called her Dr. Bennett and could read from his face he was up to something.

Agent Rife threw a look to his partner and shifted on his feet. "We'd like to have Ms. Bennett accompany us to our office. Perhaps with a bit more information, she might be able to remember." Agent Vaunt stepped forward and placed his hand on Jessica's shoulder.

That was one more indication which confirmed to Seth that something wasn't right. He reached down and pulled the Velcro cuff off his leg. A shooting pain seared up the entire side of his body, but he ignored it.

"Seth, what are you doing!?" Jessica reached her hand out to stop him.

Agent Vaunt took another step forward, wrapping his hand around Jessica's arm. "You need to come with us now."

"She's not going anywhere with you." Seth gripped her hand like he was holding on for dear life. "Take your hand off her now."

Agent Vaunt dropped his arm at the ice in Seth's command.

"Dean!" Seth yelled out.

Dean was in the doorway, with Chris right behind him. Concern etched his face as he stared into the room. Seth swung his leg over the bed, his hospital gown rising. He winced at the pain, and his voice was strained. "Escort these men out. It's time for them to leave." He stared at the agent standing beside Jessica. "I think you'll understand why I need to check your IDs."

"You don't have the authority, sir," Agent Vaunt replied.

"You don't have the right to take her with you. She's got nothing to give you, and neither do I." Seth looked at Chris. "Get their badge numbers and make sure these men are who they say they are." Now Seth realized where he'd seen them. They were the men in black he'd seen on the beach the day Jessica arrived. Wearing long black trench coats, with black sunglasses. They had reminded him of the movie "Men in Black."

Vaunt had a glare in his eyes that made Dean wonder if he was considering a fight. Seth noticed it too and used all his strength to get to his feet, while pushing Jessica behind his back.

"Seth, you can't get up!" Jessica leaned into him, wanting to help support him, worried that he'd injure his leg further. She couldn't believe he had the strength to stand.

Agent Rife set his hand on Vaunt's shoulder. "Not now," he said calmly, and smiled at both Chris and Dean. "I can see Sheriff Johnson is upset. He's been shot, and probably isn't thinking straight. We'll come back later." He turned his head to Jessica. "Ms. Bennett, we'll speak with you another time."

Seth tightened his grip on Jessica's hand, and the moment the men left the room, he sat back down on the bed, breathing heavily.

"What the hell was that about?" Dean asked, looking from Jessica to Seth.

"Chris, I'm serious, go follow them out and check their I.D.'s and badge numbers. I don't think they're legit agents. Be careful."

Chris nodded and quickly left the room.

"Seth, what's going on?" Jessica tried to make him lie back and examined his wound. "You have to lie down. Putting pressure on your leg can open this wound back up."

Releasing a long, slow breath, Seth laid back on the bed. He hated not having his strength, but there was no way he'd let them take Jessica. "Where the hell is my cell phone?" He looked at Dean. "I want you to get hold of Kyle. I don't trust those men at all. You should go back up Chris."

"Why?" Jessica asked. Her nerves were jumping while feeling for Seth's pulse.

Gunshots sounded in the distance, and Seth instinctually grabbed Jessica's arm. "Where the hell is my gun?" he roared at Dean.

Dean reached behind his back, pulled out Seth's gun, and handed it to him. "Here. I loaded it for you." His eyebrows drew together. "Seth, for the love of God…" He watched as Seth yanked out his IV. "Just stay put. I can handle this." Dean peered out the door first, glancing down the hall. Nurses and doctors were running, heading in their direction. More gunshots sounded. Dean drew his own gun and proceeded to leave the room.

"Seth," Jessica moved in front of him as he tried to stand. She pushed him back down. "Don't you dare put weight on that leg!"

"Get me my damn clothes. We're leaving."

"You're insane! You almost died! You can't leave! "

He placed all his weight on his good leg, while staring at her with steel determination. "Watch me."

She couldn't believe how strong and stubborn he was. "You can't put jeans on. They won't fit over your bandages. You need sweatpants or scrubs."

Seth ignored her and put his shirt on over the hospital gown. He felt ridiculous. Dean ran back in the room. "They shot the tires out on our cars but missed your truck. Chris is okay, they just knocked him out. The doctors are checking him out now." His words poured out in a hurry.

Jessica gasped as Seth grabbed her arm to keep her from running out the door.

"He's okay." Dean held up a flat palm to Seth. "You're not going after them."

"I know I'm not, but you are. Get Kyle Steller on the phone. I want his team monitoring the ferry."

Dean watched in amazement as Seth bent down and somehow managed to put his socks on, and then his boots. "How the hell did you know they weren't real FBI agents?" He'd sat watching those two men for hours while Seth was in recovery. "They sure as hell acted like stiff cops, and their IDs looked real."

If she hadn't been so upset, with her nerves on red alert, Jessica may have laughed at Seth's muscular bare legs in his big black snow boots. His shirt was bunched up over the hospital gown and his jacket over that. His left leg was wrapped with layers of thick white gauze. He leaned on her, and she took his weight, wrapping her arm around his waist. "You need a wheelchair. You have to keep this leg elevated." It was a bad idea for him to leave the hospital, and she looked at Dean with concern. "Can you grab a wheelchair, please?" She turned to Seth, "sit down and wait for the wheelchair. You're not walking out of here. If you're going to be stubborn and ignore doctors' orders, I'm going to sedate you."

Seth eased himself back on the bed and checked the chamber of his gun. "You're a bossy little thing," he said calmly.

"You're the most stubborn man I've ever met," she said, placing her hands on her hips.

He shot her his best smile. "Yeah, but you're safe, and I'm keeping it that way."

Half an hour later, Seth carefully got comfortable on his

couch, gritting his teeth, as Jessica raised his leg upon a pillow. She'd helped remove his boots and got him a pair of sweatpants from his bedroom. Seth got the sense she liked having something to do, and that playing nursemaid to him kept her mind off other things. He'd talked to Kyle and felt somewhat relieved that an extensive manhunt was already underway. He trusted Dean, Chris, and his buddies at the firehouse to handle the things he couldn't. They were all out on sleds in groups of two, helping in the search. Now there were three suspects hiding on the island. Seth wanted to be in on the action and hated feeling helpless. But he also knew that even if he hadn't been shot, he wouldn't leave Jessica alone. He sure as hell wasn't going to leave her alone with Chris anymore.

Jessica dropped to the floor in front of the couch, satisfied Seth's wound wasn't bleeding. "You lost a ton of blood, and it takes time for your body to recover. You have to rest, Seth." It was ridiculous she had to lecture him about something so obvious. She leaned sideways against the sofa and rested her hand on his arm. She knew he was in considerable pain and refused to take anything because he wanted to stay alert and protect her.

Flinching, Seth turned on his side so he could face her better. She was looking less peaked, but there was still weariness in her eyes. "So did you enjoy your first time snowmobiling this afternoon?"

She was surprised how easy her face lifted in a smile. She wouldn't think in her current state she would find anything funny, but the way Seth asked, with his serious face and stone-dry humor, she had to laugh. "Well, Seth," as she unsuccessfully tried to return his blank stare, "Minus being shot at, and the fake FBI agents, and having to sew you up and give you my blood, I'd say my afternoon was wonderful."

"I thought it went pretty good."

"I did love the ride, and the woods are beautiful. I also loved seeing deer."

"Yeah, the deer was a bonus. I planned that."

She laughed again, and when Seth finally smiled, she could

see the humor light up his face, and his dark eyes held an unfamiliar gleam. He was exceptionally handsome when he smiled. She felt her stomach do a little somersault, and then she grew serious. "You know, I would have gone with those men today. I thought they were actually Federal agents and would have left with them thinking I was going to the station to answer questions. God only knows what would have happened to me. How did you know?"

Seth brushed the cascade of hair covering her neck, behind her shoulder. He studied her throat where the bruises were yellowing. "I'd seen those men before on the beach. I just had a feeling based on the things they said, the way they acted." He gently ran his fingers along the side of her cheek, watching as her eyes drifted shut, and then back open to meet his. "I'm sorry I wasn't able to protect you from all the bad things that have happened to you since you arrived. I promised Mike I'd help make sure you were safe and well cared for. I'd say I've failed that request."

She gave him a look of astonishment. "Did you just say you're sorry?" His eyes stayed level with hers, and he gave no response, so she continued. "I didn't think the word sorry was in your vocabulary. I can think of several times the past few days where you could have apologized. For not returning my calls, for showing up late for dinner, for the chafed, fiery tone you've sometimes used with me. But God, Seth, you apologize for the one thing you have nothing to apologize for." She leaned closer to him, her eyes on his. "You have done nothing but provide me comfort and protection. It's not your fault what's happened due to the body and those papers. I'm alive because of you. If you hadn't shielded me at the sled, that bullet would have hit me, not you."

"I should have been more alert. I knew the guy was still running loose, and I should have protected you better."

"You took a bullet for me. You saved my life. Protection doesn't get any better than that." She thought about how he'd lain over her. "And then you kept me from going with those men at the clinic. Seth, don't apologize when all I want to do is thank you."

He looked at his hand resting on the nape of her neck. All he had to do was pull her closer. That's all he wanted.

Suddenly there was a knock at the door. Seth moved so fast, she fell back. He grabbed the gun he'd set on the coffee table next to him. He managed to stand, keeping his weight on his right leg. "Stay here."

"You can't walk!" she whispered harshly.

He ignored her and limped toward the kitchen. His leg throbbed and pain shot up his left side, but he ignored it. He cautiously moved to the door, carefully peeking through the peephole, while keeping his body close to the wall. He could see Kyle's face. Jessica was moving closer, and he glared at her. "Stay put." He couldn't trust that it was only Kyle at the door. The top chain was in place, and he had three other locks below it. He spoke through the door. "Are you alone?"

"Yeah, sorry, I should have called," Kyle yelled.

Seth opened the door a crack, keeping his gun ready. He peeked his head out just enough to see on either side of Kyle, then quickly yanked his buddy inside and shut the door, locking all three bolts. "You should have told me you were coming."

"Yeah, well, I've been busy scouring the island and talking on my cell all day. I guess I didn't think about it." He eyed Seth up and down. "You were shot in the leg, should you be standing?"

"No, he should not!" Jessica replied.

Kyle turned from Seth to Jessica. "Aww… you must be the gorgeous doctor everyone's been talking about."

"Who is everyone?" Seth asked in a tone that sounded annoyed.

"Chris… Dean… some doctor at the clinic." He waved Seth's attitude off and stretched his hand out to Jessica. "You really are pretty. You wouldn't happen to have a twin sister, would you?"

"As a matter of fact—" She caught the gleam in his eye that said he was teasing and already knew she had a twin. "Oh, funny," she laughed. Kyle was very attractive. She could tell right away he was a charmer, and probably about Seth's age. He probably handed out more broken hearts than speeding tickets in his day. He had a clean-shaven face, a devilish grin, and a buzz cut that suited the officer image. For a moment Jessica thought of Greg and realized Kyle would be Janie's type of guy. She wasn't sure what her own type was, but as she glanced at Seth's hard, indignant chiseled face, she realized tall and brooding might fit.

Seth didn't appreciate Kyle's joke, or the way he held Jessica's hand longer than necessary. "Did you catch anyone, Kyle?"

"No. But we found two dead bodies." Kyle surveyed Seth's house while Seth hobbled to the kitchen table and sat like he was pissed off. "This is a great place you've got. Did you decorate this yourself?"

Jessica placed a chair under Seth's leg and inspected his dressings for blood. "It's fabulous, right? It doesn't fit him at all. I asked the same question. But he did do it himself, and he has amazing taste."

Smiling in agreement, Kyle walked past the kitchen, and stood staring at the open family room. "It's small but has a real nice feel to it." He knew nothing about decorating so he had no idea what style the house was.

"Okay, I'm glad you guys like my home. Can we stay focused please?" Seth rubbed his aching leg, the pain making him more irritable by the moment. "Dead bodies?"

Jess took one look at him and moved quickly. She picked up the bottle of Vicodin from the counter and handed Seth a pill with a glass of water. "Since you insist on using your injured leg, you better at least stay on schedule with your pain meds. You can't keep refusing it, Seth." She wasn't taking no for an answer.

Taking the glass from her, he immediately downed the pill. "Kyle, can you explain about the two bodies?" He was eager to hear the details.

Kyle returned to the kitchen table and sat down.

"I'd offer you a beer, Kyle, but we're all out. Would you like some water?" Jessica asked.

"I'm not out of beer, Jess." Seth ran a frustrated hand through his hair. "God, a real man *never* runs out of beer."

"But you said Chris drank it all."

"I've got another case in the garage."

"Oh." She was headed to the garage door.

Seth shot Kyle a killer look. "Wait!" Kyle jumped up. "I'll get it. You sit down." Kyle ran to the garage door located to the left of the kitchen. When he came back, he was holding four bottles and a bag of chips under his arm. After he settled himself at the table, he proceeded to explain his day. "Your boys at the firehouse found the FBI fakes' car abandoned at the grocery store. By the time I arrived, they had also found both bodies in the woods. Dean and Chris confirmed they were the men who saw you at the clinic." He took a long sip of beer. "So, my theory is that when they left the clinic, they went to meet the man who shot at you, and probably attacked Jessica," shifting his gaze from her to Seth, "and probably burned the station down. My guess is, that guy shot the two men, and then took off on a snowmobile. Dean followed the tracks to the shore on the west side of the Island. We think he probably had a boat anchored there. We found the abandoned snowmobile. It was a rental under a bogus name. And Dean doesn't think the guy was shot, because we found no blood."

"If he had a boat, that would explain where he was hiding when we searched all the homes on the island." Seth wanted a beer, but instead he picked up the glass of water and downed it. He didn't want to mix alcohol and pain meds when he needed to be on guard. "Any IDs for the two bodies?"

"Yeah. Forensics is acting fast. One was an ex-con. He was known for taking various shady jobs. I've got some deputies tracing his background, trying to find out who may have hired him. The other guy had no rap sheet, lost his job in banking a while ago, and has no other work record. He obviously fell into the wrong line of work, and now he's dead."

So, no good leads from them, Seth thought.

"Okay, but we know this all relates to the dead fish and the papers we found, right?" Jessica asked. "I mean the guy that attacked me was there for the papers, and we need to make sure they end up in the hands of *real* FBI agents." Jessica stared at Kyle. "I don't understand why no one seems interested in the organism Dr. A.J. found. We saw that thing with our own eyes. It was unlike anything—"

Kyle held his hand up. "We've got nothing tangible. Dr. A.J.'s clinic was searched, and we couldn't find any wolf carcasses or anything. We've got no leads. The body that was burned in the station house has been identified. The guy's name was Mark Williams, a biologist. The only information we have on him is from a 92-year-old aunt in a nursing home, who says he's missing." Kyle popped a chip in his mouth from the bag he'd opened. "The papers are gone, and with you not really knowing for sure what was on them, I don't even know what I'd say if I called someone."

Leaning forward in his chair, Seth asked, "What do you mean *if* you called someone? I thought you did."

Kyle shook his head. "Well, I sort of indicated that because I planned to. But I was waiting to get more evidence, a lead, something more to go on than just, 'hey some Sheriff and doctor read some dead guy's science notes and they think it might possibly involve some crazy flesh-eating organism, but I don't have anything to prove it."

"But we saw it!" Jessica's voice rose a notch. "We know things that the FBI or EPA should know. We," she waved a finger from Seth to herself, "were almost killed because of it."

Seth put his hand on her arm. "Jess, he's right. The way the system works, you must have evidence. You must have something more tangible than a hunch. I have a feeling this guy that shot at us is behind everything. He's working hard to make sure all the evidence disappears. We need to find out who he is and who he's working for." Seth hated that his leg was throbbing and that he felt so exhausted he just wanted to sleep.

"I have to find him." Kyle stood up. "You, my friend, have to rest and heal that leg. I'll keep you updated, but right now you're on medical leave. Dean and I will take care of everything. I'll keep more officers on the island for a few weeks to help out. I want both of you protected also. I'll have my deputies watch the house in case this guy is dumb enough to return. I've also got the ferry covered." Kyle looked at Jessica and guessed by the look on her face she was about to protest further. "Look. The EPA knows about this organism. Don't think for a second they don't know what's going on. If you're right and Mark Williams was somehow responsible or connected, they won't be able to turn up any more leads than we can. I'm still looking into it."

Jessica turned to Seth. "Maybe we should give him the notes I wrote." She glanced back at Kyle. "You said you need something tangible, here it is." She walked to the counter and took the notes from the drawer where she'd put them when they returned from the clinic. This time, she'd taken a picture of them with her phone, and sent a backup copy to her email. She gave the notes to Kyle. "I tried to write down everything I could remember. What if the formula for how to kill this thing was included?"

He glanced at the paper. "Am I supposed to be able to read this?" It looked like chicken scratch to him. Jess rolled her eyes. "My writing isn't that bad. Seth could read it."

"Barely," Seth muttered.

"Whatever." she put her hands on her hips. "Just give it to someone with the EPA or FBI. Maybe they can figure something out."

Kyle didn't want to argue further with a clearly determined woman. "Okay. I'm going to head out and let Seth get some rest." He eyed Seth while tucking the papers in his pocket. "You look like hell, buddy."

Chapter 23

The waves smashed against the small aluminum fishing boat, and water poured over the wide beam. The wind was as furious as the waves, and Shawn resented being stuck on the water. His stomach battled unending seasickness, and if he didn't return to shore soon, he was going to freeze to death. The island was swarming with cops, and he'd therefore spent hours anchored a mile offshore, lying down on the hard, wet floor, his body sandwiched between the boat's two chairs. Malek wasn't paying him enough for this intolerable misery. He should've just found the nearest harbor, docked the damn craft, and found a motel. But he figured all the nearby marinas would be patrolled. As much as he hated the water and cold temps, he at least felt safe on the boat. But the weather wouldn't let him stay out long and beaching the craft on the shores of Marquette before the sun's grand morning appearance was perhaps his best bet.

He glanced down at his watch and thought he'd try giving his boss a call. So what if it was 3 a.m.? If for any reason he was caught on shore, this could be his last chance to update Malek. He removed his thick gloves and forced his cold stiff fingers to work the phone. He was pleased when Malek's groggy voice answered on the fourth ring.

"This better be important."

Shawn felt a moment's rage toward his boss. He might be paying him, but he didn't know the job had put him on a wet, rocking boat in the middle of winter. "It's always important," Shawn snapped, holding the phone with his shoulder so he could put his gloves back on. "Those two Johns you hired failed. They were completely worthless."

"I know they failed. Did you take care of them?"

"I did. I'm sure the cops have found their bodies, so I hope you covered your trail."

"Of course." Malek had thought sending fake FBI men might gain him more intel on whether the sheriff and doctor were a threat. The Sheriff had said neither of them could remember anything written on the papers Mark Williams had on him. The men were still supposed to kill the doctor, but the meddling sheriff had somehow seen through them. Now he'd have to cut a larger check to Shawn for killing them. Malek could hear the whisper of wind and the sound of waves. "Where the hell are you?"

"I'm on the boat. I had to get off the island and sit out on this damn infested lake. I'm going to dock somewhere near Marquette. I won't be able to get back on the island without a good plan. I shot the cop, but those two Johns said he survived."

Malek had spoken with the Johns before Shawn killed them, so he knew the Sheriff was alive. He'd learned the men had failed miserably at their orders. But not Shawn. Shawn was his best. The man was absolutely ruthless, and also knew everything about Malek. So, the last thing he needed was for Shawn to get caught. "You can forget about the sheriff and the doctor. I'm not worried about them. You destroyed any evidence Dr. Williams had, and I've gone to great lengths to make sure no one will ever know he worked for me. Just disappear for a while, and if I need you again, I'll call."

Shawn felt a twinge of relief. "Works for me." He'd make it to the mainland, steal a car and keep heading south. He couldn't wait to leave the U.P and its winter suck-ass wonderland. He put his cell back in his jacket and started up the boat. The moon was hidden somewhere in the night sky behind a wall of clouds. It was dark, and he hoped there'd be nothing in the water to hit. So, he drove slowly, his boat cutting through the waves, as his eyes fought the darkness around him, scanning for shoreline.

A long wooden dock stretched about twenty-five feet into the water. To its left was a boatlift cradling a pontoon wrapped in a tarp. Shawn slowly pulled his craft parallel to the dock, easing off on the throttle but still bumping the dock. He didn't care about the stolen boat, whose owner was probably in Florida for the winter. When the boat was close enough, he tied off the rope and proceeded to jump off. But he wasn't prepared for the dock's layer of invisible black ice. As soon has his feet hit, he slipped on the dock, falling backward. He bumped his head before splashing into the frigid water. He'd have cursed loudly had the freezing water not instantly knocked the wind out of him. His heavy, layered clothing was instantly weighing him down, pulling his face below the water. He tried to float as his boots filled with water, making them feel like lead weights. There was nothing to grab onto, so he tried to swim to shore.

His body felt like it weighed a thousand pounds, and the frigid water sent piercing needles throughout his entire body as he slowly pushed with his hands. There was a moment where he didn't think he could stay afloat from the weight of his clothes, and panic shot through him until his feet touched the bottom. He laughed. It wasn't deep where he'd fallen. He wasn't sure if the waves were helping to push him to shore or making his effort more difficult. Now he could understand how people died of hypothermia. But he wasn't going to let his life end this way. He wasn't going to freeze to death in some shitty lake. He pushed past the pain of the icy water and somehow made it to shore. He felt trickles of water torment his calf and rubbed hard at the aching spot. He used every ounce of strength to pull himself to his feet, removing his drenched jacket. Once the weight of his soggy gloves and coat was gone, he felt lighter. He wanted to remove his jeans, but that would require more effort. The pain in his leg made him stumble and his hand landed on something soft and slimy. He jolted back on his knees and wiped the water from his eyes, forcing them to focus on the dark wet sand. He was surrounded by dozens of dead fish. The knowledge of what had killed them sent a surge of adrenaline through his frozen body.

His leg was throbbing, but his fingers were so numb he couldn't bend them enough to rub the bothersome spot. He needed to find heat fast. He forced his legs to carry him, half stumbling, to the backyard of an expensive steel-glass waterfront house. The lights were out, but he assumed anyone with a home that impressive would live in it year-round. He was in no condition for a home invasion.

By the time he made it to the street he had barely enough energy to stand. His body was numb and stiff, but at least his blood was pumping, since he could practically feel his heart wanting to explode from his chest. There were plenty of cars parked on the street and driveways lining the lakefront. Shawn cursed as his eyes searched for an older model that could be hotwired. All the newer cars would have alarms and locks to prevent that. The snow beneath his soaked boots felt like pins and needles. Damn it, he was going to freeze to death. He tried to run, but his body felt too heavy, his energy completely drained. He stumbled down the road, and suddenly saw it. Parked behind a two-door jeep was what looked like a 1970's-era Mercury. It amazed him how luck was often on his side, especially when he found the car door unlocked. He always carried a knife, and that's all he needed to pull the wires down and twist them together to start the car.

Driving down the winding, snow-covered road, Shawn was becoming more aware of the pain in his leg, and the way it seemed to travel up his calf to his thigh. The heat was blaring full blast, and soon he could pull over and take his wet clothes off once he found a secluded spot. At least time was on his side. No one was on the road at 3 a.m.

Upon reaching a remote, wooded area, Shawn pulled over. After stripping off his clothes, Shawn stared down at the small hole in his leg, where blood was slowly seeping out. "No, no, no!!"

Chapter 24

"Gosh, Jess, do you really think the guy would go after your family?"

Jessica glanced at her cell and saw that the battery was at ten percent. She'd been talking to Janie for hours. The events of the week were too much for her not to share with her sister. "I don't think so. I asked Seth, and he didn't think it was likely. But I do want you to be careful. That's why I'm telling you everything that's going on. I want you to play it safe for now."

"I can't believe you could have been killed. I can't believe you were attacked and shot at." Janie shook her head, sitting in her apartment. She'd been watching the news all day. "And all this crazy fear about the water being contaminated… it's really freaking me out. The news said there's 80 fish species in Lake Superior, and they're all being affected by this. Lake Michigan and Huron seem to be okay, but they're worried whatever's in Superior will eventually make its way to the other lakes. They're saying its game over if we lose our freshwater lakes."

Jessica hadn't watched the news as much as Janie, and all she could picture were thousands of tiny flesh-eating snail-creatures.

"They're saying ducks, geese, bitterns, and many bird species will be lost, with wetlands in danger now too. People are really scared, and I can't believe you're on an island right in the middle of all that chaos. I wish you were home." Janie's voice sounded defeated.

Jessica hadn't shared her knowledge of the organism with her sister. Seth was adamant about keeping that a secret. So, she told Janie the man who attacked her was just after some evidence Seth found on the body. Janie was too upset to ask many detailed questions. "Do you guys have enough bottled water?"

"Heck yeah. Greg ordered like twenty pallets of IMH20. And I've been boiling water before I cook with it."

Seth peered into the bedroom. He wasn't supposed to be up walking around, but she noticed he was at least leaning against the crutches she insisted he use. He whispered, "Are you hungry?"

She was starving. It was 11 a.m. She hadn't slept well after Kyle left last night. Seth had been in a lot of pain, and she purposely overdosed him, so he'd sleep. Then she'd woken up at 6 a.m. to change his bandages. Since she was awake, she'd done some house-hunting, answered emails, and called her sister. She nodded her head at Seth. "Listen, Janie, my phone's almost dead. I'm going to let you go, and I'll call you again later."

When Jessica met Seth in the kitchen, she found a mile-high sandwich stacked on a plate. "I won't be able to get my mouth around that."

Seth's eyes locked with hers, and she laughed. He didn't have to say anything, because she could practically see the gears turning in his head for an easy, inappropriate comeback. "I've got no comment on that," Seth muttered.

She hadn't thought Seth had a sense of humor, but from the last two days she was learning he did in fact have one. It was a dry one, and often all he needed to give was a look. She was learning that she'd misjudged him in many ways. "Seriously Seth." She picked the sandwich up to examine the contents. "Is there anything you didn't put on this?"

He turned to sit at the kitchen table. His leg constantly ached, and he knew he was using it too much. Jessica had been waiting on him hand and foot, and he was getting tired of it. He wanted to make a sandwich the way he liked them, so that's what he did. "You were on the phone so long I figured we'd both starve to death if I didn't take matters into my own hands."

She rolled her eyes. She'd gotten to where his mood, tone, and hard facial expressions no longer fazed her. "Janie likes to talk."

"You both like to talk." He'd heard her voice a lot and knew she was telling her sister everything that happened. He didn't mind, though. It was good for her to share her feelings. She'd been melancholy, and he didn't know how to help. "How did she take the news?"

"She's also scared for her own safety now. And she doesn't want me to leave your home."

Seth didn't want her to leave either. He didn't want her out of his sight for more than a minute. "You're safe here." Christmas was next Sunday, and he was afraid she'd want to leave. He assumed it would be asking a lot to request she stay until after Christmas.

"I need to start thinking about finding a place of my own." She took a seat at the table beside him. "I can't stay here forever." The thought of leaving caused instant despair, and she glanced down sadly at her laptop. She'd saved five apartment and two condo listings in a folder on her computer. She figured at least one of them would suit her needs. They were all close to her work and looked beautiful in the pictures. "I don't want to live my life looking over my shoulder, feeling afraid. They have to catch this guy, Seth."

He set his hand on hers. "I know. They will." He wanted to convince her because he hated the weary look in her eyes. "They found a stolen, abandoned boat in Marquette, and a car was stolen nearby. They have a lead, Jess. They'll find him." He noticed that she didn't touch her sandwich. She hadn't been eating much, and her somber mood concerned him. "I need you to stay. Here. With me. I know you're probably sick of this island, and more than ready to leave but—"

"I could never be sick of this island. I see why you and Mike love it so much here. It's wonderful."

"Really?" He was surprised.

"Seth, it's beautiful! I can only imagine how awesome it is in the summer. If I lived here, I'd ride my bike to work every day, go kayaking after work, and take regular hikes through the woods." She smiled at the thought of what a different life she'd have. "I love that the island is so small you can get to everything, everywhere, within minutes."

"There's no nearby shopping malls. No big supermarkets or convenience stores." Seth remembered his wife's biggest complaint. "The closest hair salon and Target is an hour away from the ferry. There are no clubs to go dancing in. All we have is Al's diner. The ferry is old and breaks down unexpectedly. Usually at the most inconvenient times."

She rolled her eyes. "Oh Seth, you don't know me very well. I *never* go to salons. I hate shopping, and anything I need I order on Amazon. I don't care about clubs and dancing. I'm very much a homebody, and I think nature would provide me with all the entertainment I need." She watched as he sat back in his chair and folded his arms, a look of skepticism on his face. "Seth, are you trying to talk me out of liking the island?"

He studied her carefully. "I'm not sure you know what it is you want, Jess." She'd said herself that she wanted to discover what made her happy. Her confession made him extremely pleased, but he didn't dare hope. If what she was saying was true, then maybe there was a chance they could be more than just friends. But Seth wasn't looking to be someone's trial and error. He'd been down that road already.

"That's not entirely true." She felt a bit defensive. "I know I like this damn island, okay? I know I love snowmobiling, minus being shot at by lunatics. I know I love your house and would be perfectly happy having a small home of my own. I know for a fact I'm super sick of always going out to dinner, and I'd like to start making my own meals, because I like to cook." She discovered her love of cooking the day she made her first gourmet meal. "I know that you appear grumpy a lot when you're really not. I know you sound like you're mad when you're really not, and I know you're stubborn when it comes to pain medication. If I'm going to eat this giant sandwich, I need to cut it in half." She rose from the table and walked over to the silverware drawer to retrieve a knife.

He couldn't take his eyes off her as he processed every single word she'd said. "The clinic has been trying to get Doc Mike to work there for years. The position is always open for him, so I don't see why you couldn't take it, if you ever decided you did want to live on the island."

"You know… now that you mention it, I do recall Mike telling me he'd move here if he didn't have four kids who were already comfortable and happy at their schools. He told me the clinic would be a great place to work." She began to cut her sandwich. "But it would be hard to leave the practice with Mike, and of course Janie."

Seth shifted in his chair, disappointment squashing what little hope he had. "Well, I'm glad you like it here so much, because you're going to stay with me until this case gets solved and I know you'll be 100% safe." That was partly just an excuse, of course, but it was enough for now.

"Aren't you getting sick of me yet?" she teased, liking that he was insistent about her staying.

"You've managed to put up with me every day for a week, and you haven't poisoned me yet, talked about me behind my back, or tried to shoot me with my own gun."

She gave him a thoughtful stare, remembering what Chris had told her about Seth's ex-wife. How she used to 'rip' on him behind his back all the time. She couldn't think of a single negative thing to say about Seth. "I think you're wonderful." The words just came out because they couldn't be truer.

Seth's eyes raised in surprise. "Really?" He didn't think any woman could find him wonderful. His ex-wife had frequently stated his many flaws, and this was often near the surface of his subconscious. He knew he didn't have a charming personality. He wasn't flirtatious, talkative, or complimentary. He didn't personify a warm, fuzzy guy.

The way he seemed genuinely surprised saddened her. He clearly didn't know. Perhaps his ex-wife had done some serious damage. She sat back down, locking her eyes with his. "Seth, I've been in your home now for days. I know I've been helping you with your wound, but you've helped me far more. I'm not even talking about you saving my life or comforting me when I need it. I find you very agreeable. I feel safe with you in every way." She felt a trust in him far stronger than any she ever felt with Greg, and it went beyond their platonic relationship. "I feel like I know you well enough now to honestly say that you are a truly great guy."

"Is that in a purely friendship feeling kind of way?" Hope twisted in his gut again.

She knew what he was asking. He wanted to know if she looked at him as 'just a friend,' or if there was more. She wondered if she could be bold enough to move around the table and show him what she felt. She wasn't the assertive type at all. With Greg she never had to initiate anything, because he was all offhand charm and could flirt without saying a word. He left nothing to the imagination, and there was never any guesswork. But Seth was different. After a moment, realizing he was waiting for her answer, she shook her head. "I—" She paused when he took her hand in his and began to pull her over. So maybe she wouldn't have to initiate after all because he apparently read her mind. Her stomach did a little summersault and she smiled when he brought her to his good leg and pulled her down on it.

She watched his brows pulling together in a way that showed his vulnerability. He cupped the sides of her face, his eyes searching hers. He was giving her every opportunity to move away if she didn't want to kiss him. He was moving achingly slow, and she desperately wanted him.

Seth had put this moment off a long time. He'd been careful not to show his feelings. He didn't want to be her rebound, nor did he want to further complicate things in her life. But his resistance to her was completely gone, and she had a way of making him feel whole again. He didn't want to scare her off or make any mistakes with her. Even as he slowly felt her incredibly soft, supple lips, he wondered if it was too soon… if he wasn't letting the hope of what she'd said cloud his judgment. But how could anything that felt this incredible be a mistake? He heard her soft sigh, and knew the moment was right.

Chapter 25

It crawled along the mud, its narrow body extending from the soft shell it carried on its back. As its teeth plowed through the mud, the organism breathed through the walls of its quarter-inch body. It dug a hole, the dirt descending from a waste tube. Once the hole was deep enough, the organism released a sack containing a thousand eggs through its mouth, laying the eggs inside the hole. Using its head, it pressed the eggs further down to secure them, before springing up, twisting like a worm. It broke free of the lake bottom and allowed the water to carry it as it glided through the water waiting for a host… waiting to be swallowed.

In a matter of moments, a strong force was trying to suck it from its shell. The organism recoiled inside its tube, allowing tiny tarsal claws with adhesive sticky pads to protrude, latching onto the slippery skin of the prey. Once adhesion was secured, the worm-like creature emerged from its protective tube with its razor-sharp teeth in motion, chewing through the soft skin and scales straight through to tiny bones. The exterior shell shielded the creature from acid and external forces as it continued to tunnel with its teeth. The host's matter excreted from the end of the creature. It continued burrowing, chomping, and digging deeper. It made its way through the fish until it finally chewed its way out. The water sweeping it along, as it waited… waited.

"Get it off!" The creature stuck to her skin, tiny, bladed teeth, digging its way through her arm. She watched in horror, knowing it would soon be burrowed inside her flesh, eating layers of ectodermal tissue. Pain surging through her arm as it devoured muscle, bones, and ligaments, finding its way to internal organs. She raised her arm in response to the pain, screamed out, and thrashed.

"Jess, wake up!" Seth held her down, his body keeping her still. "Wake up. It's okay."

She opened her eyes, hearing her own heavy gasp and the pounding of her heart. It took her a moment to realize where she was, and it wasn't until her eyes focused on Seth's hard face that she felt safe. "It was awful."

"I know… you kicked me in the leg."

"Oh, I'm sorry." She instantly sat up to examine the bandage on Seth's leg.

He took her hand. "I'm fine." He pulled her down and wrapped his arms around her, tucking her head under his chin. "Are you okay? What were you dreaming about?"

"The organism. The way it moves through the water… It was inside me, eating me."

Seth kissed the top of her head. "In a year you won't remember this dream."

She laughed and turned to face him. "In a year we might not be here if that creature starts eating everything and everyone on the planet."

"It won't. They'll find a way to kill it. We aren't even sure yet if that's what's killing the fish. Just because superman found something we've never seen before doesn't mean there's not a logical explanation."

"I'll give you one. Dr. A.J…. okay, I'll call him Superman, because he really does look like Clark Kent. He saw how deadly and scary that creature was, so he packed up his family and went to hide out in his fortress of solitude. Or at least a pimped-out underground bunker."

Seth kissed her on the nose. "You've seen too many movies."

She snuggled closer to him. "I'm scared. I don't understand why it's not all over the news. They can't keep this from people. And I can't stop thinking about that sentence written on the papers. What was he trying to say?"

"What sentence?"

"The 'B… something… St H20 Breeding.' Breeding is a scary word, Seth. I think what he underlined was important."

Seth reached for his iPhone next to the bed. "Let's Google it." He typed in words beginning with a B and ending in ST. Jessica draped her leg over his and stared at the phone. A list of words popped up, and they both started to read. Biologist, Bicyclist, Breeziest, Brightest, Breakfast, and on and on….

None of the words made sense with "H2O breeding" following it. And Jessica could picture the way the cursive looped. "I just don't think any of these are the word."

"Honey, you can't worry about it. There was a lot of chicken-scratch on those papers, and there's no way for us to know what it all meant. It might not be important." He rolled her onto her back.

"I like the way you call me honey." It sounded special coming from him. She forgot what she was going to say next.

Seth turned the TV on as he sat back on the couch, grimacing at his leg pain. "I'll be damned." Jessica was showering, and he knew she'd want to see this. He was about to get her when his cell buzzed. He grabbed it from the coffee table and answered.

"You watching the news?"

"Yes." Seth kept his eyes on the television as more photos of the organism appeared. He'd wondered when he was going to hear from Kyle. It was three days since he'd been shot, and he was desperate for some good news.

"Don't be mad I didn't call you sooner, I've been busy dealing with all this crazy. I think the guy who shot you is the victim they found. What are the odds he was connected to this thing, and then ends up dying from it? The organism ate through his entire body, Seth." Kyle sat at his desk, looking over a report. "I've got a deputy bringing Connie in to confirm that the victim matches her sketch." The news was constantly on at the station, keeping Kyle updated on the latest findings. He leaned over his desk, resting his head in his hand. "I've got to be honest, Seth. When you first told me about the organism and the papers, I didn't really believe any of it. I mean this is straight out of a sci-fi movie."

Jessica walked into the room and gasped at the television. She noticed Seth on the phone and sat beside him. He noted her wet hair in a bun, and her yellow t-shirt that read: DOCTORS CALL THE SHOTS. The letter T in "shots" was a syringe needle. She was wearing dark jeans and fuzzy pink socks.

Kyle continued to update Seth. "They found the guy dead in a stolen car. He made it to Frankenmuth. The car was stolen in Marquette, near where the stolen boat was found. The guy's gun matches the bullets from the guys we found behind the store. Forensics can confirm he's the one who shot them. They also found wet clothes, so they think the guy fell in the water before stealing the car. Now that the guy's been linked to your case and the island, expect some real FBI agents to arrive. I've been on the phone all day with them and the State Police. They can't keep this organism a secret anymore. Everyone wants to know where it came from. Are you watching this?"

The news was finally showing photos of the organism. The President was preparing a special address to discuss the fear and concern surrounding the organisms found in Lake Superior. "Let me call you back." Seth noticed the distress on Jessica's face. He set his phone down and pulled her against his chest. "Kyle says the organism killed the guy who tried to kill us."

"Oh wow," She covered her mouth with shaking hands, glancing from the TV to Seth. "It's my dream." Tears swam in her eyes. "It's my nightmare becoming real. I can't believe this."

"Okay, but on the bright side, it killed the guy who attacked you and shot at us."

His words finally penetrated her racing mind. "How do they know?"

"They know. It's ironic, don't ya think?"

Jessica turned back to the TV. News anchors were standing

outside a hospital, confirming that the snail-looking organism did in fact kill the victim. The organism in the pictures looked bigger than the one Dr. AJ had showed them. It was longer. Wider. "How did it get him? Are the organisms outside the water now?"

"No. Don't be heading to some pimped-out underground bunker just yet." He liked that he could make her smile, though the tension didn't leave her eyes. "They think he fell in the water. He'd stolen a boat, which makes sense. I had a feeling that's how he got off the island."

"And the organism in the water latched onto him and ate him." She was almost in awe, thinking about her dream. "I can't believe this."

"One of the news reports suggested the organism was man-made. The FBI is looking into possible terrorist threats."

"If this organism killed one person, it's only a matter of time before it kills more."

"There are thousands of them. Maybe even millions."

Jessica's mouth dropped open. "What?"

He nodded at the TV. "It only takes one organism to latch on and start munching. One of these snail things can quickly cause internal bleeding. But the news was saying they are trying to analyze how many there could be. They think if you go in the water here, your chance of finding at least one is pretty good. It's why there's so much dead fish and wildlife." He'd felt sick over hearing that news. He'd never want to risk swimming in the lake again.

"I figured there was more than one, but thousands?"

Seth rubbed the goosebumps suddenly lining her arms. "The good thing is that it's winter, and the water is too cold for anyone to swim. And the organism can't survive long outside of water or living tissue. That means when it leaves the body of a fish, animal, or… whatever it's eating, it either has to find its way back to water, or immediately enter another host."

"So there could be dried-out flesh-eating snails all over the beach?" She could picture them in her mind.

"No. I don't think so. They think it usually does its damage and finds its way back to the water. The problem is that the water is loaded with the 'Invasive Flesh-Eating Snails.' Which is what they're calling it."

"So now it's out there." She didn't have to wonder if she was right, or keep it a secret anymore. She could tell her sister how it had killed the wolves, and how Dr. A.J. showed it to her before it was known. She was relieved that finally the truth was out, although it was absolutely terrifying.

Picking up the remote control, Seth switched the channel. The news was on almost every station, interrupting regular programming. He continued to flip through the channels. "The last time the news was this worked up was on 9/11, when the World Trade Towers were hit. This is probably the scariest thing to happen to our country since then."

"They think the organism could be a biological weapon?"

"It's not. I don't think this has anything to do with terrorists."

"What do you think it's about?"

"I think it has to do with that dead body we found, Mark Williams, and the papers he stuck down his pants in a zip-lock bag. The guy was a scientist… a typical American. Maybe he was experimenting, and accidently created it. He probably realized someone would kill him because of it." Seth ran a hand down her arm. "I don't know. But I think those papers are more important than ever."

Jessica didn't want to say, "I told you so," but that's how she was feeling. "Did Kyle give the papers to the right people?"

"Yes. And now that he did, we can probably expect some real agents."

Turning back to the TV, she watched a helicopter flying over Lake Superior. It was showing an aerial view of the lake. The caption under the new footage said, "All Lakes and public beaches are off-limits, and people will be arrested if they go near the water." Hundreds of freighters and other enormous vessels still traveled the Lake and St. Mary's River. The media explained the concern for the men and women onboard the ships, which were at risk for encountering the deadly organism. The Coast Guard was warning vessels to keep employees away from waves and use caution when on deck. The news mentioned all ships would need to stay anchored, to prevent ballast water from transporting the organism to other bodies of water. Jessica drew her brows together. "Oh my God!" The idea just struck her as she stared at the ships on the television.

"What?" He watched the emotions play across her face, her mind clearly working something out.

"Seth, that's it! Ballast Water!" She jumped to her feet, needing to pace. "The word on the paper... Ballast H20 breeding! He underlined it because it was happening!"

Seth leaned back on the couch, his mind racing with new ideas. "Okay, makes sense. We find the scientist's body washed up on shore because he was on a ship. He created it, and they were breeding it in ballast water." He stared at Jessica in amazement as he mentally put the pieces together. "He knows he's going in the water, so he protects the papers that he obviously wanted the world to find. Someone shoots him, and the ballast water is released."

"Exactly!" Jessica placed her hand over her stomach in an effort to calm her nerves. "Maybe those papers do have the formula for what can kill it." She stopped pacing and stared at Seth. "What? What are you thinking?"

"I'm thinking if we find the ship, we find who's responsible for this. We find who Williams was working for." Seth picked up his cell and called Kyle.

Jessica sat back down. "The ship would have a lab on it. Do ships empty all their ballast water into the lake? Their ballast might still contain the organism."

He pointed at her and nodded his agreement. The moment Kyle answered the phone, Seth said, "My gorgeous, brilliant girlfriend just figured out a major possibility in this case. If she's right..."

"Girlfriend?" Jessica smiled. She hadn't expected to hear that. It sounded nice.

"Girlfriend?" Kyle replied. "Who's your girlfriend? The hot blond doctor?"

"Yes, and only I'm allowed to call her that now," Seth warned in a tone that left no room for argument. "Pay attention. We need to search all the ships on the Lake. We think the organism was possibly created on a ship and being bred in the ballast water. One of the ships should have a room that could clearly be used as a lab. We need to search ballast water. Find the ship… find the source."

"Damn, Seth, I might just get promoted to Chief if I solve our country's biggest crime ever. I'm telling you right now, I'm taking all the credit for it."

Seth smiled at Kyle's humor. Kyle had done a lot of work while Seth was laid up with his wounded leg. He deserved some credit. "I'd love to see you make Chief. Go ahead and take the credit but get moving on this."

"I'm all over it, buddy. There might be hundreds of ships still on the waterway. Searching that many vessels is going to take time. The Coast Guard is going to need backup." Kyle knew the feds could obtain enough boats and manpower to search every ship. "Tell me you've got some proof I can give the FBI to make them jump on this theory."

"Jess realized what was written on that paper. There was a sentence that read, 'Ballast water breeding.' She didn't understand what it said at first, but just figured it out. It makes sense, Kyle." Seth continued to explain.

"Well?" Jessica asked in anticipation when he finally ended the call.

"Well, baby… it's like I said. You're gorgeous and brilliant. Kyle will handle it." He cupped the sides of her face and brought her lips to his.

Chapter 26

Christmas break had just begun, and Janie was looking forward to her vacation. She'd been glued to the TV, obsessing over the organism, just like her students and the rest of the world. It was making her depressed and extremely worried about her sister. Jessica insisted she was doing fine, but Janie knew better. Her sister didn't sound fine, and how could she be? She'd been violently attacked, almost strangled to death, shot at, and was now working with the FBI because somehow, she was the only person who could remember evidence related to the deadly Lake organism. It was all so crazy and disturbing, and Janie didn't know how to stop worrying.

The organism was described in different ways. Some doctors referred to it as a deadly flesh-eating parasite, with the ability to live inside any living host. It couldn't be killed by being eaten, which put it at the top of the food chain. Janie got a sickening feeling whenever she imagined the little snail-like parasite latching on to stomach lining and eating through whatever unlucky being was unfortunate enough to swallow it or come in contact with it.

The entire world was talking about how the deadly organism could destroy all the earth's water and wildlife, possibly ending mankind. If it made its way to the ocean, and destroyed all oceanic life, that would mean "game over." The latest news was a fisherman who'd fallen out of his boat. He was pronounced dead two hours later. He'd died the same way the first man did. And Janie still couldn't wrap her mind around the fact that the deceased man named "Shawn" was also the man who'd violently attacked her sister. His insides had been eaten through.

People were leaving Michigan, and Minnesota and the mainland along Wisconsin. Canada had gone so far as to evacuate their towns and cities along Lake Superior. The government was quickly moving to contain the creatures by building a dam across the river system which flowed into other Lakes and streams. Ships were evacuated and left anchored in the water. The extreme measures, and constant media coverage, were causing people to stockpile supplies and head for the hills. Anything to get away from lakes, beaches, and rivers. Janie felt her mind swim with worry as she decorated her four-foot Christmas tree. She was not at all in the holiday spirit, and wondered if she should even bother putting up the little tree.

She bent down, opening the box of ornaments. Inside was a picture of her parents holding a pair of babies on their laps. Even as infants Janie and Jessica were too similar to tell apart. Below the gold frame it read, BABIES' FIRST CHRISTMAS. Janie closed her eyes and tried to hear the sound of her mother's laugh and feel her dad's chin stubble against her. Tears came as fast and easy as the ache in her heart. It was so unfair that she'd been blessed with the most wonderful parents, only to have them taken from her at the age of nineteen. But at least she'd had her sister, her best friend, and her unwavering support. And Janie had actively hurt her. The guilt and regret were enough to make her nauseous.

Janie picked up the gold ornament, placing it carefully on the tree. *What the hell am I doing?* She'd never spent a Christmas away from her sister. Every year they decorated her tree together, and Jessica was always there to comfort her. They would laugh together and share their memories. Janie kneeled on the floor in front of the tree and placed a hand over her heavy heart. She had hurt the one and only person who mattered most to her. And the worst part was that her sister had not only forgiven her but offered her blessing. And for what? Janie had caused all that pain and heartache for a man who wasn't willing to fight for her. Greg was a clear disappointment. When he'd been seeing her behind Jessica's back, he'd behaved so differently. He'd convinced her he was in love with her, and she was practically insane with love for him. But now he was pulling away, and his behavior was making her fear she'd misjudged his feelings for her. He certainly wasn't acting like a man in love since Jessica left. Janie knew her behavior scared him. She was too needy, too available, and he was pushing her away. He'd been purposely working more night shifts so he could avoid her.

The only person on the planet who loved her unconditionally, and who would understand the fear and heartache she was going through, was more than eight hours away on a tiny island. The country was in fear and turmoil, and now for the first time ever, Janie was spending Christmas alone, wallowing in despair.

Jessica had admitted to having nightmares and not sleeping well. And even though she claimed she was happy staying at Seth's, and caring for him, Janie knew something was still very wrong with her sister. Jess was always the strong one. Her rock. Now she was struggling, and Janie felt partly responsible. She wanted to be there for her sister, and somehow make things right. She couldn't do it from so far away.

Picking up her cell, Janie called Greg. She was surprised when he answered. "Greg, Christmas is in four days, and I'm just wondering if you plan to spend it with me?" She spoke frankly, getting right to the point.

"I'm working. I told you, it's a busy time of year."

She sighed. Gone was his sweet, seductive voice. Gone was the flirtatious charmer she'd fallen in love with. This Greg was cold, rejecting, irritated, and breaking her heart. "Okay." She pressed "end" as she walked into her bedroom. She pulled her suitcase from the closet and opened it. Janie couldn't imagine not being with her sister on Christmas, and the thought of being alone was truly unbearable. More tears streamed down her face as she thought about how messed up her life had become. What would Greg think if she left, and acted like she didn't care? Maybe it would do him some good to spend Christmas without her and have the chance to miss her. Her biggest fear was that he wouldn't, and she'd be left with the heartache of knowing she hurt her sister for nothing.

When her suitcase was stuffed full, she picked up her iPhone, and called Mike. He was at work, but she'd get the address to Seth's house. If Jessica could drive to the U.P alone, then so could she.

Kyle cracked open a beer and sat down on his living room couch. Whenever possible he had the television on, listening to the news. Currently The Marine Environment Protection Committee (MEPC) was being interviewed on CNN. Scientists had been warning the world about invasive species in ballast water since 1903. By the 1980's, Canada and Australia were struggling with serious invasive species problems, prompting the MEPC to take action. The problem had impacted the world, but now with this deadly organism threatening mankind, the MEPC was finally gaining a voice.

It had been a very long day, and Kyle was exhausted. He looked over his small apartment. He only had two pieces of furniture. A nice leather couch and a coffee table. He didn't count the TV stand, as he'd made that himself, out of cinderblocks and wood. Maybe it was time for him to get a nicer place. Maybe if he had a girlfriend, he'd have more interest in moving. If he had a girlfriend, he'd want a larger bed. There was plenty of money, just no need to spend it.

In his mind, he pictured Jessica. Now, there was a beautiful, smart woman, the kind he wanted for himself. He was genuinely happy for Seth. Maybe a bit jealous, but nonetheless happy for him. And thanks to Jessica and Seth, the FBI had found the ship with contaminated ballast water. They found the lab. Since the FBI knew what to look for, they were able to find a garbage bin full of laboratory evidence, and hair that matched Mark Williams' DNA. The FBI was investigating the ship's ownership, but it would only be a matter of time before they found out. Terrorism had been ruled out as a result, and the FBI was beginning to think the organism was one scientist's accidental creation.

Christmas was in four days, and Kyle planned to take the ferry to Chicory Island to meet with Seth and Jessica. He wanted to shake Seth's hand, and hug Jessica. Because of her, the FBI and scientists were developing a formula to kill the organism, based on what Jessica was able to remember.

The news of Lake Superior's deadly organism had spread across the world. Homes on the lake were being sold for less than half their asking price. If there was ever an opportunity to invest in waterfront property, now was the time. Kyle had been saving his money and wouldn't mind owning one. Of course, he'd never want to go in the lake, just like the millions of Americans who would forever fear the water. He figured it would be years before anyone could trust the organisms were completely destroyed, and that required finding something that would kill it.

There was still some work he needed to do, so maybe tomorrow after work he'd take the ferry and visit Seth. He had a bottle of scotch he could bring in celebration.

Chapter 27

The young girl on the high swivel chair blew a big bubble and then popped it quickly before opening the window of the ferry booth. Janie glanced at the Ferry Schedule posted on the wall. Then she glanced at the rules: *1) Wait in line until a crew member waves you on; 2) Do not use cell phone when boarding; 3) There is no public restroom on board the ferry, there are outhouses at both ferry docks.* She smiled at the last rule—*if the ferry leaves without you, don't worry, it'll be right back.* She wasn't sure that was true, considering what Jessica had told her. The ferry was constantly breaking down.

It cost $15 to board the ferry with her red Tahoe. SUVs were charged $5 more than cars. Janie thanked the young woman, and then returned to her vehicle.

The ferry was larger than she'd imagined, as she pulled up behind a pickup truck. She was thankful the ship was large, considering the waves appeared fairly tumultuous. A young man with a bright orange parka and matching cap knocked on her window. "Please pull forward more. When the ferry starts to move, you're welcome to get out and walk around, but you're not allowed past the yellow tape," he told her in a voice that squeaked like he was going through puberty. She did as the deckhand instructed, until the front of her vehicle was almost touching the truck in front of her. The yellow tape was to keep people away from potential splashing water. No one needed to tell her to stay back.

She glanced in her rearview and saw another SUV pull up close behind her. It had taken her ten hours to reach the ferry. The weather hadn't been terrible, but she'd hit some major traffic along the way. She'd noticed lots of RV's and campers heading south. Although it was cold and windy out, she wouldn't mind stretching her legs for a bit. Her stomach growled as she glanced at the clock on her dashboard. It would be 6:00 p.m. by the time she reached Seth's house. She hadn't eaten since noon.

As soon as the ferry began to move, she stepped out of her car. The wind whipped her blonde hair, so she tied it in a bun, then reached in her pocket for her fleece headband, and put it over her ears. She stretched up on her toes, leaning back against her car.

Kyle sat in his SUV and watched the blonde woman parked in front of him get out of her red Tahoe. Her hair was long, brushing past her shoulders, and moving in the wind. When she put it up, he noticed her familiar side profile. Then she turned around, giving Kyle a clear view of her face. He laughed. "Well, I'll be damned," he said out loud, and proceeded to get out of his car. He watched Dr. Bennett walk toward the yellow tape. He thought it a funny coincidence she was on the ferry, parked in front of him, when he was on his way to see her and Seth.

He walked up beside her and said, "Don't get too close." If lake water splashed up, it could be dangerous.

Janie smiled at the stranger wearing a black knit hat and matching coat. He was handsome, with a nice smile. "I won't," she replied, taking a step back from the tape. She glanced out at the water. "It's scary now, isn't it?"

"It is," he nodded. "But thanks to a very clever woman, hopefully they'll come up with something that will kill the little creatures." Kyle flashed his best charming smile.

Janie's eyes widened in surprise. Jessica was the one person with information on how to kill the organism, but Janie didn't think people knew yet. Maybe someone had leaked to the media that a woman was helping the FBI. "Where did you hear that?"

Kyle laughed. The doctor was either extremely modest or joking around. "Oh, I have some inside connections. Thanks to this doctor being able to remember some special formulas, I've been feeling hopeful."

Janie smiled. "That's nice." She was about to tell him she happened to know the doctor in question, but Jessica made her promise not to tell anyone anything she shared with her. She hadn't even told Greg. "I haven't watched the news today, so I'm not up on the latest updates."

"You're not missing anything. Same news, different day." He tipped his head and met her eyes again. "Why are you all alone here? I'm surprised you're not with someone." He figured Seth would either go with her, or at least have a deputy guard her. Not that they felt she was still in any real danger, but Seth acted like he wouldn't let her out of his sight until the entire case was solved.

So, the man was hitting on her. It had been a while since an attractive man had tried to pick her up. She always found it flattering. "Well… my life is a bit complicated right now and my man is kind of a…" she wrinkled her nose trying to think of the right word to describe Greg. "Let's just say he's not winning any points right now."

Kyle leaned back in surprise. He'd love to ask Jessica out and pursue her for himself, but he was genuinely happy that the Sheriff had finally found a nice woman. Kyle considered Seth a friend, and unfortunately ascribed to the man code. That meant Jessica was off-limits. "Are you fighting?" he asked, feeling genuinely concerned. He could imagine Seth in an irritable mood from being laid-up with a bullet wound. Although when he'd last visited Seth last week, it appeared that Jessica didn't mind his foul mood. "Is everything okay?"

Janie sighed. The guy seemed nice, but she wasn't going into detail about her personal life. "It's okay," she replied sadly. "It's just nothing is ever easy."

"I understand." Kyle could imagine that the two were perhaps falling in love, and it would be difficult with Seth living here and her much further south. "I'm sorry to hear that."

"Thank you." The stranger appeared sincere. He spoke like a friend, and there was something about him that made her feel he wasn't just some creepy guy. "I'll be okay. I'll be even better when we no longer have to worry about this flesh-eating snail." She stared out at the vast lake, Goosebumps running down her arms. She knew this was just the beginning of learning about what lurked in the water, and as her sis had pointed out, more consequences were sure to come.

Kyle glanced at the Island Ferry dock. "We're almost to the island. I was planning to come over, so I guess I'll follow you."

"What?" Janie was confused. What the heck did that mean? Maybe he meant that once on the island, everyone had to go in the same direction. Maybe she misheard him.

Before Kyle could respond, the young man in the orange cap approached them and smiled. "Time to return to your cars now. We ask that you follow the car ahead of you slowly off the ship. Speed limit is five miles per hour until you clear the docks."

"Thank you," Janie said, feeling uneasy. "Well… bye," she added quickly to the stranger, and turned to walk toward her car.

Kyle's brows drew together, wondering what he'd missed. Jessica was acting odd. Maybe she was fighting with Seth and no longer staying at his house. He wanted to talk more, but as the boat attendants secured the ramp to the dock, he knew he needed to get in his car. In a few minutes he'd know which direction she was heading, and if it wasn't to Seth's, he'd just call her. He returned to his car.

Janie wanted to surprise her sister. She wanted to appear at Seth's front door and see the look of happiness on her sister's face, or the look of anger, depending on how she felt about an unannounced visit. But as Janie glanced in her rearview mirror, she could see that the stranger she'd spoken to on the ferry was still following her.

She had a license to carry a concealed weapon. She and Jessica had taken the eight-hour class and often went to the gun range for target practice. It was something that made her feel safe since she lived alone. Janie pulled her revolver from her purse and checked the chamber. Then she slowly pulled off to the side of the road. Her heart raced as the man behind her did the same. She'd hoped he'd pass her, but now it was obvious he was purposely following her. The guy was a creeper. She sighed, keeping an eye on him in her rearview. That's what she got for being too friendly. She should have known better. Her judgment with men has always been terrible. *Don't get out of your car, don't get out of your car.* The man was getting out of his car and walking toward hers. She stepped out of her car, holding her gun to her side. "Don't come any closer!" she yelled when he was only a few yards away. She didn't aim her gun at him, but simply held it to her side. "Look Mister, you're scaring me now. I'm sorry if it seemed like I was interested because I'm not. I was just being friendly. I'd like for you to get back in your car and drive away."

Kyle noticed the fear in her eyes and the way her hand held the gun. Her finger wasn't on the trigger. "What the hell is wrong with you?" As soon as he asked, it dawned on him. "Oh my god, you're not Jessica, are you? You're the twin."

"What?" Janie watched the man's face turn from confusion to the same charming smile he had earlier. "You know Jessica?"

"I thought you *were* Jessica," Kyle said, laughing at himself. He should've known from the way she was acting she had never met him before. "I'm sorry. It's just that you really look exactly like your sister. I'd say you're absolutely identical."

Janie felt somewhat relieved. "Okay, well, I'm not Jessica, but I'm headed to see my sister now."

"I'm headed there too, sweetheart." Kyle took a step closer and then paused. He'd thought about offering his hand but could see she was still apprehensive. "My name is Kyle Steller. I'm an officer from Dell County and sometimes work with Sheriff Johnson."

"Oh." Janie glanced to her right as three snowmobiles drove past them. "Well, that makes me feel better." Jessica had mentioned Kyle many times in their conversations.

"Do you have a license for that gun?" he asked out of curiosity.

"Yes," Janie looked down, having forgotten she was holding it.

"You scared me."

"I can see that now. We can talk when we get to the Sheriff's house. I'm also headed there. I know the way if you want to follow me."

Chapter 28

The oven beeped, and Jessica groaned. She was lying comfortably in bed beside Seth. "I have to take the pot roast out."

"Not yet."

Jessica laughed. "Seth, I have to take it out or our dinner will be burned."

He nibbled her. "Let it burn."

"Watch your leg." She was always careful of his injury. She'd already bumped it a few times by accident, and she didn't want to cause him any pain. She sat up and reached for the sweatshirt Seth had thrown aside hours ago. Putting her lounge pants on, she glanced at him, "Do you want to eat at the kitchen table, or in bed?"

Seth smiled. "Don't tempt me. I'm coming." He rolled over carefully to get dressed.

Just as Jessica was removing the large roast from the oven, she heard the knock on the door. Seth was standing on his crutches, already holding his gun. He never went anywhere in the house without it.

"Stay here." He leaned one of the crutches against the wall, so he could hold his gun up in the other hand.

Jessica was probably no longer in danger, but Seth wasn't taking any chances, and it was pointless to argue with him.

Seth glanced through the peephole before turning back to Jess with an odd expression on his face. "There's a bit of a surprise out there. It's okay," he told her. "You can open the door, babe."

"Who is it?" Jessica asked, walking to the door. She wanted to peek through the hole, but Seth covered it with his hand. "It's okay. Just open it." She did so.

"Surprise!" Janie said, hoping her sister would be happy.

"Janie!" Never in a million years would Jessica expect to see her sister standing there next to Kyle. Joy instantly overwhelmed her. "Oh my gosh, what on earth are you doing here?" She pulled Janie into a tight hug.

Kyle shook Seth's hand, and turned to shake Jessica's, but she hugged him instead. "I met your sister on the ferry. I thought she was you, and I'm pretty sure she thought I was a would-be-rapist or something."

Janie laughed. "I thought you were nice, *and then* I thought you were creepy." Janie held her hand out to Seth. "It's nice to meet you. You *are* nice and tall," she said, following Jessica into the house. Janie felt a little uneasy at the angry look on Seth's face. She hoped he wouldn't find her sudden appearance a major intrusion. "I booked a room at the bed and breakfast in town. I guess they have lots of vacancies now that everyone wants to get away from the Lake."

"Oh, don't be silly," Jessica replied. "Seth, you don't mind if my sister stays here, do you?" She couldn't tell from the deadpan look on Seth's face what he was thinking. "Christmas is in a few days, and Janie and I have never been apart on Christmas."

"Of course," Seth replied. He'd loved having Jessica all to himself, so he wasn't thrilled with the intrusion, but he wanted her to be happy.

"This is quite a surprise, so I'm glad I have a big pot roast to offer you guys. We were just about to eat." Jessica studied her sister and couldn't believe Janie had driven all the way to the U.P. to see her. "Does Greg know you're here?"

"No." Janie didn't want to talk about Greg. She'd been gone over ten hours, and he hadn't even called or texted her. She wondered how long it would take him to realize she was gone. "You cooked a pot roast?" She walked over to the counter to examine the food. "Wow, I guess you're turning into Betty Crocker."

Kyle held out a bottle of scotch to Seth. "How's the leg?" He asked.

"It's a lot better, thanks to Jessica."

Everyone sat down at the kitchen table. The conversation was constant, and there was a zestful current in the air. Jessica and Janie together set off an enthusiastic vibe that both Kyle and Seth found fascinating. The women were amazing to watch. Their identical smiles and laughter made it impossible not to feel cheerful. Janie was more energetic than Jessica, and while her voice sounded almost the same, her speech was different. Janie spoke a mile a minute, while also speaking with her hands. Seth was amazed at how many words could fall from her mouth without her taking a single breath, especially when she was talking about her job and how much she loved being on vacation.

Seth noticed that Kyle hadn't taken his eyes off Janie once, and he hadn't dropped that silly grin since he'd walked in the door. But then again, Seth found himself smiling and laughing a lot too. Seth was seeing another side to Jessica. She was different with her sister. The twins seemed to feed off each other's energy. Her eyes seemed to sparkle more, her smile was wider and deeper, and it was obvious that the two women shared an extremely close bond.

"You don't have any siblings?" Janie asked Seth.

"No."

Jessica rolled her eyes. Seth wasn't very talkative. "His mother lives in Florida and has this big social life at The Villages. Seth usually flies down every February to visit her, and she comes to stay on the island during the summer. His dad passed away eight years ago. Heart attack."

"Oh." Janie felt bad for people who didn't have siblings. "What about you, Kyle? Any brothers or sisters?"

Kyle nodded. "Oh yeah. I come from a big obnoxious family. I've got two older sisters and three younger brothers."

"Oh wow..." Jessica smiled. "Middle kid, huh?"

"Yup. I think I became a cop in the hopes I could arrest all my kid brothers one day. Jeff, Alex, and Kevin drove me completely insane growing up."

Seth started to refill Janie's wine glass. "Oh no... I can't keep drinking. I think I'm already feeling it," Janie said. "Full belly, and wine... I'll be falling asleep soon, and I need to be able to drive."

"Drive where?" Jessica asked.

"I appreciate the invite to stay, but I'd prefer the B&B for now. I'll stay here Christmas Eve, but for tonight and tomorrow, I'd like to be at the Inn."

Jessica was about to argue, but she had a feeling that Janie needed more privacy for when dealing with Greg. And as thrilled as she was to see her sister, she was enjoying her intimacy with Seth. "Well as long as you stay here Christmas Eve." She enjoyed seeing her sister laugh and smile. Things were unraveling between Janie and Greg, and Jess worried about her battling depression.

"Since you're carrying a gun, I'll follow you over to the B&B," Kyle said. "I can't have you getting scared and shooting the locals."

Janie laughed and rolled her eyes. "Hey, I was in my right to hold my gun, since I felt reasonably threatened by you."

"What did I miss?" Seth asked.

"You didn't!" Jessica laughed.

Janie faced Seth to explain. "Jess and I both have CCW permits. I don't go anywhere without my gun."

Seth looked at Jess. "You never told me that."

"Oh, I don't keep my gun in my purse. I hate guns. I only took the class to support Janie."

"Like you did with the self-defense class?" Seth was starting to approve more of Janie, because thanks to her, Jessica could carry a gun and knew how to fight.

"A woman who knows self-defense, carries a gun, and actually knows how to use it is a woman after my own heart," Kyle said, placing his hand over his chest. "Is it just me, or is it hot in here?"

Both women laughed at Kyle. "I'm actually going to get a room at the B&B tonight also." Kyle glanced down at his watch. The time had flown, and it was already eleven o'clock. If there were rooms available, he'd rather crash there than try to make the last ferry and drive home. Besides, he wasn't ready to leave Janie.

"There's a storm advisory," Seth said. "Major snow is expected tomorrow afternoon." He glanced out the window and saw it was still clear. "If you're going to be around, Kyle, why don't you come by tomorrow morning? I'd like to discuss the case more with you."

Kyle nodded. He'd expected to talk about the case tonight, but the twins took the evening in a different direction. Their reunion turned into reminiscing and a welcome opportunity for Kyle to get to know Janie.

Chapter 29

Malek slammed his iPhone down on the glass table. His father had a way of always souring his mood. And Malek had reason to be happy. Shawn's death turned out to be a major advantage. The Coast Guard had boarded Malek's vessel and found incriminating evidence. Now the FBI was investigating his crew, trying to learn who owned the ship. But his brilliant planning would presumably protect him. He was the owner of not only IMH20's million-dollar manufacturing industry, but also hundreds of other independent emergency food-storage and bottled water companies. These, along with multiple shell companies, heavily concealed his ownership of the vessel. Even if the FBI dug deep enough, they would only learn that the vessel technically belonged to Shawn Sharconnon. When they found Shawn's name, the pieces would make sense. Shawn would be blamed for killing Williams, for creating the organism, and then trying to cover it up by burning down the station and killing the hired thugs. The case would be wrapped up nice and neat, with Shawn taking the fall for everything.

His cell sounded again, blasting the song 'Can't Touch This,' by MC Hammer. Malek stood up, feeling the need to pace. Why couldn't his father just accept his genius? Nothing Malek did was ever good enough. His father still sought out flaws and fixated on them. But Malek wasn't worried. Even with the information Mark Williams leaked, the damage was already done. His plan worked, and he'd become a billionaire as a result. More importantly, he had proved himself God-like. A power that his father should admire and respect.

He'd proven he was far superior to his wretched father.

He'd hired a new right-hand man to replace Shawn. The new guy, Adam, made Shawn look like a kitten. Malek paused thoughtfully. It still amazed him that Shawn was eaten by the magnificent snail.

Malek's house was like a museum. Expensive art adorned the walls, statues decorated the vast space, and authentic leopard-skin rugs warmed the black marble floor. He didn't care that the organism killed people. He found it humorous the first human it killed was Shawn. It was like karma was laughing at him.

Soon Malek would be leaving the country. His home in Italy was waiting. He was just ensuring that his business here was complete. Feeling confident the FBI would never be able to find him, he held up the tiny portable aquarium, and marveled at the small snail-like creature creeping along the sand.

"Adam!" Malek called out.

Adam arrived in the door, wearing a $4000 three-piece suit, compliments of Malek. "Sir?"

"Take my most prized possession to the plane. Make sure it's safely on board, along with the rest of my luggage."

"Sir, I thought you wanted a few more days to finish getting your affairs in order." Adam took the small tank, holding it carefully.

"There's nothing more for me to do here."

Adam glanced at the tank. "Are you concerned they'll find a way to kill it?" He'd been watching TV in the elaborate library. He was intrigued that his boss was the creator of the deadly flesh-eating organism. The news was constantly discussing the future implications of the creature that could potentially destroy humanity.

"They'll find a way." Malek knew what the answer was. Dr. Williams had found the one thing that would kill it, and he knew eventually other scientists would to. "I'll make sure the organism is never completely eliminated, as will others. Now that it's been created, people will try and use it for their own purposes." Pride etched his voice. "But I was the one who introduced a true fear of Armageddon. People will look to the only things that really matter when the survival of humanity is at stake… food and water." His eyes sparkled. "Food and water are all anyone currently cares about having. The country has turned to my companies to provide them." He controlled the industry. He owned every freeze-dried food company there was. No one could get their hands on bottled water Malek didn't own. Even the government was dependent on him. "If this organism continues to kill people, they'll hide out. People will be afraid to go anywhere. It will be like a plague, evoking fear and panic." He smiled, knowing he held the power. And power was everything.

The next day, snow began falling in sheets. Kyle was driving Janie back to Seth's house. She'd left her car there last night, as he'd offered to drive her to the B&B and bring her back in the morning. He noticed she wasn't in quite the same elated mood as last night.

"Are you okay?" he asked her, noticing her eyes were red and slightly swollen. It was clear she'd been crying.

Janie enjoyed getting to know Kyle last night. He seemed like a really nice guy, in addition to being attractive, and she appreciated how he made her feel desirable. The way he looked at her and subtly flirted with her. "I'm okay, but this snow is scary." It was causing whiteout conditions and she couldn't see the road. "I think we should pull over."

"I was just thinking the same thing." The windshield wipers couldn't push the snow fast enough, and the blizzard offered zero visibility. "Why don't you call your sister and tell her we're okay, so she won't worry. Tell them we're just going to wait this out a bit, until we can see enough to drive."

Luckily there was a signal, and Janie was able to reach Jessica. After she ended the call, she turned to see how much gas was left in the Explorer.

"We won't run out of gas. I've got some extra blankets in the back if we need them, along with bottled water and food."

Janie felt a twist of alarm. "Do you think we could be stranded here?" She had thought they would only need to pull over for a minute, but now she realized it could be much longer. Perhaps hours.

"No." Kyle heard the concern in her voice. "Don't worry, I'm used to these winter storms. It's no big deal." He was more concerned with what had made her cry. "Your eyes are red."

Pulling down the visor, Janie looked at herself in the mirror. "Yeah, I guess they are." She sighed. They could be stuck here for a while, so maybe it wouldn't kill her to talk about Greg. He was the reason her eyes were red. The reason her heart ached. "Did my sister or Seth tell you what happened with Jessica and her ex-fiancé?"

"No. I didn't even know Jessica had an ex-fiancé. Last night was the first time I spoke to Seth and Jessica about anything other than the case. Seth and I are friends, but we mostly talk about work."

"Weeks ago, Jessica came home from work sick with the flu. When she walked in the door, she found me and her fiancé, Greg… together."

Kyle felt both surprise and disappointment but kept his face from showing any emotion. He simply watched her, waiting for her to explain.

"I fell in love with Greg two years ago. I kept it a secret and tried to get over it. I even considered moving to California so I wouldn't have to be around him and Jess so much." She looked down sadly at her hands. "It bothered me that Jessica didn't seem completely in love with him. She'd tell me all the time she thought about ending it with him. She was always on the fence. When he proposed to her, it secretly killed me. I wanted to tell him my sister wasn't really in love with him. And honestly, I was mad at Jessica for accepting his proposal." She glanced up, reading something in Kyle's eyes. "But I never said or did anything because it wasn't my place. Jessica seemed happy to be engaged, and it made me think that maybe I was wrong. But then soon, she started complaining about him again. He worked too much. He never liked to do anything but go out to dinner. She wondered if he liked kids… blah blah blah."

"I'm listening," Kyle said, wanting to hear the rest of the story.

Janie took a deep breath. "One day, I was dropping off some

extra produce I bought at the store. I was used to walking in Greg's house all the time. I'd normally just call out to one of them. I expected Jess to be home, but I guess she had some appointments that day after work." Her stomach felt sick at having to confess the next part. "I was in the kitchen, putting carrots in the refrigerator. Greg walked in wearing a towel. He'd just gotten out of the shower and obviously thought I was Jess."

"Oh boy," Kyle said, realizing how easy a mistake that could be. But then it would only take a second to know it was the wrong sister. "Go on."

"I think he knew pretty quickly it was me. I could almost tell the minute he figured it out, but he kept going. He could have just laughed and told me how embarrassed he was. It was an honest mistake. We could have joked about it, and no harm would have come. But he looked at me with this intense…" She shook her head. "No one that hears this will understand. I was already in love with him. He made it clear he wanted me."

Greg sounded like a total creep, but Kyle didn't comment. Instead, he set his hand on Janie's, gave her a sympathetic pat and said, "Go on."

She hated how awful the confession sounded. "I didn't want to keep seeing him. I tried to tell him it was a one-time mistake. I'd never do anything to hurt Jess, and it literally made me sick knowing that I had."

"He's the one to blame," Kyle said.

"No, I'm to blame. I didn't believe Jessica was really in love with him, and I didn't believe she'd be happy with him. I held on to that belief and kept seeing him. Gosh, you must think I'm awful." She reached over and turned the heat down.

"Jessica obviously forgives you." He could see last night that the women were closer than any two ordinary siblings could be. He hadn't seen a trace of resentment or animosity, and he was a good judge of people.

"She did forgive me. But only because she knows how sorry I

am. She knows I didn't mean to do it. I was sick over it."

"Maybe she also knows you actually did her a favor?" Kyle said, thinking Greg was a player who didn't deserve a woman like Jess or Janie.

"She actually said that too. But what I did is unforgivable and so wrong," she said sadly.

It wasn't hard to feel sympathy for her, and he didn't like seeing her normal vibrant face so downcast. "If Jess can forgive you, maybe you should forgive yourself. You didn't intend to hurt her. Sometimes things just happen."

"You really think so?" Janie asked. It was good to get someone else's perspective. She hadn't spoken to anyone but Jessica about this, so to hear a stranger's point of view was helpful.

"It sounds to me like you and Jess were victims of a sleazebag. So why are you here, and not with Mr. two-timer?"

She furrowed her brows. "He's not a two-timer. He's… confused." She appreciated Kyle's perspective and was relieved he wasn't shaming her. But she still wasn't sure she qualified as a victim.

Kyle didn't think he should say what he was really thinking. She didn't appreciate his "two-timer" comment, so he decided to keep his mouth shut. But he'd grown up with sisters and had arrested plenty of sleazebags. He knew the "Greg" type, and what they were capable of.

Janie wondered what she was doing, confessing her sins to a cop she just met yesterday. When she realized that Christmas Eve was in two days, and she was sitting in a car on a remote island in the middle of a blizzard, she realized her life had taken a serious detour. She glanced sideways at Kyle and couldn't read his blank expression. "I have to say I'm surprised by your response to my situation. I thought you'd think a lot less of me."

Kyle turned the engine off, to spare the gas and cut the heat in the warm car. "I think you and your sister fell in love with the wrong guy." He shrugged his shoulders. "Are you still in love with him?" He already knew the answer.

"I am." She said, letting out a long, slow breath. "But I'm afraid it's not going to work out." She feared the pain of that. She studied Kyle's understanding face, and realized she had a knack for choosing the wrong men. "Thanks for listening to my Jerry Springer story."

Kyle laughed. "It's not that bad. It's probably not juicy enough for Springer." He put his hand on hers. "For whatever it's worth, you and Jess seem like exceptional women, and you both deserve exceptional men. If you have doubts about this Greg guy, don't ignore them. You're not in a position to be desperate. There are plenty of men who'd truly value you."

"That means a lot," Janie replied, feeling her face warm from the clearly sincere compliment. Kyle was right and hearing it from another man made her feel better.

"The snow is letting up," Kyle noted as he turned the windshield wipers on and stared out the window.

He needed to drop Janie off and put her from his mind. She was in love with another man, so he didn't want to like her more than he already did. He felt a sharp stab of disappointment from the situation. Apparently, all the good ones were taken. His phone sounded, and he pulled it from his pocket. "It's Seth." He listened carefully.

"What's wrong?" Janie asked, watching the look on his face. Kyle sounded concerned. "What?" She asked impatiently when he ended the call.

He turned his car back on. "The mayor is holding an emergency meeting at the firehouse. They're thinking of evacuating the island."

"Can they do that?"

"Depends."

"On what?"

"How big the threat is." He began to drive slowly through the snow. They finally got into town, where snowmobiles were lined up outside the firehouse. Of course, the island locals wouldn't let a blizzard stop them from attending a meeting. They just hopped on their sleds, probably enjoying the snowy ride.

Chapter 30

The Mayor of Chicory Island, Rick Heelson, was younger than Jessica expected at age 37. He'd been elected the previous year because his father and grandfather both owned stores on the Island, and all the residents knew his name. Heelson lived permanently there with his wife and daughter.

Around thirty people stood gathered in one room, some huddled in smaller groups. Janie and Kyle weaved through the townsfolk, finding Seth and Jessica at the front of the open room. The firehouse was spacious, with a large chalkboard at the front near a long wide window. Obviously, classes or meetings were held there, and Janie noticed a pallet of IMH2O wrapped in the corner.

"Please be seated, or stand off to the side," Mayor Heelson announced, holding a microphone to his mouth. He had a deep, commanding voice that didn't seem to fit his round, friendly face, and wide smile. He wore jeans with a button-down black shirt, and large black snow boots.

Jessica gave Janie a hug and led her to the chairs she'd saved near the corner of the room. A wooden desk was kitty-corner to their left, with boxes piled high beside it.

Seth stood beside Mayor Heelson, crossing his arms over his chest. His leg was throbbing, but he ignored it. "Quiet down, people. Let the Mayor talk." He glanced at the twins who had just sat down, and Kyle, who stood by the wall next to them. Everyone hushed at his command.

"I know people are concerned about this deadly organism,

and the implications for our island. I'm here to put your minds at ease. I've spoken with government officials, and they will not be evacuating the island." At the Mayor's words, everyone began speaking at once. A few people replied, 'thank God.'

"Listen up!" Seth shouted, and the room again fell silent.

Mayor Heelson sighed and gave a look of appreciation to Seth. "There are legitimate concerns about the lack of food, and the safety of our well-water. I'm aware that most of the residents have already cleared out the store shelves, and you're worried about surviving the winter if supplies don't come in. I've been told that supplies to the grocery store should not be a problem. And the owners are planning to stay and maintain their business."

Claire stood up, tucking her white hair behind her ears. "My husband has not been well. We're staying because this is our home, and we have nowhere else to go. But if they close the clinic, it won't be safe for us. We heard the doctor and nurses have left. Without the clinic, we'd have nowhere to go if we had a medical emergency."

Seth had just been in the hospital and hadn't heard any talk of the staff leaving. He started to reassure Claire, but the mayor spoke first.

"That's why we're having this meeting. We'll find out who's planning to leave or stay. Most of the tourists have left, and yes, some residents are planning to leave as well. There's a chance that if Bob has a heart attack or needs surgery, there won't be a surgeon on the island. And there's a chance that the ferry won't be running then. However, I'll have the police boat ready at all times to transport residents off in emergencies. These are all things residents need to take into consideration."

Janie grabbed Jessica's hand. "This is terrible," she whispered. She felt for the sweet, elderly woman and her husband. She'd been upset about her relationship with Greg, but the meeting reminded her there were more important things than her man troubles.

Another resident stood and asked, "What about Al's Diner?" He looked directly at Al himself, who was sitting with his wife in the middle of the room. "Someone said you might leave? You know I don't cook much, so if your place shuts down, I won't be staying."

The mayor put his hand up as more people began speaking. "Look. We'll answer all your questions when the surveys have been filled out. We plan to find out who's leaving and who can stay. Once we have all the information, you and your families can make an informed decision on whether or not to stay."

"Are you staying, Sheriff?" another man called out.

"I am." Seth glanced at Jessica. "I know most of you have stockpiled food. Most of us do for the long winters. I'm not that concerned about food and water at this point." Seth trusted that his well was not contaminated, and he had a garage full of emergency food. "I'm also not concerned about the ability to get off the island should anyone need to. We've got two police boats, and many of you have fishing boats." He walked over to Jessica and took her hand, pulling her to her feet. "This is Doctor Jessica Bennett. She's not a surgeon, even though she did a damn good job on my leg, but she is a doctor, and I'm planning on keeping her here for a few more weeks."

Glancing around the room nervously, Jessica noticed some people smiled and nodded, while others just stared. She tried to hide her discomfort while Seth returned to the front of the room. He had no right to tell the residents she could help. She didn't have access to medical supplies, and she couldn't just take on new patients by herself. She was unhappy he hadn't discussed this with her first. Just because they'd slept together didn't mean she was automatically staying. She hadn't decided that yet.

Feeling her sister's unease, Janie rested her hand on Jessica's leg.

The mayor continued to speak, but Jessica tuned out his words, feeling a pounding in her chest. By the time everyone started asking more questions, she had worked herself up to a slow, simmering rage. She stood quietly and left the room.

Kyle noticed the look on her face and then glanced at Janie, who began to follow her sister. He caught Seth staring and shrugged his shoulders. He didn't know what was wrong.

"Excuse me," Seth said, and walked out of the room to the hallway. "Wait up!" he shouted to Jessica and Janie, who were heading toward the exit doors. When he caught up to Jessica outside, she turned on him, anger flushing her pretty face.

"Seth, how dare you!" She was shaking, she was so angry. "You go back in there and tell those people you misspoke! I'm not here to help these people. Just because I'm a doctor doesn't mean I can just write scripts or examine anyone. I don't work here!" She put her hands on her hips. "I never once told you I was staying here! If food is running out and there's a chance things are shutting down and everyone's leaving, I'm not going to stay!"

Janie touched her sister's arm. "Calm down, Jess." It wasn't often Jess lost her temper, but when she did, Janie knew to watch out. She knew Seth didn't mean any harm, but her sister was fuming. "Seth can tell everyone—"

"You're right." Seth spoke calmly, even though his pulse was suddenly racing. "I shouldn't have introduced you the way I did. I didn't mean to imply you'd be the next island doctor. People are scared, and I thought maybe knowing there's a doctor on the island in case of emergencies would help ease their fears." Hell, she'd saved his life, and he knew she was extremely capable. "I should have discussed that with you first." He glanced at Janie, and then took Jessica by the arm to speak privately. He dragged her to the side of the building and was glad when Janie stayed put. His heart was hammering inside his chest. "Do you want to leave?" He had to know.

Jessica heard anger in his voice, but the look in his eyes was something else. His eyes were searching hers, demanding an answer.

"Tell me right now. Are you going to stay here and trust me to keep you safe, no matter what happens, or are you going to leave?" He didn't want to accidently squeeze her too tight, so he let her go, and jammed his hands in his pockets.

"Seth…"

"I need to know now."

"I..." She couldn't imagine walking away from him. Just that morning they'd stayed in bed wrapped up in each other for hours. It was her favorite place in the world to be. "I don't want to leave you."

He took a deep breath and slowly exhaled with relief. He saw tears swimming in her eyes and pulled her to his chest, wrapping his arms around her tightly. "I'm sorry I upset you. I made a mistake, and I'll fix it." He kissed the top of her head. "I want you to stay with me, Jess. I need you to stay with me."

Kyle pushed open the doors and saw Janie a few feet away on the sidewalk. Her arms were folded over her chest, and she was staring down at the ground. The snow had stopped, but the wind was still bitter. Janie wasn't dressed warmly enough, and he was about to drag her back inside when suddenly a red pickup truck came speeding into the parking lot. The parking lot was plowed, but as the driver slammed on the brakes, the truck kept going, sliding across the lot, heading straight for Janie.

Seth and Jessica heard a loud scream and turned in time to see Kyle diving on top of Janie, pushing her clear of the truck that smashed into a bush along the sidewalk where Janie had been standing. "Janie!" Jessica yelled out and ran toward her sister lying on the ground.

Kyle leaned up and stared down at Janie. "Are you hurt?" He'd tried to protect her head with his arm, but she'd still hit it against the sidewalk.

Janie had the wind knocked out of her, and her head hurt. She flinched as she tried to sit up.

"You idiot!" Kyle jumped to his feet as the driver stepped out of the truck.

"Kyle, no!" Seth grabbed Kyle's arm before he could confront the young man.

"I need help! My wife's in trouble! She fell in the water!" The driver grabbed Seth's arm, pleading for help before running to the passenger door. "Help me, please!"

Kyle glanced at Janie as Jessica knelt over her, examining her head. Jessica looked up with alarm before helping Janie to her feet.

The young woman in the passenger seat was breathing heavily. Tears streaked down her face, and she appeared in agony. "It's in my chest! I can feel it!" She practically collapsed into Seth's arms as he helped her down from the truck. "Please," she cried, "Get it out of me!"

Seth helped hold the young brunette up. The couple was probably only in their early twenties. "You need to get to the clinic."

"We went there, but it's closed. We came here because someone said there was an EMT here."

"Please help me! It's inside me! It hurts!"

The man quickly helped walk his wife inside the firehouse. He was wearing a wet blue parka and matching snow pants. His black boots were squeaky with water, and his hands were as red as his face. "Is there a doctor here?" he called out frantically.

"In here," Seth said, guiding them into a small room and holding the door open. People had heard the screaming and commotion outside. They were starting to approach with questions.

The woman was crying and becoming more hysterical, as she screamed out.

Dean entered the room, as Seth glanced at him. "They say the clinic is closed. Get someone to call the staff and find out what's going on." He was furious that the medical staff would leave without notifying anyone. There was only one surgeon, two nurses, and a few medical assistants that remained on the island over the winter. They worked as a team. If the surgeon left, he could see where the clinic might close entirely. The woman screamed in pain as Seth and her husband eased her down onto a black leather couch. They were in the Chief's office. The only furniture was a big brown desk, the couch, and a filing cabinet.

Chapter 31

Jessica asked Kyle to find ice for Janie's head as she eased her down against the hallway wall. She heard the other woman yell out in pain again but was concerned Janie might have a concussion.

"I'm fine," Janie said. "Go help that poor woman." She waved her sister away, watching people from the meeting stream into the hall and chief's office in response to the commotion.

Seth examined the woman's chest. Her pink shirt was soaked and torn at the shoulder. Blood trickled from an apparent hole in her skin beneath the tear. He glanced at the woman's frightened face as she cried and grabbed Seth's arm. Behind Seth, her husband was begging them to do something fast.

"Please it hurts so bad. Just cut it out of me!" The girl screamed again.

He started pulling back the fabric to get a better look, but she just ripped the shirt off, screaming "Get it out!" She was wearing a black bra, and her hands were shaking as she pointed to where the organism was moving in her chest.

"Get Logan in here," Seth told Chris, who had entered the office. "Everyone else needs to leave, now!"

Mayor Heelson began clearing the room, gently pushing people out. "It's all right. Just give the Sheriff some room."

Logan was the EMT for the island ambulance. He soon entered, opening his medical bag beside the couch. "Maybe we should get her off the island?" he suggested. "I'm not a doctor, I'm limited here."

"It's okay, Logan." Seth calmly reassured him. There wouldn't be time to move the woman anywhere. The organism was already eating through her. He looked up as Jessica entered the office.

The woman screamed out again. "Cut it out of me!" She stared frantically at her husband. "Dylan, cut it out! My God, get it out!"

Gently, Seth pushed the woman down on the couch, trying to calm her. "Look!" He glanced at her chest and saw the skin rise. "It's close to the surface."

Logan gave the woman an IV of anesthesia. "What's your name?" he asked her calmly.

"Becky," The woman replied with wide eyes and fear in her voice.

"Becky, try and calm down."

"I can't calm down! It's going to kill me!" All Becky could think about was what she'd seen on the news, and how two men had already been killed by the flesh-eating snail. She was terrified and began to cry.

A round, raised lump could be seen again under Becky's skin. "We need to cut her open and grab it now, while we can still see it." Jessica moved quickly, kneeling beside Logan, and reaching in his bag for gloves and a scalpel.

"Yes, hurry!" Dylan said frantically, holding his wife's hand.

"We can't wait for the anesthesia. It has to be now." Jessica glanced from Logan to Seth. The only hope to remove it was when you could see its raised outline, and she didn't want to lose it. "You'll have to hold her down."

"Hurry! Just do it!" Becky yelled, closing her eyes tight. "It already hurts! Just don't lose it!"

The cut was just deep enough that the blood did not flow right away. Becky began to scream as Jessica focused on pulling apart the skin. "Hand me the tweezers," she told Logan.

Logan was relieved he didn't have to cut the poor woman open, and that the anesthesia was starting to put Becky out. He watched as Jessica dug her fingers into the sliced open skin. He tried to help by mopping up the blood with gauze pads.

"I don't see it!" Jessica fought the panic making her hands shake. "I don't want to keep cutting this poor woman." She wiped sweat from her forehead and looked up at Seth and Dylan.

"It's okay," Dylan replied with a pained expression. "Do what you have to. It will kill her if you don't."

Seth nodded, and Jessica tried to steady her hand. She angled the scalpel to cut deeper and continued to look for the pea-sized organism. There was a lot of blood, and she knew it would be difficult to spot, but then she saw a speck of black. "I think I see it!" She pressed her knee into the couch as she leaned over the woman and used the tweezers to try and grab the shell. "It's moving faster now." Her heart pounded. "Oh god, it's…" She looked up, reached for the scalpel, and dug hard and deep between the left clavicle and rib. "I can't let it reach the thoracic organs." Ignoring the tweezers, she stuck her fingers deep and pinched the snail, feeling the hard outer shell between her fingers. She pulled at it. "I've got it, but it's really gripping," she groaned as she pulled. Not wanting to let it go, she kept her thumb and forefinger pressed around it, and slid the scalpel blade up under the snail. "I'm going to lose it," she feared aloud.

"No, you're not. You can do this, Jess. Just keep at it." Seth tried to pull the skin apart more as he encouraged her.

"Got it!" She felt the hard, tiny pea-size snail between her fingers. "It's… Oh!" She fell back and quickly whipped her glove off, feeling the pain in her fingertip.

Seth grabbed her hand to examine the finger. "Are you okay?" He glanced at the floor where her glove was lying. "Where'd it go?"

Dylan jumped to his feet. "Help Becky, she's bleeding!"

Jessica looked from the floor to Becky.

Seth checked under the couch for the organism. He turned to Jessica, "You sure it's not on you?"

"No. I dropped it." The creature had instantly tried to latch onto her finger.

"It's here!" The mayor said, pointing to the bottom of the wall.

"Don't touch it!" Seth picked up the tweezers and moved to the tiny shell. He carefully picked it up and dropped it inside a glass coffee cup he grabbed from the desk. Jessica was wiping blood from Becky's chest while Logan stitched together the cuts.

"She's going to be in a lot of pain when she wakes. I cut a lot of tissue."

Dylan set his hand on Jessica's shoulder. "You saved her life." Tears swam in his eyes. "Thank you."

Kyle was standing in the doorway, keeping an eye on Janie while he watched Jessica carve into the poor woman's chest. He felt a little nauseous. "What can I do to help?" He asked as Seth approached him.

"We need to write up a report." Seth turned to Dylan. "How did she end up in the water?"

Dylan released his wife's hand and walked over to them. "We were snowmobiling. We're renting a cabin here. Becky wanted a picture of her standing on the rocks with water in the background." Dylan ran a shaky hand through his hair. "I knew it was stupid. She was surrounded by dead fish, but Becky started climbing onto the rocks. She only got a few feet offshore when one of the rocks shifted. She lost her balance and fell in. The waves washed over her, and by the time I got to her she was drenched. She didn't feel the pain in her shoulder till we were back on our sleds. When she stopped in the woods, she started screaming. I knew. I knew right away and so did she." His voice quivered.

"So, you knew there was something deadly in the lake, but your wife still wanted to risk going near it for a damn picture?" Kyle hated stupidity. He couldn't keep the irritation from his tone.

"I know it was dumb." Dylan glanced at his wife. "She didn't think she'd fall in, obviously."

"The news is telling everyone to stay away from the water. The beaches are closed. Maybe—"

"Kyle," Seth interrupted him, placing his hand on his shoulder. He pulled Kyle out of the room, glancing down the hall at Janie, holding an icepack on her head. "This is why they were discussing evacuation. When this gets out, it's going to make things worse. People will be afraid to be anywhere near the water."

"Why does it have to get out?" Kyle asked. He didn't give a crap about stupid people dumb enough to risk their lives for a picture.

"All the residents who were here know what happened. This is probably already on Facebook and Twitter. If we can't keep the tourists and locals safe, the outside government will step in. They'll forcibly evacuate us." Seth didn't want that.

Kyle rubbed the stubble on his chin. "Have the mayor call everyone back. People need to know how serious this is, and how deadly these things can be. Maybe it'll scare people enough to keep them away from the water. Use this incident to warn the island residents."

"It's a good idea," the mayor said behind Seth's back. "I'll have my wife report this on the island website. I've already got a list of departing residents. This island may be a ghost town soon."

"Are you staying?" Seth asked the mayor.

"I am. I've got no problem waiting out the winter and staying home. My wife is excited about it. She's been into canning for years. She's looking forward to using our supplies."

Seth nodded at the Mayor as Janie approached him. "How's your head?" he asked, as she rubbed her neck.

"I'm okay." Kyle moved to her side, resting his hand on the small of her back.

Jessica walked out of the office, wiping blood from her arm with a white towel. The mayor turned to her, offering his hand.

"You did good work in there. I'm glad to hear you're staying. The clinic is yours if you want the job. I'm working on getting replacements for the staff that left." The mayor glanced at Janie. "I'm seeing double." His smile was wide and charming as he turned to Seth. "How on earth do you tell them apart?"

"Oh, trust me, I can tell them apart," Seth replied, with just a hint of a smile.

"I couldn't at first," Kyle laughed.

"Are you a doctor, or perhaps a nurse?" The mayor asked Janie. "You're welcome at the clinic as well."

"I'm a teacher."

"Jessica won't be staying, mayor. I'm sorry I indicated otherwise. She's just here to visit." Seth tried to undo the damage he'd done. "I misspoke when I introduced her earlier. I'm—"

"I'll think about it," Jessica said, interrupting him with a smile. "I seem to be needed."

Chapter 32

Dr. Armando dropped high concentrations of salt into a 35-gallon fish tank containing fifteen of the flesh-eating organisms. He was a chemist studying the Dr. Bennet's notes. Some of her formulas couldn't be correct, but the iodine one was interesting. He was about to test a theory.

A few hours later, Federal agent Jason Tyndell entered the lab. "Have you gotten anywhere?" he asked Armando. The moment the doctor turned around, Jason had his answer.

"Oh yes!" Armando held a test tube in his hand, a wide smile on his face. "They can't survive in saltwater, and salt alone will kill them. It appears to have incredible immunity to almost everything, with two protective systems. The tubular skin acts as a shield, difficult for anything to penetrate, and that's located inside the hard outer shell." He held the test tube up as proof.

"I'm not sure salt is the answer. We need a chemical that won't hurt the Lake." Tyndell stared at the dead organism in the bottom of the test tube.

"There are no chemicals. The creature's system filters out poisons. It recognizes anything artificial or non-mineralized. But that's why salt works. Its body doesn't recognize salt as a poison, so it absorbs it. If the levels are too high, the same thing happens to the organism that happens to humans." Armando sat down in his chair, dumping the dead organism into a petri dish. "If humans consume too much salt, it ruins the fluid balance in the body's cells, preventing the kidneys from removing water. The organism eats through things because the consumed flesh literally goes right through it. It doesn't digest it. But salt doesn't filter through its body the same way. The organism perceives salt as a nutrient and absorbs it." He spun around in his chair to face the agent. "The creature gets high blood pressure, its organs shut down, and it dies."

Tyndell rubbed the back of his neck. "It would be impossible to dump enough salt in the Lake to take out all the organisms."

Armando shook his head. "Did you know that salt deposits exist under most of the state? The city of Detroit is built over salt mines. They spread out over 1500 acres and have over a hundred miles of underground roads. 1.2 ounces of salt poured into one liter of water will give you the average salinity of sea water. That's what I used, and it killed the organism within two hours."

"Okay…" Tyndell pulled out his cell to google how much water was in Lake Superior.

"We're talking about changing the entire lake ecosystem. The salt will have many consequences, but then…" Armando glanced at the tank containing the deadly organism. "If we don't kill these things, they will kill everything anyway, and change the ecosystem permanently."

"So, either way, the country's in trouble?"

"The entire world's in trouble because scientists have learned to create new life forms. The moment we created a living cell with 'foreign' DNA, we set the human race on a path to destruction. Marine life cells can now be engineered without any of the four DNA bases used by all natural organisms on earth. And my belief is that this is just the beginning." He stared down at the organism in the petri dish. "This is an extraordinary creation, and the fact that man has genetically engineered plants and animals is only the beginning of our troubles."

Tyndell rocked back on his feet, putting his phone back in his pocket. "I hadn't really thought of it that way. I haven't even heard of genetically engineered cells."

"Ha!" Armando looked at him scornfully. "You can Google

it."

"Just tell me how we can kill it."

Chapter 33

About fifty hangers filled Seth's closet, and there was little space left for anything else. Jessica stood in the door, thinking about all her clothes packed in Mike's garage. She was still living out of her suitcase and missing the items she didn't have. Had her frame of mind been better, she would've participated in the packing, rather than letting Maria and her girls do it all. Then again, she did have two fully stuffed suitcases.

"What are you thinking?" Seth limped from the bathroom with a towel around his waist. His leg was still sore, but the wound was healing.

"I have a lot of clothes and a ton of shoes."

Seth turned Jessica in his arms. "If you stay, I'll build you a walk-in closet. Hell, I'll add another bedroom to the back of this house and turn this entire bedroom into your closet if that's what you need." He'd do anything he could to make her happy.

She smiled and leaned in. "I'd love to tell you that won't be necessary, but I can't. I don't want to give up my clothes." And she'd never part with a single pair of shoes, not even the ones she hardly ever wore.

"I told you, you can hang some up in here, just to get them out of your suitcase." He didn't like that her suitcases were still packed. "I'll move my clothes out temporarily. We'll make it work for now, unless you're still thinking of jetting off this deserted island."

Though he was teasing, she could still see a bit of apprehension in his eyes. Two days ago, she'd really scared him when she'd gotten mad during the town meeting. It was probably her fault he was a tad insecure now. "I'd be a fool to ever leave this little paradise. I'm no fool."

"Ha," Seth hugged her tight. "Still thinking this is paradise, are we?"

"Nothing has changed," she laughed.

The news station played on the television as Janie sipped her coffee. It was 10:30 a.m. Christmas morning. It didn't feel like Christmas. It didn't look like Christmas. There wasn't a single decoration, and even the television didn't acknowledge Jesus's birthday, other than a few lame commercials that reminded the world it was time to buy presents. Janie had given Jessica her present on Christmas Eve. A pair of earrings and a scarf. She hadn't been in the Christmas spirit this year. Jessica had Janie's favorite perfume shipped to her house from Amazon, not knowing she was coming to the island.

Janie heard her sister laughing and leaned back in the sofa. She was happy Jess had found a man to replace Greg— the man she didn't really love. Jessica had better luck with men and also managed to avoid heartache. She didn't have to suffer over losing Greg the way Janie was. Seth was a handsome man, though rough around the edges. And the only thing that mattered was that he made Jess happy. Jessica finally seemed like a woman in love. Janie knew right off her sister had fallen harder and faster for Seth than she ever had for Greg.

Thinking of Greg, Janie picked up her cell. It was Christmas day, and she hadn't heard from him since the day before she left. He hadn't even bothered to wish her a Merry Christmas. Her heart ached, knowing it was over. She'd been a fool in love. She thought about what Kyle said to her when they were sitting in his car. 'You fell in love with the wrong guy.' Yes, she had. She was always falling in love with the wrong men. A tear fell down her cheek.

"I could use a nap." Jessica finished straightening up the bedroom. "But I feel I'm being rude leaving Janie out there by herself."

Seth changed into a pair of jeans. The wound on his leg was

healing nicely. In a year, he should have a perfectly round scar. He walked around the bed and sat beside Jessica, taking her hand in his. "I have a Christmas present for you."

"What?" She watched as he reached in the bottom drawer of his nightstand and pulled out a small box. "No, Seth. I didn't think we'd exchange gifts, because neither of us had time to shop."

"It's okay, I don't care. I had an advantage because I've got connections on the island. Besides, you might not even like it." He handed her the box with gold wrapping paper.

She began to unwrap it, feeling guilty that she hadn't put any thought into Christmas. She lifted the lid and stared down at the breathtaking necklace.

"It's white gold."

"Oh, Seth." She held up the necklace. It was a beautiful thin chain and hanging from it was a small clear glass pendant with bright blue flower petals inside.

"It's the real petals of a chicory flower. They're blue and grow on the island. That's how Chicory Island got its name. I happen to know a sweet old lady who makes these glass pendants."

"Who?" Jessica looked at him in surprise. "Claire?"

He nodded. "She used to own a store in town and made all her own jewelry. But she's retired now, and only does it upon request." Seth took the necklace from her and placed it around her neck, clasping it together. "I thought if you ever decide to leave, you'd always have a piece of the island with you."

It was the most thoughtful, sweetest gift she'd ever been given. The necklace was not only unique and beautiful, but incredibly sentimental. She couldn't think of a more romantic gift. "I love it, Seth." She turned and set her hand over the stubble on his face. When his eyes met hers, she was overwhelmed by emotion. "I love you."

He studied her a moment, feeling his heart explode with those three precious words. She'd said them first, and he could see from the look in her eyes that she meant it. He cupped her face. "I'm very much in love with you." He couldn't think of a better Christmas present than those three words, and what they meant. He'd never forget this moment.

She laughed when he touched the button on her flannel. "Seth, we can't."

He remembered Janie in the living room and sighed.

Chapter 34

Red roses adorned a $5,000 mahogany casket, lined with burgundy velvet and satin. It seemed out of place in the old Kentucky church graveyard, where some of the gravestones dated back to the seventeenth century. But this was the graveyard where Malek's great-grandfather was buried. Malek glanced down at his great-grandfather's plain grave marker, which simply stated his name, and birth/death dates. He smiled knowing his father had purposely placed his own elaborate/impressive stone monument right beside his grandfather's plot. Malek's father had purchased the plot years ago, with the idea he'd be buried beside the 'best' family member. He respected his grandfather, who'd been a successful entrepreneur. A man with vision who died owning sizable tracts of land in Kentucky.

A few elderly gentlemen stood to the left of the 8-foot grave, as the cemetery caretakers began to lower the casket into the cold ground. A crisp breeze stirred the air and swirled the soft snow that layered the grass. Malek glanced around the empty cemetery. The men standing nearby meant nothing. They were not family or friends, but simply business associates. No one was there to mourn, say words of kindness, or display sorrow. Not even Laurence Senior's house staff would attend the funeral, unless Malek insisted, which he had not.

There was no sound as the casket was lowered into the earth. Malek expected a thud or something once it reached the bottom, but instead it was silent, making his mind wander to thoughts of his childhood. Silence had been an important part of his younger years. He'd learned early on that his father would not tolerate noise, which included a child's laughter or talking too loudly. He'd left for college the moment he graduated high school. He hadn't liked the noisy parties, or the loud, obnoxious students who couldn't speak in quiet tones. He'd enjoyed the science lab, though. For some reason, the science room felt serene. The students had their heads in books and held quiet thoughts as they peered through microscopes. Maybe it was just his interest in science and biology that made him prefer those classes over business courses. He would've chosen a field in science had his father not pushed him into business. Business was an obsession for Malek's father. In his mind, the only thing that mattered in life was accounting, finance, and management skills. Malek was raised with the strict discipline needed to create a strong, successful entrepreneur.

However, the love of science was still there. Malek loved articles explaining how scientists were creating genetically modified human embryos. He was fascinated with the scientific advancements occurring every day that were transforming the world. From physics, to medicine, to biology, each related story would blow his mind. It amazed him that people went about their daily lives, focused on their basic needs for money, with no idea of the myriad new technologies that were growing and shaping the future. But Malek knew. Malek could see his father's million-dollar companies and loaded off-shore bank accounts and envision something bigger and more powerful than anything his father had achieved. Malek, like his grandfather, had a vision. But his vision was far superior, and unlike his father, he would not be laid to rest beside inferior family members.

From his jacket pocket he removed the article he kept as a reminder. The article that had sparked his ultimate vision. He carefully unfolded the paper titled, 'Scientists Create New Synthetic Life Form.' The article discussed how scientists had created an entirely new lifeform that was capable of carrying and passing down to future generations an expanded genetic code. Cells which could carry synthetic DNA nothing like the normal code of natural organisms.

Highlighted in yellow were the names of the brilliant scientists who'd worked on the breakthrough technology. They'd been restricted in their research, with limited funding for their labs. Malek remembered another article that discussed the first man-made artificial chromosome, and the successful transplant of mycoplasma bacteria into a different species of bacteria. But continuing research funds were limited, due to dwindling grants and lack of government funds. Underlined at the bottom of the article was Dr. Mark Williams's name. The scientist who'd been extremely easy to hire. The scientist who designed his own computer, capable of determining which trait/gene of a species would be selected and then crossbred to introduce a new genetic background for an entirely different species. With marine life, there seemed to be hundreds of options. And it was Malek who'd given Williams the support and opportunity to make those options viable.

Taking a deep breath and closing his eyes, Malek slowly refolded the article. He stretched his arm out over the grave and let go of the paper, watching it fall to his father's casket. His private jet waited for his return so he could leave the country and be forever safe from the destruction he had caused. His plan had worked, and all that mattered was that his father had lived long enough to see the product of his brilliant vision. The world feared fresh water was endangered and that human life was threatened. Where there was fear, there was opportunity, and where there were scarce resources, there was money to be made. Above all, where there was scientific creativity, there was immense power.

Chapter 35

Jessica pulled her red sweater over her black leggings, and then slipped on her black UGGs. She picked her cell up again, seeing if Janie had responded to her text.

"Damn him." Jessica shoved her phone in her pocket. Yesterday no one had been in the Christmas spirit. Kyle stopped by for dinner, which seemed to cheer Janie up a little, but everyone was still melancholy, and Janie definitely wasn't herself. Jessica knew something was wrong. It wasn't just the doom and gloom on TV, or the experience with Becky and the flesh-eating snail that had Janie so blue. It was Greg.

"Hope you're not talking about me," Seth said, leaning on the door frame with his arms folded over his chest. He'd just come to bring her coffee.

Reaching for the mug after placing a kiss on his lips, concern etched her eyes. "My sister hasn't responded to her texts all morning. She was sad last night, and now I'm worried about her. I know she's depressed about Greg."

"She must have checked her phone at least fifty times last night." Seth assumed she was expecting a call that never came. "She seemed okay to me. I think there might be something between her and Kyle."

Jess shook her head. "Greg never called her, and she was upset." She knew Janie was putting on an act for Kyle and Seth. She'd mastered the ability to hide her pain from everyone except Jessica. "She likes Kyle, but she's in love with Greg. The bastard is doing a number on her. I'm going to go to the Bed and Breakfast she's staying at. I called there, and they said she hasn't checked out yet. When she didn't answer the room phone, I had them check if she was still there. They told me her 'do not disturb' sign is on the door."

"So, she's just ignoring you?" Seth followed her from the bedroom into the kitchen. He limped to the garage door where he kept his boots and began putting them on.

"It's complicated, Seth." She picked up her purse. "What are you doing?"

"I'm coming with you." He didn't want her driving alone. The roads were slick from last night's snowfall, and if Janie was suicidal, he didn't want Jess finding her sister alone. "Don't argue, babe. Once I know everything is okay, I'll be happy to leave you alone with her and give you privacy, but I'm going with you."

Jessica sighed, staring at him as he put his jacket on. His leg was still sore, and any other man would still be lying on a couch. But not Seth. He didn't let a bullet wound slow him down or stop him from taking care of her. He was a good man, and there wasn't anything he wouldn't do for her. But his behavior could be construed as controlling, or at least over-protective. She decided to test the waters. "Seth," She walked over to stand in front of him. "I need to go see my sister alone. I'll drive slowly and be very careful, and I'll text you as soon as I get there to let you know I'm safe. But I don't want you to come." She didn't feel she should have to explain herself any more than that.

"I'm worried about you finding her… hurt. Alone."

Suddenly she understood what his concern was. "Oh." So, his wanting to go made a little more sense. "That's not going to happen. She promised me she'd never hurt herself again. I'll be fine."

He began to take his jacket off. "Just text me to let me know you're both okay." He kissed her on the forehead. "And drive careful."

And just like that, he was willing to let her have her way. Jessica noticed the twitch in his jaw when he bent to take his boots off.

He was still in pain, and bending his leg hurt. She put her hands on his shoulders and waited till his eyes met hers. "You're a really good man, Seth." He wasn't controlling or over-protective. He was caring and reasonable. She moved her hands to the back of his neck. "I'm very much in love with you."

Seth stared into her eyes. He'd been criticized a lot by his first wife, so hearing compliments from Jessica wasn't something he took lightly. Her happiness was important to him. "I don't want to screw this up." He was scared to admit how much he needed her, and how perfect he thought she was. And his biggest fear was that he'd end up being her rebound. A temporary fix after a painful breakup. But looking in her eyes, he didn't care about any of that. "You're the best thing that's ever happened to me." He leaned his forehead against hers, and took a deep breath, feeling more love for her than he'd ever felt in his life.

She didn't want to leave him. Or for the moment to end, because the way he kissed her and made her feel made it extremely difficult to pull away. "Seth…"

"I know." He held her close and smiled. "Go make sure Janie is okay."

Janie didn't answer the door when Jessica pounded on it. "If you're in there, you better open up, or I'll get security to do it," Jessica hollered through the door. Her anxiety was building. "You're scaring me, Janie!" she shouted, and then turned to walk to the lobby.

The door opened, and Janie stuck her head out. "Come in," she said in a hoarse voice.

One look at her and Jessica could see that things were as bad as the week they'd lost their parents. She followed Janie into the dark room and shut the door behind her. "Where's the light?" She felt along the wall until she found a switch. A chandelier instantly lit the room, casting shadows on the pale-yellow striped wallpaper. The bedroom was pretty but had an ominous feel from the pile of wadded-up Kleenex on the floor, the drawn curtains, and the sorrow on

Janie's face.

"Don't do this." Jessica sat down next to her sister, curled up in a ball on the large king-sized bed. The yellow comforter was balled up at the foot of the bed, and Janie lay on the white sheet, tears soaking a wet spot on the pillow.

"I can't help it. I can't stop crying." And even as Janie tried to get the words out, her face contorted with pain and tears fell from her eyes. Her body shook with sobs. "I thought he loved me. I don't want to feel this heartache."

Jessica brushed a strand of Janie's hair behind her ear. "He does love you. I saw the way he held your hand in the hospital."

Janie sniffed and sucked in air. "He loves me, he loves you, and he loves a nurse named Elizabeth."

"What?"

"He's cheating on me!" Janie sat up and reached for the Kleenex from the nightstand. "I'm such an idiot! A pathetic fool!"

"How do you know he's cheating?"

Janie blew her nose and tried to calm herself enough to speak. "I called him last night after I left. It was Christmas for Pete's sake, and he hadn't even bothered to call me. Jess, I hadn't spoken to him since the day before I left." She sniffed again, trying to catch her breath. "A woman answered his phone. When I asked where he was, she said he was in the shower."

"Oh God." Jessica leaned her head back against the white headboard.

"He called me back. When I confronted him, at lease he was honest with me. He said he started seeing Elizabeth the day after I overdosed. He claims he was distraught over losing you and confused about whether or not he wanted to be with me. Elizabeth was trying to comfort him and offer support. He said he didn't mean for it to happen, but it did."

Jessica felt sick. Part of her suspected Greg was the kind of man incapable of true commitment. Maybe that was why she hadn't felt shocked over finding him with Janie. And she hadn't been devastated over losing him, because her trust had never run that deep, nor her love. But Janie was fooled by him. "He didn't mean for it to happen, but it did. Where have I heard that before?"

"I know. I know. And the worst part is that he told me he's still in love with you. And he can't be with me, because I look like you, and that's just too painful for him." Janie set her hand on Jessica's leg. "It's what I get. He's doing to me what we did to you, and it's my punishment. It's what I deserve." She sobbed and curled back into a ball.

"Janie, can you look at this another way? Can't you just see the kind of man Greg is, and accept that he's a player? Can you see that this has nothing to do with us, or what we do or don't deserve? Greg is dishonest. He's egotistical, self-centered, and likes to be with different women. He loves the power of being a handsome surgeon, and his head's the size of Mount Rushmore."

"But I love him. And he made me believe he loved me too."

"He does love you. He loves me. He loves any beautiful woman who will stroke his ego." Jessica stared at the ceiling in frustration. "You'll never be able to trust him. You couldn't have built a future with him because he can't offer you solid ground. He can't offer the commitment and trust you deserve. I'm sorry you fell in love with him. I'm sorry that I cared enough about him to bring him into our life. He's not a good man, Janie." She closed her eyes and pictured Seth. Seth was the complete opposite of Greg in every way, and she felt extremely fortunate to have him.

"I know." Janie rolled over and looked wearily at her sister. "I know all this, but it doesn't make the pain go away. I'm so sick of falling for the wrong men. I don't know how to fall out of love. It hurts so badly, I can barely breathe."

"I need to know you're not going to do anything to hurt yourself."

"I won't."

"Sitting in a dark room, ignoring my texts, and refusing to open the door is unacceptable. I can't keep worrying about your state of mind. I'm afraid of losing you." Her phone vibrated in her coat pocket, and Jessica pulled it out, glancing at the text from Seth: *I'm making lunch, bring your sister over if you want. Let me know you're okay.*

"He's very good to you," Janie said, nodding at her sister's phone.

"Yes, he is. I'm crazy about him."

Janie set her hand on Jessica's glass pendant, admiring it. "I know. I'm happy for you."

"But things are complicated right now."

"Because of the case?" Janie sat up again, reaching for another Kleenex. Last night Kyle had told them the FBI had closed the case. The man who'd paid to create the organism had died by the organism. He'd tried to kill Jessica, so in Janie's opinion, the man got what he deserved.

"No. Not just because of the case. You heard Kyle last night. He thinks I'm completely safe now. Things are complicated because I'm not sure I want to give up working with Mike. I like my practice. I'd have to move here."

"You love it here. And the Mayor offered you a job."

"I do love it, but still… the Island could change. If the organism scares everyone away, especially the tourists, we could eventually be living on a deserted island." Jessica swept away a tear about to fall from Janie's chin. "And I don't want to live that far away from you."

"You can't worry about me. I promise I'll be fine."

"I know, but moving here is a huge decision, and I don't know what to do."

"You found a great man. Seth loves you… and he's tall," Janie smiled, laughing when Jessica did.

"Janie, one day you're going to find a good man too. One day you'll barely remember this."

"You sound like Dad." She leaned over and wrapped her arms around her sister's waist.

"We don't really need men, ya know. We are strong, capable women with thriving careers. What do we need a man for?" Jessica looked in her sister's eyes. "My coming here was the best thing I could have ever done. I know who I am, Janie. I know what I want, and how to have a happy life even without a man."

"Yes, but you *have* a man."

"One day you will too, but don't let a man have this much control over your life."

Janie understood exactly what her sister was saying, and she was right. She remembered Kyle's words, "You're not in a position to be desperate." She knew in her heart Greg didn't deserve her. "Thanks for coming here." She hugged her sister tight and decided to be strong.

It felt good to hold Janie for a few moments. "You know, the news is trying to convince people that the water is safe to drink. Kyle told Seth the government has a plan to kill the organism, but in the meantime, people are scared. There's no way to know if the government's plan will even work. I'm worried about you being alone and so far away. Is there any chance you could take some time off work and stay here awhile?" She wanted Janie to stay. Kyle had mentioned there were plenty of houses for rent. She felt safer on the island, where Seth had his own well and plenty of food.

"Reply to Seth's text so he won't worry." Janie stood up and thought about Jessica's proposal. She didn't like being many hours from her sister either. When Jessica finished her text, Janie wiped the tears from her cheeks and gathered her thoughts. "I can't stay here. I know you love this island, and the peace and quiet of the forest. But I'm not like you. I could never live here, Jess. I need my job and to be around people. I like the city life."

"I know. You always hated camping."

"I *hated* camping," Janie laughed emphasizing the word.

"Will you at least stay till Christmas break is over?"

Janie thought for a moment before she responded. "I'll stay if you can talk Kyle into taking me for a snowmobile ride."

"Deal."

"Are you going to move here, Jess?"

Jessica stood up. "I know that I can't leave him."

"Then let's go have lunch with the love of your life, and hope to God the snails don't eat the only good men left on this planet."

Chapter 36

The Lilacs were in full bloom. The sugar maples were sprouting leaves, and the forest was turning green with a rich mix of shrubs, wildflowers, and evergreens. The rain had finally let up, and the sun was welcoming the warmth of spring.

The National Guard continued patrolling the Lake Superior beaches. The President hadn't lifted the State of Emergency, implemented before Christmas. It funded the immediate creation of cement dams sealing off the entire Lake from all other bodies of water. The dams were built in record speed, as time was a major concern. Nearby lakes were constantly monitored to determine if the organism had already spread to connected waterways. The government had a plan to dump large quantities of salt into Lake Superior but was first waiting to see how far the organism had spread. The media discussed the concept of making Lake Superior saltwater, and the consequences it would have on the region's ecosystem.

The State of Emergency prevented further stockpiling of food and water, and a 6:00 p.m. curfew was imposed upon all cities bordering Superior, in both Michigan and Minnesota. Canada had taken similar actions. Luckily, because of frigid winter temps, there had only been two human deaths from the organism. Dead fish and wildlife continued to litter the beaches, but the threat from the organism was apparently contained. No one dared go near the water.

Seth listened as Dean's voice came on the radio attached to his shirt. Dean was reporting he'd installed a four-way stop sign to replace the broken traffic light near town. The electric company was already en route to the island to make repairs. At least the world was continuing to function, since most people now believed the country would survive some maniac creating a deadly new organism. The island would suffer from fewer tourists, but Seth had seen many wildlife enthusiasts coming on the ferry to admire the spring growth. There wouldn't be any boaters, but people still wanted to the see the beauty of Chicory Island. "Look at this plant," Jessica said, standing with her camera. "Oh Seth, it looks so unusual."

He turned to see her take another picture. He'd brought her to his favorite spot on the East side of the island, where unique plants and wildflowers were reborn after the long cold winter. The trail they were on was a thin dirt path hikers enjoyed all summer long. She'd taken the day off work to be with him. She was now a permanent resident of Chicory Island, working at the local clinic. Though Seth was starting to think she was more interested in photography. Seth was always on duty but had the luxury of roaming anywhere he wanted on the island.

"I'm going to have these pictures put on canvas for Janie. Our birthday is next month, and I think they'll make a beautiful wall hanging." Jessica marveled at the plant as she snapped another picture of the wildflowers blowing softly in the breeze.

Seth felt in his pocket for the ring. He had brought her to his favorite spot for a reason. He glanced around at the empty forest and thought now was as good a time as any. He walked over to her and pulled her towards his chest. He kissed her softly and looked into her eyes. "You might get tired of seeing all this nature."

She leaned back. "Are you kidding? I'm so excited for summer I can hardly stand it. I'm not even scared to go near the water. I can't wait to see the caves you've been talking about." She liked working at the clinic and having more free time to enjoy doing things. She'd taken up new hobbies, including painting. She had more time to spend cooking, and Seth seemed to love everything she made. She frequently took walks with him on the island and loved spending time with him outdoors.

"There's something I want to ask you." He cupped the sides of her face to draw her attention. "You and I have been together almost six months. I know that's not long, but what we've been through together makes me know we're a good fit."

She wrapped her arms around his waist. "We're a great fit."

He laughed at her playful innuendo. "Let me say this."

She realized he wanted to say something important and became serious.

"When you moved in with me, and I didn't have enough closet space for your shoes, I was nervous." He'd built her a walk-in closet by adding a wall and making the master bedroom a bit smaller, but she seemed to love it. "I was afraid you'd realize life with me is simple, less extravagant, and perhaps a little boring."

She immediately went to contradict him, but he set a finger on her lips. "Hold on a sec and hear me out." When she smiled, he continued. "I know you're happy here. I know you don't need or want anything more than what we have. You've told me too many times for me to think otherwise. But I want more, Jess." He stepped back from her and bent down to one knee while taking the box from his pocket. "I want a life with you forever. I promise you I'll never need or want anything more than you." He opened the box to display the simple princess cut ring. "I need you to be my wife, because I want to have children with you, and grow old with you. Will you marry me?"

Tears welled in her eyes, as she stared down at the man she loved with all her heart. "Yes." She bent down and wrapped her arms around his neck.

He fell back as her body pushed him into the soft plants along the path. "Hey, you better hope we aren't lying in poison ivy," he laughed as she brushed rapid kisses along his cheeks and neck.

Dean's voice came on the radio, interrupting Jessica's assault. "We've got reports of kids at the beach throwing dead fish at each other."

"Kids are dumb," Seth muttered, against Jessica's mouth. "We have to go. I'll drop you off at home."

Jessica laughed. "Our kids won't be dumb."

"Of course not." Seth helped her to her feet. He took the ring and carefully placed it on her finger. "I want to marry you as soon as possible. Whatever you want, we'll do." He took her hand and began to walk back to the car. "Do you want to elope or have a wedding?"

She already knew what she wanted. "I just want to have a small wedding here, surrounded by all this beautiful Chicory." She stopped and looked around the forest. "*Right* here, Seth." She placed her hand around the pendant he'd given her, and her heart swelled with emotion. "Just Janie, Mike, Maria, Kyle, Dean, and your mom. I want to stand right here in the middle of July when the entire forest is alive with color. And then I want to take a fantastic honeymoon!"

Seth pulled her into his arms and held her tight. "My God, you're perfect." He wanted the exact same thing. She was everything he wanted.

Chapter 37

The case file was open on Kyle's desk. He sat with coffee in hand, reading the final report. The FBI had added greatly to the Mark Williams' murder investigation. It appears he'd been hired by the man named Shawn Sharconnon. The two fake FBI agents, whose bodies were found in the woods, were also hired by Shawn. The FBI confirmed that Shawn shot the men. Sharconnon was apparently a businessman who invested in numerous companies. He'd been one of the owners of the Visionary vessel. That was the ship they found containing the organism in the ballast water. The Visionary had a long history of ownership turnover, starting out as a merchant vessel in the early 1960's. Sharconnon was the only owner linked to Doctor Williams's death. Crew member interviews confirmed that Sharconnon was in charge and had hired Williams to experiment with crossbreeding organisms.

Kyle raised his head when he heard a few men whistle. A slow smile curled his lips as he watched the lovely blonde approach his desk. He immediately thought of Janie, but it would make more sense for the woman to be Jessica.

"Hi, Kyle." She stood in front of his desk. "Front desk said I could come back here."

He stood up and walked around his desk to offer her a hug. The moment he inhaled her scent, his smile widened. "I thought for a second you were Jessica. This is a pleasant surprise, Janie. What are you doing here?"

Janie was thrilled that Kyle somehow knew it was her. She

laughed. "Darn, I was going to mess with you. How did you know it was me?"

"I'm a detective now, so perhaps my skills improved with my latest job promotion." He held her shoulders a little longer than he would with Jessica. "Have a seat. What brings you here?"

"Well first, congratulations on your promotion. Jess told me it's exactly what you wanted." She sat down in the brown leather chair and faced him, feeling a little flutter in her belly. He looked good. His hair was buzzed shorter than the last time she'd seen him.

"Yes. I'm happy." He glanced down at the file on his desk and swept the papers into a neat pile. Janie made his hands a bit shaky. "You look great, Janie. Jessica tells me you've been well." He hadn't seen her since New Year's Eve dinner at Seth's house. She'd been dealing with a fresh breakup and a broken heart from the cheating surgeon. He'd have asked if she was seeing anyone new, but Jessica had kept him up to date. Janie had sworn off men for now and was getting her life on track. "Are you visiting your sister for the weekend?"

Janie shifted in her chair and pulled her white skirt down over her knees. Her soft blue blouse was slightly untucked, but she saw that the delicate buttons hadn't come undone. "Yes. I'm on summer break now, which I love. I'm going to spend a few weeks on the island. I brought the last of Jessica's boxes from Mike's house. She and I are going gown shopping this weekend. I was headed to the ferry, but Jess called to tell me it was broken down again. Seth won't be able to pick me up in the police boat for a couple hours, so I thought I'd kill time and pay you a visit."

"I'm so glad you did." He couldn't take his eyes off her. "You look good, Janie. You look happy."

She tipped her head a little and sighed. "It's taken me some time, but I'm getting there. I've been taking a lot of self-help classes. It's really good for the soul."

He smiled. "I'm glad."

"Will you be attending the wedding in July?" She knew he was but wanted to hear him say it.

"I wouldn't miss it for the world. Your sister has made that big guy very happy. Some people are even saying he doesn't look as pissed off these days."

Laughter helped to ease Janie's nerves. "Jess tells me you bought a new house on the Lake."

"I did. It's a fixer-upper, so it's been keeping me busy. I love it though." He couldn't pass up the opportunity since lake homes were now selling so cheaply.

"Any chance you'll brave the water in the future?"

"Probably. I did buy a boat. I'll wait for the all-clear from the government first." The government had started dumping the salt two weeks ago, at the start of June. Testing on the Visionary ballast water had proven effective at killing all the organisms there, but it was an enormous project, and the National Guard was still keeping people away from the water. Green fences were also installed along the shore to keep homeowners a safe distance away. It was highly illegal to cross the fences. "I'd love to show you what I've done with the place."

"I'd love to see it." Janie reached in her purse and pulled out an envelope and handed it to him. "I'm throwing Jessica and Seth a little bridal shower. It's a couples' thing, and I'm hoping men will come too. Jess and I don't have a lot of family. Most of our friends are men, so…"

Kyle understood what she was saying. There would be no one to invite if it was only for women. "I'll be there. You might have to give me some gift ideas. I've never been very good at that sort of thing."

"I will."

Kyle didn't want her to leave. "Hey, I've got some interesting news to share with Seth. I was going to call him, but I know how much he appreciates my unannounced pop-overs," he said with a grin. Seth always seemed grumpy when Kyle showed up at his house unexpectedly. "How about we get a bite to eat, and then grab the ferry together? Whenever it breaks down, it's never for more than an hour or two."

"I'd like that." She wasn't at all hungry, because she'd just eaten, but Kyle didn't need to know that.

Chapter 38

When Janie and Kyle knocked on Seth's front door, no one answered. "Let me call her," Janie said, reaching in her purse for her cell. Just then the door opened, and Jessica was standing in the doorway, wearing a bathrobe.

"Is this all you guys do?" Kyle asked, as he patted Jess on the shoulder in greeting, and then offered his hand to Seth. Seth was shirtless wearing a pair of grey sweatpants.

A lovely red flush filled Jessica's cheeks. "Actually, Seth just got home from rehab, and I was just changing my clothes because I was working in the garden."

"No need to explain," Kyle waved his hand in the air.

"Hi Seth!" Janie greeted her future brother-in-law with a high five. She could see why her sister would want Seth's shirt off on a daily basis. "You should put a shirt on, that's way too much muscle for us women. Jess, how do you focus on anything?"

"Hey…" Kyle turned as the women were laughing. Then he glanced at Seth and said, "Yeah, I've got to agree, buddy. Put a damn shirt on."

Seth growled and turned to walk to the bedroom.

"He still growls?" Kyle asked Jessica.

"Yes." She laughed and walked to the fridge to offer Janie lemonade and Kyle a beer. "Janie, did you bring my boxes?"

"Of course." Janie took a seat at the barstool in the kitchen and glanced at Kyle as he sat on the stool right beside her.

"I've got some news for you and Seth," Kyle said, taking the beer from Jessica, and tipping his head in thanks.

Seth walked out of the bedroom. "Let's hear it." He was wearing a pair of worn jeans with his brown button-down Sheriff's shirt.

"We found where Dr. A.J. has been the past six months."

Jessica leaned over the counter with wide eyes. "You did? Is he okay?"

Kyle nodded. "He burned the bodies of the wolves in his back yard and then buried them. That's why we weren't able to find them. Then he packed up his family and drove to his underground bunker. Apparently, he has a tricked-out fallout shelter that they spent the winter in. He thought it was going to be the end of the world."

Seth wrapped his arms around Jessica, as they both laughed. "Don't say anything, babe."

Jessica couldn't resist. "I told you so!" she yelled out from under his arm. She couldn't stop laughing. "I knew it!"

Seth ruffled her hair and kept squeezing her close as he explained to Kyle. "Jess actually joked about him being in a fortress of solitude when he first disappeared. It's pretty funny."

She poked her head out from Seth's arm, still unable to get her laughter under control. "I'm always right!" She tickled Seth's stomach to get him to let go.

"She IS always right," Kyle agreed, watching the two play affectionately with each other. "Anyway, he decided it was safe to come out of hiding since the government has things under control, and now he's back in business."

"Is that the doctor you said looks exactly like Superman?" Janie asked.

"Exactly. The guy could pass as Christopher Reeve's twin." Kyle took another swig of beer. "I've got the casefile on Dr. Williams wrapped up. I'm not entirely convinced no one else was involved, but the FBI hasn't found any more leads for now. I guess Shawn Sharconnon is getting the blame. He's going to go down in history as the evil bastard who unleashed the world's first deadly manmade creature."

"Speaking of that," Janie jumped off her barstool and ran to the door where she'd left her shoulder bag. She pulled out a medium-sized package wrapped in silver paper, and then handed it to her sister. "I got you each a little engagement gift."

Jessica shook the box, having an idea what would be inside.

"Go on, open it!" Janie was excited.

Seth helped Jessica pull the paper off the box, and then chuckled when he saw what was in it. Jessica held up a small white t-shirt that read, I SURVIVED THE SNAILS, WHAT'S EATING YOU? Seth picked up the same shirt, size XL, and held it to his chest. "Is this what I have to look forward to for the rest of my life?" Seth leaned around Jessica and planted a kiss on Janie's cheek. "Thanks." He shook his head with a soft, easy smile.

CPSIA information can be obtained
at www.ICGtesting.com
Printed in the USA
BVHW052142200722
642672BV00004B/51

9 781612 254753